Skylark Farm

Antonia Arslan, who lives in Padua, has a degree in archaeology and was a Professor of Modern and Contemporary Italian Literature at the University of Padua. *Skylark Farm* is her first novel.

Skylark Farm

ANTONIA ARSLAN

Translated from the Italian
by Geoffrey Brock

Atlantic Books
LONDON

Originally published in Italy in 2004 as *La masseria delle allodole* by Rizzoli, an imprint of RCS Libri S.p.A., Milan.

First published in English in the United States of America in 2006 by Alfred A. Knopf, a division of Random House, Inc., New York, and in Canada by Random House of Canada Limited, Toronto.

This edition published by arrangement with Alfred A. Knopf, a division of Random House, Inc. and with Agenzia Letteraria Roberto Santachiara.

First published in Great Britain in 2008 by Atlantic Books, an imprint of Grove Atlantic Ltd.

This paperback edition published in Great Britain in 2008 by Atlantic Books, an imprint of Grove Atlantic Ltd.

9 8 7 6 5 4 3 2 1

A CIP catalogue record for this book is available from the British Library.

978 1 84354 674 0

Printed in Great Britain, by CPD

Atlantic Books
An imprint of Grove Atlantic Ltd
Ormond House
26–27 Boswell Street
London WC1N 3JZ

www.atlantic-books.co.uk

For Enrica-Henriette, the little girl who didn't grow

Prologue

WE MADE OUR WAY beneath the arcades toward the Basilica of the Saint. It was June 13, my name day. It was raining, and I had no desire to go anywhere, but my grandfather, Yerwant, the patriarch whom no one disobeyed, had said, "It is time the child met her saint. It is nearly too late; she is five years old. It is not good to make the saints wait. And you must bring her on foot." He would meet us in his Lancia, with Antonio, his driver.

And so I walked down the two long arcaded streets that led to the Saint, with my aunt Henriette, tiniest of women, with her large Armenian nose and shiny black pageboy hair, she who had many secrets and held them tight, who never wore low heels or let me open her purse. She was not happy, either, with my grandfather's edict: she was hot, had a "near headache," thought that going to the basilica on one's saint day was unrefined, for provincials and tourists, and was afraid she would lose me; she worried for nothing, as always.

Aunt Henriette was a survivor of the genocide of 1915. A creature of the diaspora, she no longer had a mother tongue. She spoke many languages, including her own, Armenian, in a wooden, unnatural fashion: like a foreigner. In all of them she made poignant mistakes, and she would never tell the story of her survival. She had even forgotten how old she was (when she arrived in Italy she was so tiny and sickly that two or three years were taken off her age). But every evening, she came to our house for dinner bearing a tray of Austrian cookies, great tubs of homemade yogurt, and *paklava* brimming with nuts and honey, and her presence filled the house with obscure memories.

I loved her immensely, and she spoiled me. Edith Piaf records played all day at her house, and we danced in cloth shoes. Thus I was being dragged toward the Saint with a feeling of lazy curiosity, hoping for a gelato, or a trinket, or perhaps a picture book. I was open to all manner of gifts—and expected one, confidently.

And when Via del Santo deposited us in the vast piazza, I received my gift. The rain had stopped a few minutes earlier, and suddenly the clouds parted, like a curtain, and a warm shaft of sunlight turned the piazza into a theater, where countless colorful little figures began shaking themselves off and closing their umbrellas, as they scurried toward the entrance. Tante Aide, Nives, Esterine, and Gigie were calling to one another, happily and hurriedly, and they were accompanied by contrite little boys dressed like miniature monks and by thick-set, serious men in elegant black suits. In their midst, a solemn, stately group stood out, thanks to their showy garb, the women's long skirts and proud hats, and the men's thick mustaches. They gazed, motionless, at the basilica's great door, which stood ajar.

"You see? The gypsies are here, too," said my aunt, nervously. "Don't let go of my hand." I had no thought of letting go. Their eyes were enough. I was enchanted and confused. These, then, were gypsies? The ones who were always on the go, who never stayed in one place; who lived in gaudy caravans that were like tiny houses, with everything they needed inside? We Armenians, too, had traveled to every country, but once we reached a place, we stayed there; that is why we have relatives all over the world. And I began repeating the list of cities where we had relatives and the relatives' names, turning the words over in my mouth like candies.

My aunt always used to say, "When I've finally had it with all of you, when you get too mean, I'm leaving. I'll go stay with Arussiag in Beirut, with Uncle Zareh in Aleppo, with Philip and Mildred in Boston, with my sister Nevart in Fresno, with Ani* in New York, or even with Cousin Michel in Copacabana—him last, though, because he married an Assyrian." I was fascinated by this Assyrian aunt. I had seen, in an illustrated book, the costumes and the beards of the ancient Assyrians, had been told the

---

* Armenian words, like French words, are accented on the final syllable. Thus all the proper names are stressed on the final vowel (Aní, Arussiág, Sempád, Shushaníg, and so on). Turkish names are pronounced in the same way.

story of Nebuchadnezzar and the great cities of Babylon and Nineveh, and I pictured this aunt pacing, wrapped in sumptuous fabrics, back and forth through the hanging gardens of Babylon (which sounded a little like Copacabana). They should hardly be last on the list, as Aunt Henriette had said; this splendid Brazilian connection, in my opinion, should have come first. But the fact was that no one asked for my opinion.

Still squeezing my hand nervously, my aunt looked all around. Small, pathetic, and instantly ill at ease, she was seeking the reassuring presence of my grandfather, who indeed arrived at just that moment. In a flawless arc, the silver car glided around the perimeter of the piazza and came to a silent stop right beside us. Antonio the driver stepped down and ran to open the door for my grandfather, who was also tiny—yet so much more authoritative than my aunt! From his completely bald head, carefully shaved each morning, to his small, imperious goatee, to his shiny ankle boots and precisely buttoned spats, my grandfather exuded self-assurance and inner strength, qualities not unrelated to his capricious authority, which no one disputed and which delighted us children precisely because he often contradicted, in utterly incomprehensible ways, the sensible decisions of the other adults in the family.

My grandfather understood the situation at once, including the disquieting presence of the gypsies, and declared, "Henriette, you enter the basilica by the side

door, have a seat, and begin your prayers. A rosary, perhaps, because this will take some time. We will come for
you afterward. The girl will stay with me. You, Antonio,
spend some time inside—today is the Saint's day, and he
is your saint, too. Surely there is something you need to
ask of him. A nice prayer will do even you some good.
Then, afterward, go sit behind my niece and the two of
you can wait together."

He took me by the hand and led me straight toward
the gypsies, who were still standing in the same place in
the middle of the piazza. Their leader, out front, was a
large, beautiful man. But when he saw my little, rotund
grandfather, with his glinting watch fob stretched across
his paunch, he greeted him and immediately turned to his
cohorts, who to my enchanted eyes were all as beautiful as
he was, and said, "It's the doctor, the one who saved the
baby. He's coming into the basilica with us, coming to
pray with us." And my grandfather said, "This is my
granddaughter. Her name is Antonia."

At that moment, the great central doors began to
swing slowly open. I glimpsed, between the heavy drapes
on either side of the entry, the vast dark cavity beyond,
from which emerged the potent fragrance of incense,
the indistinct buzz of a large, respectful crowd, and—
occasionally—gusts of song. My grandfather took one of
my hands, the gypsy leader took the other, and we
advanced together at the head of the group, with solemn
step and slow, toward the entrance. The crowd parted

around us, whispering. The group's particular odor is fixed forever in my memory, like the scent of the soul's nest, to which we will all return: horse and leather, bronzed skin and road dust.

The gypsies were singing, in their mysterious language. And then my grandfather, in his mysterious language, was also singing, as if to himself, his voice deep, his words so sweet they seemed to issue from some other mouth; and I—beneath him, near him—hung on those words, feeling at home, as though I had returned to a warm nest. "God of mercy, Christ our savior, have pity on us. O holiest trinity, grant peace to the world and glory to the Church; love and unity to our Armenian nation; health to the sick; and the kingdom to the sleepers."

Then there came a loud, resolute voice (which seemed to emanate from some mysterious Allwhere, rather than from a preacher in the pulpit I could not see): "From the Holy Brother Anthony. Christ compares himself to a mother hen: *As a hen gathers her brood beneath her wings* . . . He observes that the hen falls ill whenever her chicks do; she calls them to feed until her voice is hoarse; she protects them beneath her wings and defends them with stiffened feathers from the chicken hawk. Thus Christ, God's Wisdom, made himself sick for us, who are sick, as Isaiah says: *We have observed him: he is despised and least among men, that is to say the greatest outcast; a man of sorrows who is well acquainted with suffering.*"

I liked the mother hen idea: I knew mother hens, knew how they behaved, had even had a chick once. Though my mother, I reflected, young and brash as she was, was certainly no mother hen. And in my mind the healing of the sick from my grandfather's prayer, the Armenian see, the attentiveness of the God-hen about whom the voice spoke, the odor of the gypsies, and the vast protective cavity beneath the basilica's heavenly domes—all these things fused into a sensation of total security, of happiness so intense that I began to weep.

My grandfather then took my hand in both of his and said, "This church is like a ship, and it is your saint who steers it. This church is a harbor, and it is your saint who gathers us here inside, and he dictates the words you've been listening to, and evil remains beyond the door." (I looked at the great entrance: it shimmered with the outside light, and it didn't look like a guard. But my grandfather knew everything.) "This is the visible house that leads to the house that is invisible. You will always be at home here. You heard what the Saint said: God is solace and knowledge; He is nearby in sickness, a warm heart beating close to yours. All our dead are here: your grandmother Antonietta, my dear young mother"—and thus I learned to my amazement that my grandfather had had a mother—"all my brothers lost in the deportation . . .

"But now," he continued, "we shall go say hello. One must not neglect one's host." And so, after many warm goodbyes, we left the gypsies and went to stand in line amid the sweaty throng that wanted to touch the black slab, behind which, my grandfather explained, lay the body of Saint Anthony.

"But is he there really, and can he actually feel us?" I asked. "And does he know our thoughts?"

"You have to put your hand on the marble," he said, "and say a prayer, the one you know best and that comes to mind first. He will see inside your heart." I was not at all sure that there was much to see inside my heart, stuffed as it was with childish things. Nothing that I thought would be of interest to a saint. On the other hand, I was fascinated by the silver hearts, the delicate lacework of glittering metal hanging everywhere, together with little silver arms and legs and tiny colorful paintings. But there was no time to linger on anything. The dense crowd pressed on all sides, around my grandfather and me, jostling us, confounding us.

At last a large man behind us took note of the old man and the little girl: he shielded him, and he lifted me, pressing me against the black slab for a moment. I quickly thought, "First of all, my name is Antonia. I'm telling you my name right away, because with all these people how else will you remember me later?" But the Saint did not reply. "Too many people," I thought. "Perhaps I should have spoken louder." But I had done my duty, I had behaved well, and besides, he probably already knew who I was. My grandfather would have told him.

And the happiness surged back, like a current sweep-

ing me along with the moving crowd. I do not recall the
rest of the visit, only that my grandfather was holding me
firmly by the hand, as if we shared some secret emotion,
and that at a certain point (perhaps in the relatively calm
darkness behind the main altar) he sat down on a step, he
who was usually so fastidious, as if beaten down by some
thought that set him apart, and I stood before him, quiet
and full of joy, and waited for him. Today I know it was in
that moment that his dead rejoined him, and suddenly he
seemed a tired old tradesman, one who had dreamed in
vain of returning to live out his final days on his native
Eastern soil but had now resigned himself to dying here,
in an exile that wasn't really exile, since all peoples called it
home, his ancient fatherland lost.

I recall vividly, however, his recovery. Suddenly cheerful and lively again, he said, "Now we shall go say hello to
the provincial priest. Your aunt and Antonio can pray a
little longer. I am sure he will give you an orange soda and
a cookie." In fact, my cookie was accompanied by a tiny
glass of a delicious rosolio liqueur, hot pink in color,
whose sweet rose savor seemed to me sublime (something
to crow about, back home, to my envious brothers), and a
cartoon version of *The Story of Joseph*, for when I learned to
read. But I preferred to listen, and to look at that table
with its thick cover, at the portraits of holy men on the
walls, and at the two old men in friendly conversation: my
grandfather with his dull, yellowish skin, calmly stroking
his goatee, and the friar, calm too, and powerful, with rosy

skin and a bushy gray beard he occasionally tamed with his hands. He told me, "You'll have to come visit me again soon, with your grandfather, on a more peaceful day than the Saint's day. Because you're named after him, and because you're a woman, you have special duties. There are lots of Antonios, but few Antonias." I immediately felt very flattered by his words.

I absorbed all these things that June afternoon, like a curious sponge or an ardent girl.

My grandfather died a few months later. We never went to visit the old friar again, and I never learned the "special duties" inherent in being named Antonia. Many years have passed, but I have not forgotten. Still today, the basilica's great cupolas are, for me, like powerful ships, ships that sail majestic from the West to the East, following the prophecy, coming to rest above that distant little city. I am still moved, each time I pass through those great doors, by the smell of incense, the chanting of the Laurentian litanies (or their memory), the present echo of the shuffling feet of millions upon millions of pilgrims, coming and going like a sea, each of their souls watched over by the great Saint whose name I bear.

After so many years, that fragrant interior, teeming with people, is where I feel at home, in the warm nest of that distant day: neither a foreigner nor a guest, but a passenger waiting for a train whose schedule I do not know. I know only that it will stop here, at this great station where no one is a foreigner, and that a great heart still beats to show us the way. This is where I would like to end my days, resting on a step worn away by the feet of men, waiting for Someone to accept me, so that instead of vanishing into nothing I will travel toward the light, hand in hand with Antonio, my Portuguese friend, the one you call Anthony of Padua, the Saint with the lily in his hand.

FIRST PART

Uncle Sempad

UNCLE SEMPAD is only a legend, for us—but a legend that has made us all cry. He was my grandfather's younger brother, his only uterine brother; their mother, Iskuhi, the little princess, died at nineteen giving birth to him. My great-grandfather then remarried an "evil stepmother," who bore him many other children; my grandfather couldn't stand her, and so, at the age of thirteen, he requested and was granted permission to leave the little city and go to Venice, to study at Moorat-Raphael, the boarding school for Armenian children.

But Uncle Sempad was much sweeter and more easy-going than his brother, and he loved his little city, his lazy, sleepy province, the café chats with his friends, the fierce games of backgammon, the hunting. He went off to Constantinople to become a pharmacist, but always knew he would return home. At the university, he read the papers, joined a political party, dreamed like others of the rebirth of the ancient Armenian homeland, kicked up his heels a little, and kidded himself. Back home, he made his peace with the stepmother, amused himself by coddling his little brothers and pulling his sisters' braids, and began to think of marriage.

Every so often he went riding, with a friend from the Laz country. Together they felt like crusaders and knights, imagined heading off to battle in the direction of the sun, like Alexander, free men with swords at their sides. Goodbye to exhausting negotiations for every permission, to imperial bureaucracy, to the necessarily servile deference of the Armenian, of the merchant, of those who make requests that are easily denied and have no weapon but the vassal's tricks. And yet: to be riding toward the East, the conquered, but to be men of the West, the conquering. To speak French, to subscribe to the *Revue des deux mondes*, to visit Paris . . .

They often spoke of Paris, or of Italy, a friendly country, where Yerwant was making his fortune. But Sempad had no desire, his promises notwithstanding, to go visit his brother: he was timid and Eastern. If only his brother would come home, if only he would bring his Frankish* wife with him, and their children Yetwart and Khayël, and introduce them to their family. He had left with honor, and with honor he would be welcomed back. But in his heart of hearts, Sempad feared that this would never happen; Yerwant had gone away for good, and his sons—despite their names—did not speak the ancestral

---

* From the country of the "Franks"—a typical term for Westerners.

language and had been educated in German or Italian schools. Anatolia, for them, was a far-off fairy tale.

"Perhaps," thought Sempad, "one of my sons will find his way to Yerwant, and perhaps we will all trade this place, a few at a time, for places where we'll no longer be afraid." But he didn't really want that. Many were leaving, it was true. From the most dangerous regions, the boldest youths, the brightest, the most intrepid, those who couldn't bear the strict confines of the Ermeni Millet— the Armenian administrative unit—within the Empire, were flowing out in a continuous stream.

For Europe, for the coveted culture: to become doctors, dentists, architects, poets—or for America, to become utterly new, to forget. His half brother, Rupen, lived in Boston and was quite content. But Sempad, in his simple heart, understood Rupen's solitude and sent him a fine wooden backgammon set, with a decidedly affectionate inscription engraved all around it in Armenian characters, the same set he had at home. He never would have imagined that that set—relic or icon from a terrible shipwreck—would for two of his children be the only sign, aside from a solemn ceremonial photograph, of their father's lively existence.

Sempad loved his pharmacy. He was a slow-moving man, not particularly witty, and profoundly good. As a boy he protected his younger sisters, Veron and Azniv, from their tumultuous, harassing brothers, Rupen and Zareh. And he loved to send telegrams.

"The pharmacist," he used to say, "ought to be equipped to send and receive telegrams. There could be an *urgency*."

Everyone teased Sempad, both at home and at the pharmacy, for the elaborate way the word *urgency* rolled off his tongue. How it resounded in his mouth, that Westernism: symptom of progress, symbol of haste, of the shaking off of Eastern indolence.

"People," he used to say, "are not going to put off death so that we can finish our card game. We intellectual Armenians need to set an example, of precision, of modernity, of punctuality: for both the average Armenian and the average Turk. Why else did we bother studying?"

But he himself no longer studied anything; he observed the holidays and stroked his mustache—counting his seven children. He barely glanced at the paper with the news from Constantinople, though he was proud that the Armenians up there were beginning to gain respect; some had even become delegates, and Krikor Zohrab, poet and delegate, played *tavli*—the Turkish version of backgammon—with the supremely powerful minister of the interior, Talat Pasha.

Zohrab's *tavli*! His friendship with Talat had become, for the gentle, daydreaming Armenian people, an omen of good fortune, a symbol of the new day of prosperity and progress that was about to dawn with the political collaboration between the Young Turks and the Armenian millet. A powerful, disarming symbol: "He goes to his home, he's received like family, they drink tea together." For Sempad, and all the others like him, it was literally inconceivable that a man could deceive—much less kill—someone with whom he drank tea *in his own home:* a guest!

For Sempad and those like him, worldliness included neither duplicity or deception; it was grounded, rather, in the application of a careful mercantile etiquette of earnings, profits, and losses, calculated generously and with due respect to the community's poor. And moreover, the pharmacist had a moral code to uphold. He was practically a doctor and practically a man of letters: the guardian of health, the keeper of poisons, the bearer of newspapers, the telegram man—a pillar of the community.

Everyone knew that Shushanig, his boisterous and fertile wife, though she professed to have nothing to do with her husband's affairs, happily controlled him down to his last whisker, as the proverb says. And he happily allowed himself to be controlled, even when, with her tacit consent, he ran off in a wretched pair of leather pants with his Lazian friend, rifle over his shoulder, proudly returning with a couple of hares. Sometimes one of his sons accompanied him.

The eldest, the tight-lipped Suren, dreamed of Europe, and was on the verge of departure. But he adored his simple father and had no desire to leave him. His preference would be perversely respected by destiny.

Suren read a lot, and thought a lot. He smelled blood in the air, caught the scent of evil. But who pays attention to a boy of fourteen, who speaks rarely and grudgingly, who cries alone at night, dreaming of a woman's lap, a maternal refuge in which to disappear and hide?

Garo, the second son, also spoke little and thought even less. He acted out of a loving instinct, without reflecting, with a perfect economy of gestures. He could calm any crying, whining, or shrieking baby; his fleeting presence alone lulled and soothed a helpless, insecure community, for which each day might take a bad turn, where the elders tell stories not of witches and ogres but of the slaughters of twenty years before, or ten, counting as a kind of rosary the list of massacred or vanished relatives.

The third son was Leslie the Brit, who was "conceived on a stormy night," according to Sempad; it was "a calm night with a full moon," joked Shushanig. His parents claimed not to know why he had always been called the Brit. "Did the name come first, or the nickname?" their friends would slyly ask, recalling Sempad's epic binge. He was typically a very restrained drinker—at most, alcohol made him a bit sad—but once an American missionary gave the pharmacy a bottle of medicinal Scotch, resulting in Shushanig's being chased around the courtyard and winding up, indecorously, in the henhouse, the outcome being, of course, Leslie.

It was pleasing, that liquid, sibilant, exotic name, written in white letters on the bottle that the contrite parents kept as a souvenir. (An old soldier, a veteran of the

Balkan wars, later built a magnificent sailing ship inside it, even providing it with a nostalgic cartouche that recalled Nelson's battles and his own dream of sailing the open seas; but he would be among the first to die, in May 1915, surrounded by his smashed ships.)

The bottle on top of the cupboard—that beautiful Italian walnut that Yerwant sent from Italy on the birth of his first nephew—and Leslie beneath the cupboard. Leslie grew up alone: fought over at first like a doll by his two older brothers, he was quickly forgotten at the birth, ten months later, of a cute, sweet, and very normal baby girl, Aunt Nevart, who would later live in Fresno, who did not care for children. Leslie laughed all the time, asked if he could play with the others, was not offended when the answer was no: he just went under his cupboard, back to his secret lair.

Then the rest: Arussiag, Henriette, and Nubar, two girls and a little boy dressed as a girl. Along with Nevart they are the numb survivors who will, after escaping Aleppo, come to the West. These children now look out at me from a snapshot taken in Aleppo in 1916, one year after their rescue, just before they embarked for Italy: their grave, childish eyes are turned mysteriously inward, opaque and glacial, having accepted—after too many unanswered questions—the blind selection that has allowed them to survive. They are wearing decent orphan clothes, but they seem dressed in uniforms of rags, and at a quick glance the eye sees prison stripes. Their dark Eastern eyes, with their thick brows tracing a single line across their foreheads, repeat four times, wordlessly, the fear of a future that will be inexorable and the hidden nucleus of a secret guilt.

WAR HAS BROKEN OUT in Europe. Balkan anguish strikes again. The Ottomans align themselves with the Central Powers, Germany and Austria-Hungary. People hope they've picked right this time—but it's never a good idea to act on the heels of old resentments, out of a sense of national humiliation strong enough to become a flag. The little city is abuzz. Many locals are consulting the American missionary, the one who opened, with great success, the Protestant boarding school. They like this new way of approaching the old faith, without the glut of sentiment and emotionalism found in the long, traditional services, which are comforting but never change. They like this austere God who requires self-control and punctuality, responsible devotion, modern prayer. Armenians' feelings of guilt are purged, the myth of America reinforced.

Deep in her simple heart, Aunt Veron, who eagerly converted and became a devoted supporter, wonders if this God might also be more powerful, might know how to defend the Armenians next time. Veron is short and chubby, with a curiously Parisian nose (*retroussé*, she calls it) of which she is quite proud, and harbors certain notions about women's liberation. She is also quite proud of the little Protestant chapel, where she goes by herself on Sundays, wearing a bonnet that actually is French. She finds the chapel to be in excellent taste, exquisitely furnished in the latest style; but her soul, having remained, without her realizing it, pleasantly retrograde, runs into some emotional difficulties: she finds herself unable to weep freely so far from the solemn gaze of the Mother of God.

Because sometimes, of an evening, Veron weeps. She would like a real boyfriend, one who doesn't find her name laughable. (*Veron, Veron, vrai pompon,* her nephews sang to make her mad; no one now recalls who first came up with that infamous refrain.) Maybe an American, Veron daydreams. What if she went to visit Rupen in Boston and stayed? She could work, be a shopgirl or a milliner, design bonnets . . .

In a secret box, beneath the yellow leather gloves that Rupen himself sent her for Christmas, Veron sets aside a little money for her American wedding. She'd rather not go alone, however, and now and again she confides in Aunt Azniv, her rose-lipped younger sister, who loves her but sometimes makes fun of her behind her back. Azniv wears a long braid down her back and puts a fresh geranium behind her ear each morning. ("We need to revive the traditions of Armenian women," she read in a Social Revolutionary Party bulletin; she also read, in the *Illustration Parisienne,* about the gypsy Carmen and her tragic loves.)

Azniv has absolutely no intention of leaving. The little city suits her to a tee, and she feels important there, nestles girlishly into it, certain of the future that awaits a pretty, intelligent young woman. She speaks French quite well and has an Armenian boyfriend with whom she dances spiritedly at all the parties. And she has a Turkish suitor, too: a young officer who follows her with his gaze whenever she's near, meekly, with smitten eyes. He has more than once sent her poetry, which she wisely shows no one. But her heart races a little when she sees him, thrilled by the gauntlet she has taken up just by allowing him to write. He is a refined, romantic young man, and she furthermore finds him quite handsome.

But Azniv would never actually get involved with him; the rift between Capulets and Montagues is nothing compared with what separates these two. Above all, above all: only in the world of literature, in the paper world of Western novels, could such a liaison be possible, even thrilling. To pretend to believe in blind passion, to repudiate the future . . .

Azniv is too practical in her carnal exuberance. And besides, she feels superior to Muslim wives, who are sometimes forced to share their husbands with other women. Azniv is free to choose her own path, and she likes to imagine herself doing so and her father listening to her wishes.

That's how it has always been in her family. Yerwant was thirteen when he decided to go to Italy, and Rupen only slightly older when he left for America—and if Veron can afford to pay her own way, no one will stop her. Old Hamparzum can't bring himself to stand in the way of his children's choices, choices that might mean salvation. And no matter where in the wide world a son or a young daughter might go, some Armenian will be waiting there to lend a hand.

But out in the Syrian desert, Azniv and Veron will have only each other to cling to, will take turns gently rocking each other and singing in low, spent voices "Ov sirun sirun," their song, and "Veron, pompon," their hard, secret joke during the deportations; they are not animals scrapping for the last mouthful of bread, but women, still, with one final source of strength: the thought of saving the children.

Zareh, on the other hand, lives in Aleppo. Like his big brother Yerwant, he is a doctor. Educated, skeptical, proud, Zareh can play backgammon like everyone else, but his passion is bridge. There are always a couple of games, with Arab waiters bearing spirits circling the tables solicitously. And it is certainly not insignificant that ladies play bridge, too.

Zareh is twenty-six, with a thick mustache and a little goatee, in imitation of Yerwant. He likes to think he resembles Yerwant, but he has a stouter, somewhat coarser physique. (His mother was not the little princess, Iskuhi, but the solid daughter of merchants; Hamparzum had chosen his second wife according to logic and social rank.) Watching the ladies in their colorful dresses, in their utterly artificial (yet so agreeable) gaiety, Zareh believes that he has been forgiven, that he is no longer Armenian—how nice it would be to have two distinguished French parents behind him, a good Western provincial upbringing: to be Western, not merely to seem so.

But you, poor Zareh, with your olive skin and your strong wide fingers, your large nose and liquid brown eyes—how would you be seen in the West if not as another hungry child of the East?

Zareh, however, thinks that he has managed to make a clean break, distancing himself a little more each day from all those cumbersome, faraway relatives, from that cumbersome femininity: those stocky aunts; those silly, naïve, nosy sisters who have yet to find husbands; those vain nieces made happy with ribbons. Twice a year he sends them all a suitcase of brocades from Aleppo. The owner of the Aleppine factory is his patient and gives him discounts on fine cuts of heavy silk with only the slightest of defects. In his last shipment, Zareh added—for Azniv, his favorite sister, his near twin, only eleven months younger than he—a perfect piece of garnet-colored silk with velvet roses accented with pure gold thread: a splendid thing.

This silk will end up in the desert and serve as a blanket, and each evening Azniv will laugh, yellow teeth showing in her shrunken face, when Veron, doubled over with hunger, asks her, Are you dressing for your prince, my little dove, with your silk and your gold? But she will not hesitate to trade it, in the end, for a little bread and water.

. . .

ZAREH WILL BECOME CRUCIAL to this story. But not because of his life, or his death. He will marry a good Assyrian girl, Aunt Alice, and his French, nearly perfect by then, will serve him well in the years of the French protectorates in Lebanon and Syria. He will live quietly in a beautiful house with a view of the Citadel and balconies overlooking a courtyard, in a quiet nineteenth-century neighborhood. He will have a single child, named Juliette, who will die as a young bride of a mysterious illness, shortly after the death of her husband, also Syrian, a boy from Damascus with dark, quiet eyes.

But it will be Zareh the skeptic, the European, who will save the family legacy, the children, and the photographs: the four little malnourished bodies curled together like dying birds, their small skulls all eyes, and the precious packet of family portraits, sewn up along with Gregory of Narek's prayer book inside a velvet rag and passed from hand to hand, from the dying to the survivors. Parched, dried skeletons— memorials of a life that had been cordial and boisterous, with plenty of water, plenty of hospitality and mirth.

AND SO THE WAR broke out in Europe. August 1914. Old Hamparzum is about to die. He has seen everything, has worked hard, and has thought at great length about his family and the Church. Now, with faith and honor, he blesses everyone and makes his goodbyes. And he entrusts to his children his fine wife, the wise and cantankerous Nevart Alexanian.

Now he is able to turn inward and to cast off his heavy age, his burdens, and his belongings. Now he can return to his pretty young princess, Iskuhi Kardiashian, with her fishlike cheeks and her dresses of fire, she who seduced him forever one July afternoon in 1865. It's she he thinks of when he sees Azniv with a geranium in her hair. But Iskuhi was so much lovelier! As if wrapped in sunlight, as if dipped in flame. He still sees her smiling, her black eyes liquid and misty, her mouth sullen, in her golden cloud in the presence of God.

He knows, old Hamparzum does, that she is waiting for him, that she is looking down on him already from the balconies of heaven, reaching her lovely round arms toward him, and so he is able to savor his final days. He doesn't suffer; an unutterable, grateful languor simply spreads little by little through his bones. He enjoys sips of yogurt and cucumbers, sucks a piece of bread, and feels his mind grow ever more acute and prophetic, honing to an edge.

"Grandpa, want a grape?" says Nubar as he toddles in, engrossed in the task of walking, of showing off his first steps. He's the youngest grandchild, Sempad and Shushanig's last-born son—the amusing, chubby, sonorously named Nubar.

The grapes from the small vineyards of the little city are large and sweet; the old man takes one and detects the dense scent of the flesh of Iskuhi, his radiant doe. "To be reunited in the lost homeland, with she who will not die again," he thinks—and then, "A few more days . . . "

And now of a sudden his brain sends him a lucid, crystal-clear vision of horror and despair: his heart begins to beat erratically, the steel fingers of anguish grip his throat, and his life begins to transform, to flow down into despair. The steady vision of the beloved vanishes; in its place appear the black horsemen of the Apocalypse, giving rise to inauspicious images of annihilation, in the obscure absence of any God.

Hamparzum in that moment understands that he is seeing the future; that all these luminous lives that have branched off from his will be cut short; and that thanks to evil's supreme mockery, he alone, the old trunk, will be permitted to die in his bed, knowing what will come to pass.

Heaven has turned metallic and empty, God doesn't exist, whoever dies disappears forever, and Iskuhi never existed, nor will she reappear to his faithful heart. To give himself over to panic, and then to die: nothing else is left for him to do.

But Nubar is still in the room, transfixed by the play of sunlight over the blue and pink and green of the tile floor. Shadows dance, and he watches them with wonder. He is still holding his bunch of grapes. His grandfather and he are alone in the room. Suddenly a soft noise makes him turn. It's the grape he gave his grandfather, fallen from his open hand. There is something helpless and imploring about that hand, and his grandfather is not dozing, as he has spent most of the last days doing, but gazing at some elsewhere, his eyes wide and fearful.

Nubar quickly decides what to do: he won't call anyone, he will help his grandfather himself. He knows he is the only one who can help him now; and he feels very brave. He runs toward the bed, clambers onto it, and lies atop his grandfather's motionless body, rubbing his face with his hands, with his sticky cluster of crushed grapes.

He doesn't speak, he acts. Through Nubar's warm little body and his wet hands, the old man smells the scent of grapes (which is the scent of life) and feels the heat of young hands and of a fishlike face. Thus Nubar takes part in his battle, without knowing it.

And through him returns Iskuhi the beautiful, coming from the fields of heaven down to the wet earth, to a room heavy with sickness and odors, routing dissolution and madness. She consoles him.

Rocking in her arms, the old man now knows. It's his last duty, his last labor: to warn them. "Sempad, Nevart," he calls breathlessly in his mind, but his mouth forms no words, only a menacing sputter. Frightened, Nubar slides off the bed and stands there holding his grandfather's grim, fixed gaze, over which a veil is descending. And finally the cry "Flee!" forms on his worn-out lips; his hand hangs, gripping the little boy's sticky hand with a deathly vigor.

"Flee, flee!" repeats Hamparzum to the boy, but his voice becomes a shrill rattle, a grievous leave-taking.

Ah, death cannot be happiness. "May the life of this little boy, at least, be saved," asks Hamparzum with his last thought, and Iskuhi and Mary nod. The old man entrusts his spirit to them. Nubar, not moving or making a sound, continues to watch him and squeeze his hand.

That's how they found them, grandfather and grandson. Motionless in their reciprocal, silent communion, balanced between the past and the future in a miraculously dilated present: a red evening that wasn't falling, a mysterious epiphany. The Virgin had walked upon the earth, among the poppies and the golden grain, and she had liked the bunch of grapes.

"In, out, in, out": the children quickly separate the peas and lentils. Tomorrow is their grandfather's funeral. The church bells toll the hours; all is peaceful, quiet bustle. The baking pans line up on the large marble table, ready for the funeral supper; the children laugh quietly and nibble on currants and sunflower seeds.

Everyone has a precise task, is carrying out his or her duty. In the air, not sadness—perhaps a slight nip of arrogance. The family is important, has many relatives abroad, making their fortunes: it will be a beautiful funeral. The bishop will come to preside, the choir of priests from the cathedral has been hired, and the wailing women are already at work—and frequently come to the kitchen to cool their throats. They love Shushanig and her generosity but fear Sempad and his science, so they keep themselves busy.

The whole quarter (the whole city) is talking about Hamparzum's death in the tones reserved for amazing events—about how he was kept company by his smallest grandchild, about how grandfather and grandson were so still, both of them, and calm, looking into each other's eyes and holding hands.

It isn't long before the wailers seize on this story and call Nubar a chosen one: he was found there bathed in light, and an angel had clearly been in the room, Ismene adds, because you could smell the ambrosia. Ismene is Greek, from Chios. In her mouth she always has a wad of *masticha*, and in the deep pockets of her frock mysterious colored handkerchiefs, which she sometimes knots and unknots rapidly in a show of amazing dexterity. Thick gray whiskers adorn her upper lip.

The Armenians like Ismene, but so do the Turks, who often invite her to ceremonies and funerals, because she knows lamentations and songs in many exotic languages, and because she lived in America when she was young: she took part in the gold rush in the wilds of the

Klondike, knew Indians, and even lived with one. "Like a wife, a real wife," she always says, "and he showed me great respect!" (Who could not respect Ismene?) Then she utters mysterious words, and her shrewd eyes flash.

But no one would dare criticize this family in her presence. She is fiercely devoted to Sempad and Shushanig, a devotion that extends to all their children—though not to the aunts and uncles, nor to the old man's widow, whom she derisively calls "Madame Nevart."

On the special occasion of this funeral, Ismene will outdo herself, because Sempad is becoming the head of the family, since Yerwant will of course not return to Anatolia. As soon as he heard the news, Yerwant sent telegrams and also wrote his brother a letter, a statement of investiture, which arrived two months after the funeral and gave Sempad ample authority on every family question: from the girls' marriages to their dowries, from the pension of the old servant, Hagop, to the fate of Skylark Farm, their ancient house in the hills.

Sempad is thinking of turning it into the sort of country house that so many Westerners have, and then inviting Yerwant and his Italian family. Behind the main building, near the crusade tower and the large dovecote, there's a clearing surrounded by whitethorn hedges that would be ideal for a tennis lawn, in the English style, and there's space, too, for a toolshed and a nice round gazebo for afternoon tea. For years he and his brother have been talking about a visit, which was impossible as long as the old man was alive: he never would have agreed to Sempad's renovations, nor did he care to see Yerwant again.

In his obscure way, deep down in his imperious, competitive nature, Yerwant retained an almost involuntary veneration for the father who—patriarch to primogenitor—had granted his wish when he was a headstrong thirteen-year-old and allowed him to emigrate on his own, supporting him, however, only until he was eighteen. They never saw each other again, and Hamparzum never spoke of his distant son and merely accepted Sempad's fraternal pride and the enthusiasm of his other children, for whom Yerwant was an icon, a living legend.

But because of the war, Sempad never got farther than leveling the ground for the tennis lawn, and in that pretty rectangular pit, fresh with newly dug earth, he and his sons will rest forever.

HALF THE CITY is out in the street. Dignitaries of the Armenian Church, the bishop, and many priests, wait solemnly at the top of the cathedral steps, as if posing for a photograph (which indeed is taken, with the latest in German cameras, by Levon Yakovlian, the Armenian quarter's faithful inspector-postman, proud father of the man who, having emigrated years ago to Munich, where he now runs a respected brewery, sent him the camera).

At the same time, another photograph is being taken. Around Hamparzum's body, lying placidly on its bier, his children and grandchildren take their places quietly, as if for a new rite. In the main hallway on the second floor, there's a nineteenth-century lithograph, *The Death of the Good Paterfamilias*, which captures in a bourgeois interior the ancient rituality of the public deaths of kings: all the relatives kneel around the solemn four-poster bed upon which lies the dying man, who is receiving extreme unction.

That picture may have offered Sempad a model, but a negative one. It wasn't for some didactic image that he called in the photographer, but rather for proof that modernity and progress had come even to the little city. He thinks it elegant and in Western good taste to compose this new kind of family holy picture. Because nowadays, since modern cameras exist, mementos must be sent to his brothers. And so the photographer arranges everyone, alternating children and adults, women and men, without separating husbands and wives. No one, of course, smiles openly, but they all have bright, happy eyes. Nubar has been seated near his grandfather's head.

So many pairs of eyes, so many restless little shoes! Black velvet drapes the long table supporting the bier, hanging to the ground. And it's on the lower levels that impatience with the long pose can be seen. Boys are kicking girls, hands and feet are touching, sharp pinches are being exchanged: the game is that on their faces nothing can show, nothing but the grave composure of this mournful occasion.

And finally they are finished posing. Aunts chase after children, carrying them to bathrooms to get them ready for the ceremony. The photographer drinks coffee in the kitchen and eats one of the sweets that have been prepared for the funeral supper. He doesn't earn much, so he slips a few cookies into his pocket, to sweeten the account he'll later give his children.

Then come the uncles. They heave the open casket onto their shoulders, carry it slowly out the large open door. They're wearing dark clothes, impressive ties, and pomade in their hair. They don't look at anyone.

Nubar senses that his moment of glory has passed, but he doesn't want to stay home, as he has been told to do. I'm not too little, he thinks. But he needs a protector, so as not to get lost in the city.

Behind the coffin, which has been placed on an magnificent carriage, pulled by four plumed horses, the pallbearers now flank the widow and Sempad, the eldest son. Behind them, in a long line, other aunts and uncles and cousins, relatives and friends and officials, and the family's poor, which include a gimpy Turkish beggar named Nazim. Among the spectators are two Turkish officers: Azniv's admirer has brought a friend so as not to find himself alone.

When Azniv passes, gravely, with a lovely black veil, she acts as if she doesn't see him. But in fact everyone sees him, and a murmur snakes through the long line of people.

Bringing up the rear, the wailers advance with liturgical dignity. At the group's center is Ismene, wrapped in her many-colored rags, waving a large black shawl, which she holds in her outstretched hands like a flag. Everyone knows that the science of mourning must be respected; it must be handled with care, by experts. Every aspect of the clamor made by these women has a meaning—the cries, the shrieks, the exclamations; together they shape the lacerating harmony of mourning, rebuilding human patience and the faith in the hidden God whom these priestesses alone are authorized to call on, as they do with provocative familiarity.

Their clamor sustains and accompanies the family on the road toward the future, toward the unknown—unknown because the one who protects them from evil, who represents them and absolves them, is gone.

Nubar is with Ismene, behind her black shawl. He moves back and forth with the women and loses himself in their metallic, rhythmic shrieking. He is happy, drunk on noise and motion. And this will remain his first memory: the vigil with his grandfather has already been forgotten.

THE GRAPES OF AUGUST! In his later years, while overseeing with rigid authority his granddaughter's convalescence, Yerwant recalls how as a boy he and his cousins Ohannes and Vahan helped with the grape harvest: from the vineyard on the hill they would bring home enormous bunches of grapes, hanging from poles that were each shouldered by two boys. He's cold, tight-lipped, and authoritarian, this grandfather, but it's a natural authority that enchants children. And the little girl won't forget the emotion he masked with irony, as they dined beneath the dense pergola of wisteria at the Doglioni Brothers Alpine Hotel: "These are not real grapes. They are pale, nearly tasteless. In my far country, the bunches were enormous, and milk and honey tasted like the ark of the East."

"Don't interrupt him while he's telling these stories," the girl is thinking—and luckily the old gentleman continues, as if to himself, "There is no other flavor like that. I used to make yogurt with Aunt Mariam, and I was so good at it they allowed me to help prepare the *paklava*." And thus the girl gets her first glimpse through the window that opens onto the Lost Country, via the sweet sense of taste, the dream of distant flavor.

Of course she knows *lokhum, paklava, kurabia, shakarlokma*, as well as the Italian curly tart and the Viennese *kipfel*—all the sweets of the East and the West that Aunt Henriette brings each evening, crossing the street with her faithful Maria. But the girl's grandfather has given her something else: the living echo of aromas and flavors, true nourishment, and the birth of nostalgia (*for a country that no longer exists, for the columns of deportees, for a family dying beneath a poisonous sun, for the unmarked graves along the dusty roads and paths of Anatolia; and for everything that disappeared with them,*

*everything alive and fragrant, exhausted and joyous, painful and con-
soling: the country's soul).*

"Later they invited me to come back."

"Yes, grandfather, they invited you, but why didn't
you go?"

The little girl would learn the answer only many
years later.

NOW THE HEAD of the family, Sempad, with joy in his
simple heart, thinks that at last Yerwant will be unable to
refuse to return. For a visit, of course; next summer: and
Skylark Farm will be ready to receive him.

Yerwant, who has conversations with himself, and
who trusts no one but himself, is pondering such a journey, too. He feels new pleasure at the thought. He was
among the first, in the city he now calls home, to buy an
automobile, and he helped begin the tradition of the
Sunday outing, the whole family and two drivers heading
to Recoaro, Thiene, the Berici Hills, the Pre-Alps. His
wife pleads migraines, his sons homework, but it isn't easy
to disobey him, and so they make their outings, and the
resentment flows beneath the surface. On the car doors,
the silver coat of arms features an intertwined *Y* and *A*.

A mysterious zone of darkness separates Yerwant
from his sons, a mutual fear, a circumspect exchange of
glances that never becomes trust. The eldest, Yetwart, is
sixteen and is always at boarding school, has always been

at boarding school, since he was little. The youngest, Khayël, is eleven; he's his mother's son and takes the side of the woman who seems to him so helpless against her tyrannical husband, the Eastern despot.

Yerwant never says where he's going when he goes out, sometimes disappears for days, invites Armenian friends over, and speaks that obscure, barbaric language that he never asked his wife to learn. She defends her boys from that blood, those ways, those rites—when they get older they'll even change their first names.

But she, Teresa dei Conti Sartena, doesn't realize that in fact she is fulfilling her husband's great wish. She has, without realizing it, undertaken to do what he cannot: to estrange his sons, to annihilate their every curiosity about the Far Country. (Only as an old man, after the dust has settled, will Yerwant open the reliquary of his nostalgia, for his granddaughter.)

Yetwart and Khayël see their cousins, Sempad's children, as alien, utterly foreign, and Sempad himself as a relative of whom to be vaguely ashamed—that bushy mustache, that simple air, that fez on his head. (How their Sartena cousins laughed at those photos, behind Yerwant's nouveau-riche back.)

Yerwant, meanwhile, is making careful plans. He wants to return in style. To sink back down, for a while, into the warm womb of his country, to enjoy the admiration, the esteem, and—why not?—the envy of those for whom he won't allow nostalgia. He hopes Italy won't enter the war. (In his heart of hearts, he's actually completely neutral.) He mistrusts the masses when they get worked up, animated by hazy nationalisms. He knows, and always has known, that every crowd can kill, that every crowd is looking for a sacrificial victim and has a taste for blood.

Yet when asked, he offers nothing but the blandest of opinions, always ready to change his mind, to agree with his interlocutor, to blend in, to disappear. Italy is the country that welcomed him, gave him success and respect, and his loyalty is beyond question. But with a peculiarly Eastern diffidence, Yerwant still feels himself a vassal— an Italian one now rather than an Ottoman one. And since a vassal has no rights that cannot be taken away, he is wise to avoid politics. He is free only within a narrow zone, whose borders are invisible but palpable: within them, such a man can exert his authority; beyond them, bets are off. For Yerwant, the zone is medicine, where everyone obeys him.

Elsewhere, he is careful to hide his weakness, which no one sees. He strives to give his children what seems to him the greatest gift: complete belonging to the new country, without the weight of memory, without the burden of nostalgia. In their place, strong maternal roots in a welcoming provincial setting: a tight-knit community, and the liquid speech of the Veneto region by which they all recognize one another—nobles, clergymen, officials, lawyers . . .

But the sons, the sons: When they have become men, to whom will they reveal their disquieting weaknesses, the strange attacks of kindness that will devastate them? That savage shyness before girls, and that inability ever to feel truly accepted?

IN MID-OCTOBER, Yerwant finally decides. He orders a red Isotta Fraschini, with his monogram in silver on the doors. Six seats, leather and velvet jump seats, curtains, a small icebox with miniature bottles of liquor and cut-crystal glasses, silver flatware, and a set of dishes bearing his initials. Well-concealed, a small strongbox encrusted with mother-of-pearl, with an English combination mechanism. (*During World War II, the elaborate key to that safe hung in the hallway with the blue silk walls, allusion and mysterious invitation to the automobiles walled away in the granary.*)

For the big family visit, Yerwant falls back on elaborate Eastern etiquette: to make a show is crucial; to go too far would be an egregious offense. Thus he orders a great number of small gold and silver objects from a superior London firm: cigar cutters, lighters, cigarette cases, mustache trimmers, all with geometric designs in green and gold enamel, for the men; for the ladies, enamel and gold compacts, little scissors in the shape of herons or cranes, evening bags and silver-plated vanity cases with semi-

precious stones as clasps (onyx, amber, chrysoprase, tour-
maline, lapis lazuli); brooches and small gold rings for
the children, with the word *Remember* or *Souvenir* in blue
enamel.

He orders many more gifts than he needs for the
family members Sempad has listed in his letters. Who
knows how many friends of his father or of his family
knew him in those distant, luminous years? Yerwant begins
thinking of his childhood again, thoughts that weaken
and perplex him. But at the same time, as the memories
and joys return, an ancient serenity returns, too, filling an
immense void that he is only now discovering.

In 1915, Yerwant enters his fiftieth year, and he is
satisfied—and alone. Slyly, randomly, his memories return,
crowd his mind, fluidly, never overly urgent, between one
appointment and the next, between one operation and the
next. "I'm now a citizen of Italy; the Ottomans can't
touch me anymore," he thinks. And, "Why not buy
myself a villa, near the Farm, near the falls?"

With that thought, he is filled with an infinite peace
and everything seems possible—that his wife might agree
to retire there with him, that his children might learn the
old language, that an Armenian nation might someday
exist . . . "Perhaps," reflects Yerwant, "the war itself will
provide the opportunity; the Germans will probably win,
and the Armenians are fighting vigorously, on the front
and in Parliament, in support of the government; our peo-

ple took part in the revolution along with the Unionists,* and Enver has personally thanked the patriarch for the Armenian nation's loyalty. And Talat, after all, plays backgammon with Zohrab."

A doctor friend of his, Aram Kardiashian, who also happens to be a distant cousin on his mother's side, has sent him a 1915 almanac from the capital, along with a very optimistic letter recounting the Armenians' enthusiastic rediscovery of themselves; the respect and friendship shown them by many Unionist leaders; the intellectual fervor of the poets, artists, and writers as they rediscover the ancient culture, explore the majestic language of their forefathers, publish, meet. "The old days of the Red Sultan are finished," writes Aram. "Finally we too will have a future. When the war is over, we will have won the right to be considered full citizens, both autonomous and loyal."

Yerwant's wariness recedes somewhat. He turns the pages of the almanac, smiles at the sketches of daily life as described by a perky young journalist. And though he is usually too busy to read anything beyond the news, he becomes immensely fond of a short poem, a sort of lullaby, called "Antasdan," or "The Blessing of the Fields of the Four Corners of the World." Written by a celebrated

* The members of the Union and Progress Party (Ittihad ve Terakki Cemiyeti)—called "Unionists" or "Ittihadists" (or simply "Young Turks")—took control of the Ottoman Empire in 1908, deposing the sultan. Enver Pasha, the minister of war, and Talat Pasha, the minister of the interior, were the primary architects of the Armenian exterminations.

poet, Daniel Varoujan, and dedicated to children, it is a song of peace and harmony that mysteriously seduces Yerwant's troubled heart. He cuts it out and folds it up and puts it in his wallet, like an prophecy or a promise:

> *In the regions of the East*
> *Let there be peace through the land . . .*
> *Let sweat instead of blood*
> *Flow through the veins of the fields,*
> *and whenever town bells ring,*
> *let there be songs of blessing.*

His granddaughter will find it there after his death, in May 1949.

AND THUS IT WAS THAT, between October 1914 and March 1915, the correspondence between the two brothers piled high; and thus it was that both of them, as though caught in an all-consuming vortex of mutual acknowledgment, gave too much rein to softhearted memories and too little to levelheaded knowledge of the times. Life had always smiled on Sempad's natural optimism; in those months literally everything gave him joy, and his bright round face glowed with satisfaction and expectation. At the pharmacy, the usual joking now sometimes centered on Yerwant, and on speculation regarding the impending meeting of the two sisters-in-law: the merry authoritarian Shushanig and Teresa, the little Italian countess who always wore purple.

The bets fly in the pharmacy, accompanied by the rhythmic clacking of backgammon dice. Armenag Mardirossian, Sempad's longtime dear friend, needles him: "What will those two ladies say to each other when they meet? And the countess, will she eat our food?"

"She'll spit it out, every bite," interjects Krikor—doctor, obstetrician, confidant—as he rolls a cigarette. "You'll have to call on my services, and they won't be free. Our food will make her ill, she'll get migraines, she'll look us up and down, she'll be too hot, and you can hardly have her sleep on the roof." (Everyone knows that on summer nights that's precisely what Sempad and Shushanig and everyone else does—and they don't limit themselves to sleeping, this serene, shameless couple.)

At the wicked comment about the roof, Sempad's heart skips a beat. But he recovers at once: "I've already drawn up plans at the Farm for an open balcony facing Falls Valley, and in the middle I'll make an English-style bow window, with stained glass with cast-iron frames. And I've even ordered the latest fans from France."

"But she'll be too hot just the same—care to bet?" laughs Krikor, rubbing his hands. They quickly agreed to a "nine-month" bet, amid much laughter: "At the end of September, when 'they' have gone back, you'll pay us all through the nose."

Sempad is too happy to be annoyed. "They" are his personal gilded icon, his connection to the twentieth century and to Progress. "I'll never see Paris, but I have an important brother," he thinks. And he begins, in the back of his mind, to savor the notion that his brother will reciprocate the invitation the following year, as his letters have suggested—and perhaps he will find the courage to accept. His eldest son, Suren, will be in Italy by then, as he will be studying, beginning in September 1915, at Moorat-Raphael, the Armenian boarding school in Venice, under his uncle's watchful eye.

Sempad chose Venice precisely because of its proximity to the city where Yerwant lives: he worries about this sad boy who follows him wherever he goes, asks the elders to recount the massacres of 1894–96, reads the papers, but isn't combative. Sempad would understand better, though he would also worry more, if Suren—like so many other youths in their city and district—aligned himself with a particular party, participated in the endless late-evening political discussions that drag on over countless cups of coffee, sweets, and alcohol. But Suren would rather stay home and read or, better still, follow his father around, as if he never tired of seeing him. "Or of judging me?" wonders Sempad, slightly discomfited by this focused attention, this childish behavior that gets in the way of his usual jokes and embarrasses him a little in front of his friends.

"I'm not going," Suren says one windy February day, as he rides with his father to the Farm. The work has begun, and Ohannes, his father's trusted expert, is supervising the construction of the elegant balcony and the bow window. The stained glass has arrived from England, featuring two full-length Romantic figures, a knight and his lady, along with charming designs of unfamiliar flowers—English morning glory and heather—for the small side windows.

"We've never seen such things," observes Ohannes proudly, and Sempad thinks that his wispy little sister-in-law could not help but feel at ease here.

"I can't go," Suren suddenly repeats, as if by way of explanation, yet explaining nothing.

"You don't want to go?" Sempad asks, a little annoyed, disturbed in his naïve contemplation of those unheard-of marvels that his labor and money have procured. He was just imagining the inaugural feast with the entire family, friends, dependents, distant relatives, even the less likable ones. Perhaps he'll even invite Khalil Effendi (the district governor, or *kaimakam*) and the chief of police (his customer and good friend, who sometimes comes to the pharmacy for a game—they always let him win).

Eventually, tearing himself away from his dreams and plans, Sempad takes Suren by the arm, affectionately, and sits down with him in a corner of the garden, where the tennis-lawn excavations are set to begin. They sit in two white wrought-iron armchairs that have seen better days. ("I should order some Vienna straw garden furniture," Sempad suddenly thinks.)

"Why did you say you're not going?" he asks, finally posing the question directly. At first Suren looks down, visibly paling. Then he slowly lifts his head and stares at his father with such searing pain in his tearful, ashamed eyes that his father turns away, feeling a sudden inner void, a cold interior space that expands frightfully.

There is neither panic in Suren's eyes nor rage—simply emptiness and pain. Sempad suffers for his son, and he suffers from not knowing, as one might before a thick veil that hides an unseen nightmare, the Beast of Beasts, the Apocalypse. This is the moment when his inner vision could come into focus, when he has the chance to grasp images of a real future. But his simple heart cannot bear ill omens, and he refuses to read what his mind's eye already sees, what his unwitting son is showing him.

Sempad rubs a hand over his eyes, a hand that is trembling a little, and he forgets. He looks at his son with eyes that are happy again, full of hope—and he forgets. Rising, taking Suren by the arm, he says, "Don't be scared. You'll see how beautiful Venice is, and your boarding school. And what's more, your uncle will invite you to lunch on Sundays." Suren looks at his father with gentle, loving eyes, and says nothing.

.   .   .

YERWANT WRITES FEVERISHLY, describes the automobile, the preparations, his sons, the gifts they are bringing. He is silent, however, when it comes to the sulking of his wife Teresa, whose migraines are flaring up prodigiously.

The date of departure is fixed for the end of May. Missing a few days of school will hurt neither the sixteen-year-old Yetwart, a brilliant, hardworking pupil at the Benedictine boarding school in Einsiedeln, in the Swiss canton of Schwyz, nor the lively and affectionate Khayël, who at eleven is a year ahead and also very bright, except on certain oppressive days when he is assailed by a precocious and irreversible melancholy—such days he spends alone, crying, ashamed of his weakness. They will depart with two drivers and an escort car laden with gifts, tires, and spare parts.

" 'We'll pass through Trieste' "—Sempad is reading the letter aloud to his friends—" 'and then proceed to Athens. Then Salonika, Kavala, Alexandroupolis, Constantinople . . . Why don't you come meet us there with Shushanig?' "

The listeners shudder at the idea that the encounter between the sisters-in-law might happen somewhere else. But Shushanig never goes anywhere; she reigns supreme at home, and she certainly wouldn't want to lose her advantage in this situation.

"I'll go with you to meet them," offers Veron, who has just come in. "We can take the train." Sempad, as a general enthusiast of modernity, embraces the idea at once: with the new railway one departs and arrives according to a schedule, one has a ticket stamped with times—not as in Yerwant's day, when trains left only when full. (According to family legend, Hamparzum entrusted his son to some bandits, to whom he gave, as payment, one half of a banknote. They received the other half "on proof of delivery," when Yerwant wrote his first letter home from Venice.) Further, the family considers trains a safe way of traveling, since many of the railway men are Armenian. Veron is already deciding what color hat to wear and choosing a matching veil.

The chief of police is also there that evening at the Pharmacie Hayastane, for one of his friendly games. Suddenly his thin voice rises amid the hubbub, and everyone listens: "That might not be a good time to travel north," he says calmly. Each man senses something like distant thunder, a nagging thought, perhaps, and later, back home, each will have a long discussion with his wife in the warm, secret conventicle of their bed, where everything beyond the covers seems both familiar and strange. As always, the talk will lead nowhere; instead of listening to the distant voices in their hearts, they will exorcise them with sweeping signs of the cross.

MEANWHILE, THE WAR is not going so well on the Eastern front. The frigid end of winter is shot through with whispers and strange proclamations; spring seems delayed.

But the cathedral's golden dome shines with new splendor. Armen and Hrayr Sarkissian, the carpenter twins, made a vow last year: they would repaint all the worn spots with fresh, shiny gold if their father, Haroutiun, wrote from America saying he had found work for them—the same work for both of them, as they insist on spending all their time together, which is why they married two sisters (one bossy, the other obedient).

Their father did write. And now people look up at them, perched high in their basket over one spot or another of that vast golden surface, and wonder whether they'll finish in time, given that their father has also sent their tickets for New York, leaving the first day of June. Three months are not much, and a vow is a vow: betting flourishes, especially since the twins must do it all themselves. Sempad, who has wagered a considerable sum in their favor, would gladly cheat by giving them a hand, but that wouldn't do: a vow is a vow. The twins accept only the substantial basket of food that Shushanig prepares; they find it in the quiet shade of the sexton's house when they come down for lunch. The sexton is named Garo, like Sempad's second son, and he is a simple man of God.

Indeed, he speaks with God every day and is surprised that others don't do the same. The green fields of heaven are as familiar to him as the green fields of earth. His protracted childhood plays as serenely up there as down here, and colored angels are always present. Garo sees colors coming through his angels—everyone knows this about him.

"A green one told me," he tells his public in all seriousness on a cool April afternoon, "that soon we'll all be playing with him, and that they are inventing special games just for us." His public is the usual threesome: the twins come down from their scaffolding, which is so close to the vault of heaven that they see angels, too, and little Garo, who has brought the lunch basket. He never doubts anything and loves all living creatures.

"What are the fragrances of heaven like?" Armen wonders. And Hrayr replies at once (the twins are perfectly self-sufficient in their never-ending dialogue): "Like the ones here, only more intense. And we'll no longer have any desire to go away."

"But why *are* you going away?" asks little Garo. "You won't find skies like these anywhere else."

Big Garo corrects him: "The skies are inhabited by angels everywhere, even on the other side of the world. They might just be different colors."

The debate on the color of American angels becomes animated. Each advances details in support of his own opinion, and time passes gaily. Then the twins go back to painting, and the sexton goes for a walk with little Garo. They have a secret destination, a gazebo built long ago by an emigrant on his return to the town. It's made entirely of carved wood, in the style of a Swiss chalet, and over-looks the falls.

A stone table in the shape of a large mushroom and two stone chairs in the shape of smaller mushrooms command the pair's full admiration, as they sit calmly together, hands on knees, in silence. Big Garo and little Garo would die for each other. They live in a suspended time all their own, amid colorful, tangible visions of bustling ranks of angels, which they can communicate to virtually no one.

Little Garo has round eyes and a big head topped with wild hair. He's affectionate with everyone, indiscriminately, and his big voice is surprising in such a small body. His poorly articulated speech conveys a sense of peace and thoughts of oblivion. All mothers entrust their babies to him. But his secret sorrow is that his own mother, Shushanig, hasn't fully trusted him since he lost his little sister Henriette in the market; she was found mysteriously asleep in one of shops owned by the Jewish jeweler, Elia Samuelson, a man unable to have children of his own.

No one knows how Henriette—who is three, wobbles when she walks, whines readily, and has a huge nose—wound up there. The shop was closed and the girl was sleeping peacefully inside. Samuelson, a man of culture, a learned man, carried her back to Sempad's house, weeping.

"She turned up in my closed shop. An angel of God brought her to me. If you were to leave her with me, I'd raise her respectably," he timidly whispers, as the little girl reaches toward him, smiling serenely. And then, his voice even lower, "You have seven, seven children, in these dangerous times. . . . I'd raise her as a Christian."

Shushanig, gasping, doesn't even reply. Sempad hears, in his simple heart, the rude tolling of another bell, and suddenly surprises himself by thinking, without knowing why, "I ought to let him." But this, too, he soon forgets.

HOLY SATURDAY. The patient trap, agleam with barbed wire and congealed blood, is about to be sprung. But life, impassive, continues on.

Djelal Djemin, the young officer who is courting Azniv, hasn't been seen for two weeks, and Azniv feels a little tightness in her heart. She has grown used to his solicitous, reticent presence, to the fire in those velvety eyes that followed her with respectful insistence. But she can hardly ask around, and her sister Veron is too busy getting ready for her trip to Constantinople to discuss it with her. On the other hand, Azniv doesn't really feel his absence so much as the slight sting of vanity. The officer would be a fine catch for any girl—imagine for an Armenian.

As Azniv's thoughts wander, she hums a tune and helps old Serpuhi roll the dough for the *paklava*. She's good at this; her sister lacks the patience, though no one has her touch when it comes to measuring out the filling for *bereks*.

In the Armenian quarter of the little city, joy spreads from house to house with the approach of Easter, the biggest feast day of the year. On every table the ranks of hard-boiled eggs increase: they are colored with herbs, then painted patiently by hand, in the evening, when the children aren't around to see. The *shakar-lokma*, with its intense, crumbly flavor of almonds and butter, is boxed and ready to eat.

From house to house dash the girls in their fresh aprons, to borrow or return a little sugar or salt, some flour, some Smyrna grapes or almond water; from house to house children chase one another, excited swarms of them appearing here and there, pecking away at small leftovers—dough trimmings, cookies that didn't turn out.

The adults are ostensibly fasting for Lent, which the women strictly observe. A few strong souls, like Krikor the doctor, make a show of ordering meat sauce on Good Friday, or a nice pair of roast pigeons—a small sin, which God barely notices, and which Krikor shrewdly performs in order to buttress his Westernizing image and his less-than-recent degree from Berlin.

Hamparzum's large house is now divided in two,

with Sempad's family on one side and the widow Nevart and her daughters Azniv and Veron on the other—though they share a yard, and the communicating door between the two kitchens is always open. Behind the house, full of evening whispers and the eager calm that precedes a feast day, stretch the extensive gardens: vegetables, fruit trees, flowers.

The vegetable plot is oddly restricted to a ribbon of bare earth in the back, running along the high boundary wall, which is clearly visible from every room of the house: a mighty wall, much older than the house, it sternly encloses and protects the grounds. Rows of fruit trees—espaliered apples, peaches, and pears—alternate with tall plane trees and climbing roses imported thirty years ago from England, which interlace to form an elegant promenade leading to a round pergola, a masterpiece of vegetal engineering by Nerses the gardener. Not a single ray of sun filters through that perfumed vault, from which hang large blood-red roses that bloom only at this time of year, in late April.

The trees of the pergola hide several meters of the wall from view, and there, protected and partially concealed by the tumbling vegetation, is a small door that exits directly onto the Street of the Holy Apostles, a narrow alley flanking the cathedral.

In the faint, restful melancholy of a spring evening, as children flit about like swallows and shouts and shrieks bounce up and down and up again, Azniv sits on the wooden bench in the back of the pergola with a French novel—a rather risqué story that all the girls are passing around. They read it with passionate innocence and torment themselves with the cruel tale of Parisian love.

But Azniv is distracted this evening. She wears no flower in her hair, and her damp palms smell of cinnamon and walnuts. Suddenly she hears a voice from over the wall, calling her urgently, speaking quickly: "Miss Azniv, I know you're there. I saw you. I beg you, please, let me in for a minute. Hear me out." All her day's restiveness coalesces into a single quick motion. She knows it's the Turkish officer and—against all rules—runs to the door, pushes the tumbling rosebush aside, and opens it. (The key is always in the lock, for anyone rushing to mass, anyone running late, anyone needing to escape the sharp eyes of Shushanig and Nevart.)

He hurries in, a little furtively, as though not wanting to be seen by someone outside. Then he clasps her hand and solemnly kneels: "I beg you, Miss Azniv, please, don't be upset, don't be afraid. Hear me out."

Azniv isn't afraid. Tomorrow is Easter, and she's at home in the enchanted realm of her garden, beneath the green dome and the perfumed roses. The young man seems to her to have entered her private dream; it seems natural that he should kneel. She sits back down on the bench, delicately abandoning her hands to his nervous grip. She's expecting a great romantic moment—everyone deserves at least one in their lives; they're useful in the dark times, for reheating memories.

Yet Djelal continues squeezing her hands and repeating, "Hear me out, don't be afraid." Azniv is not afraid, but she is starting to become annoyed. Why does he not explain himself? Why has he come?

"Please, my rose of May," the young man finally begins, "hear me out, listen to my plan. Come away with me, at once. I promise not to have any other wives, and I won't insist that you convert. We'll go to Europe together, I'll get a job, we'll live in Paris . . ."

Azniv does not understand. She only recently learned this man's name, her curious friends having discovered it, and she has received a few of his flowery letters; she has never spoken to him, and he has never attempted to speak to her, much less declared his love. Nor does he do so now, as if some unknown urgency were pushing him beyond that, as if everything were already understood between them.

Azniv is speechless, forced by surprise into unwilling silence. The more worried he seems, kneeling uncomfortably on the fine gravel, the less she understands, nor do the young man's speeches shed any light: "I don't want you to suffer, my rose of May, my little princess. I'll save you. We'll go to Paris, to London, to Vienna—wherever you want. I'll get a job. . . ."

These sentences stick like a refrain in Azniv's mind, plunging her into a bewildered torpor. For long, long minutes, the young man keeps on speaking, until Azniv suddenly snaps out of it and blurts a shrill "Why?" that startles him.

Meanwhile, evening has fallen, the children have disappeared. The sky is purple and black; lightning flashes in the distance. "Why are you saying these things?" she repeats. "We don't even know each other."

"Because I want to save you," he blurts, before looking around furtively. "You, my dear girl, you must believe me. I can, I must save you. Come away with me, at once. I'll desert the army. I have two fast horses." And kneeling even farther down, he presses her hands into his face and kisses her knees.

A shudder of despair rocks her to the core, and suddenly Azniv grasps the danger, the looming horror, and her youthful blood surges with luxurious hope. A blind instinct pushes her to leave that place, where the roses now seem to smell of death and the garden wall hides unknown tombs. She stands, and so he stands with her, having grasped nothing, and pulls her to him for a kiss. The kiss barely grazes her, but it echoes darkly within her: shame, dishonor, madness, in her own father's house . . .

Azniv clasps her arms across her chest, blushes, and with the same rapidity with which she opened the door to let him in, she opens it again and pushes him out, with silent fury. Her body has shown her what her mind has not yet come to grips with: the ever-reddening sea of difference between them, with her on one shore and him on the other, the sea that divides their peoples.

"I beg you, think it over; I'll come back tomorrow," he somehow manages to whisper, breathlessly, from behind the door, but Azniv goes on crying disconsolately, rubbing her burning cheeks. Before this evening, she was dreaming, a child among children. Now she has become a woman.

But when she goes back inside the darkened house, she quickly climbs the stairs and hurries to the mirror. She moistens her lashes and eyebrows with saliva, wraps her face with a veil of red gauze, leaving only her eyes uncovered, and gazes at herself admiringly.

In the words of the popular song, "Here comes the proud-eyed daughter of Armenia." Her thick, heavy eyebrows nearly meet above her strong, straight nose. Beneath them, her eyes are beautiful, unnaturally bright, excited by her adventure. She's dying to tell someone. Not Veron; perhaps Sempad? Her older brother has authority but doesn't use it, and he has a soft spot for her. "Yes, that's what I'll do," she decides. Then, succumbing to a wave of drowsiness, she goes to bed with a happy sigh, having had her first kiss. She sleeps calm and contented through the poisonous night.

The next day is Easter. Azniv, who has already forgiven herself for her near sin (merely an imprudence, she tells herself), feels a little nervous, a little guilty, especially because he said he would return this evening. But she is soon caught up in a thousand pleasant holiday tasks, and she forgets.

In any case, she has had no chance to speak to Sempad, who left early in the morning, on horseback, for the Farm, to make sure everything there was ready for Easter dinner. The main room on the ground floor has just been redecorated for the occasion, with garlands of flowers, round putti, and fruit baskets, by Melkon the ikon painter, who claims to have learned his trade in Paris. (*The blood sprayed across those putti will resemble happy nuptial festoons, and someone will try to erase the pink clouds, above, with broad strokes of charcoal.*)

The Day of Resurrection begins beautifully. Ismene is, as always, the first to arrive, carrying a basket of fresh lettuce on which rest the consecrated eggs. She also brings a loaf of bread, blessed by the Greek priest, Elias Isaac Christoyannis. Sadly, Isaac doesn't have many followers in this little city, and he always goes about in a stained blue cassock, wearing what little hair he has pulled tightly back into a pigtail.

Isaac's wife, Katerina, is a day seamstress, and his only son died of pneumonia two years ago, despite the medicine and aid lavished on him by Sempad. But neither Isaac nor Katerina (nor Ismene) ever forgot the care the boy received, or how little Garo held his hand throughout his entire final night, not sleeping, staring at him.

"Christ is risen. May you be blessed!" Ismene says.

"Yes, he's risen!" replies Azniv brightly, opening the door for them. She then turns her attention to her coiffure, humming *"Ov sirun sirun"* with her mouth full of hairpins.

But instead of lingering for the usual small talk ("How did you sleep, my rosebud?" or "May the pillow you lay your head on tell me your thoughts"), Ismene leaves her basket in the kitchen, brusquely greets Nevart, who's watching her from the front window, and then runs to her beloved Shushanig. Her head is full of thoughts of death, and she feels blasphemous on this morning of the Resurrection: "Christ, O dead Christ, how will you rise this year?" This question shoots through her mind, to the tune of one of her lamentation melodies, like a wrathful profanity.

Ismene doesn't know much, but she perceives thoughts. Yesterday, as she was arranging the garments of the *kaimakam*'s aunt, recently dead of old age, and braiding her sparse hair and praying to the Virgin on her behalf (under her breath—what harm could it do?), the *kaimakam* himself stopped by to view the body. His opaque eyes said nothing, but Ismene could hear his thoughts. *Death, death in the making; loot, loot for the taking.* But for whom, by whom? There are many kinds of people in the little city. Ismene needs to consult the calm wisdom of Shushanig, who always knows what to tell her, who clears the fog from around her head.

"Ah, Shushanig, if you were truly wise . . ." But

Shushanig's mind in focused on the Easter feast, and besides she knows that Ismene hears thoughts, having comforted her countless times. That's what she does this time, too, and to cheer her up she invites her to the feast, along with Father Isaac and his sad-eyed wife ("but make him change his cassock, please; important people will be there, don't let him cut a poor figure").

Recalled to a more feminine and familiar task, Ismene forgets. And the day will be a completely happy one: she'll be treated as an equal, gathered into the warm embrace of that big family, taking her place among them, helping compose something like a gilded triptych, with customers and friends garnishing the side panels, all of them framed in a sacred order so ancient that nothing, it seems, could ever sunder it.

THE AFTERNOON LIFTS Veron's spirits. After attending her Anglican service by herself, as usual, she goes to meet the others at the Farm. Krikor the doctor, who has long courted her, gives her a ride in his cabriolet.

Arriving thus—like a lady, in a new hat with a purple veil and a man who bows when proffering his arm to help her down—smooths her knitted brow, and as she watches her sister's mood worsen over the course of the afternoon, her own barometer rises even farther. She has no idea what's troubling Azniv, who never tells her anything, never gives her the respect due an older sister, and is prettier to boot. But something has happened, and Veron would like to be able to advise her.

Suddenly Azniv asks Ohannes whether he can give her a ride back to the city. But this thought saddens Sempad, even though she has an excuse at the ready, and he says he still needs Ohannes. The French violinist, Gerard, has arrived and will present a few Romantic pieces, taking turns with Hrant Agopian, a shepherd and a virtuoso of the *duduk*. Someone must offer afternoon refreshments and tea for the ladies, along with the pastries from the Confiserie Viennoise, which, a couple of years ago, introduced the locals to the delights of Western confectionery; Ohannes must therefore make Azniv wait for an hour or so. Usually so quick to stand up for herself, this time she says nothing.

Nor does she join the musicians, as she usually does, or dance, or offer to sing, in her robust, melodious contralto, any of the many songs that inspire joy and the desire to dance. She remains seated, as if a little cold, watching the setting sun, saying nothing. Her round, expressive face is blank; the music slips over her, shutting her in.

Azniv seems elsewhere, and her posture suggests fatigue, but in her feverish heart she repeats, "I wonder if he'll come today. I did everything I could; perhaps it's better like this. But would he really marry me, and not make me convert, and take me to Europe? And what if *he* were to convert? That would be the last impediment." Azniv can already imagine herself as an important lady, the one who converted an officer, in Armenian (or progressive Turkish) circles in London or Paris.

She never considered leaving before; she's a calm girl, she likes everybody. But this would indeed be a valid reason—she's not naïve enough to think that life would be easy for a mixed couple in the Ottoman Empire. It might well be the first case where it isn't the Turkish man who carries off the Christian girl to add her to his harem, but rather the Armenian virgin (she smiles to herself) who is so strong and beautiful that the Turkish man cannot escape her.

Her mind is full of vague images drawn from the terrible stories she has heard so often, from warnings, from the ever-present atmosphere of attention and nervous vigilance surrounding girls in the bloom of youth. And of a mild anxiety, like the feeling that everything before her was a dream. And then there's the joke of falling in love, when you're still aware of a person's defects but they don't seem to matter anymore, and languor pervades you.

Returning to town no longer seems so urgent. Azniv is now convinced that if he comes back to the door this afternoon and doesn't find her waiting, he'll certainly try again. How could he not, after yesterday's impassioned love scene?

Indeed, Djelal has already come back, and he knocked in vain at the little garden door. No one saw him, except Nazim, the gimpy Turkish beggar, who during the Easter holidays visits the houses of all the Armenians, filling his pockets with better-than-usual tidbits and alms.

Nevart treats him well, and Shushanig, too, but today they are all gone. He doesn't know that they are celebrating Easter at the Farm; he thinks they must be at a neighbor's house, exchanging greetings, and so he waits, in the nook by the main gate. He sees Djelal arrive furtively, hears him call Azniv with supplicating and then brusque tones, tender and then vehement. Djelal spends half an hour knocking, and as Nazim listens, silent and flat against the wall, he comes to understand much more than is said. Speaking doesn't do a beggar much good, but he might get rich on silence. Every crumb may prove useful.

Thus, when Azniv returns, Djelal has already left, as has Nazim, who, brimming with news, continues on his rounds. In vain Azniv sits, novel in hand, beneath the rosebushes, in the same spot as yesterday; in vain she tries to convince herself that it's better this way, and that in any case he'll come back tomorrow, especially as he knows today is Easter. A wordless dismay, a nameless fear snakes through the garden and wraps itself around her simple heart. She is unable to read, and so she waits for nightfall, nostalgic for lost opportunities—an acute nostalgia, and yet so familiar to a woman's heart.

.   .   .

A FEW DAYS LATER: early morning, April 24. A letter has arrived from Yerwant, and Levon Yakovlian, the inspector-postman, has rushed it to Sempad. Yerwant's plans are growing: he has now decided to get a piano, a Heitzmann baby grand trimmed with mahogany and gilded bronze, for the parlor at the Farm. He approves, he writes, of all of Sempad's renovation plans: the bow window with the stained glass, the tennis lawn, and the Viennese garden furniture. He is adding the piano for family evenings, so that his sisters will have something to remember him by. He likes to monogram things, so he is having their monograms put on the lid in silver.

Yerwant has thought of everything. Since Austria-Hungary is allied with the Empire in the war, he has chosen a Viennese instrument, avoiding potential snags. The piano will be shipped directly by the factory, which will send a telegram to Sempad to make sure everything's ready at the Farm. And it will come with a chaperone, a technician who will set it up and remain there until Yerwant arrives and sees it all for himself; only then will payment be made. Will Sempad promise this Austrian his hospitality?

Sempad certainly will. He can't wait. Overjoyed, he runs off to read the letter to Krikor, his wary friend, the doctor people trust precisely because he doesn't take anyone too seriously and doesn't mince words, so that in his care illness seems slighter. In his consulting room, which smells of tobacco and sundry humanity, Krikor smiles indulgently at his friend. More than wary or ironic, he is wise, with that particular Eastern wisdom possessed only by Easterners who have studied in Europe, and he understands Yerwant.

His degree from Berlin was well deserved. He was asked to stay on, make his career there. But Krikor had an elderly mother and three sisters who were not yet married, and he was acutely shy. So he came back to the little city, and now he treats everyone, impartially, skeptically. He subscribes to many journals, and he would lay down his life for Sempad, whose lighthearted tenderness he loves.

"Look at the postscript," he barks as he finishes the letter. "Maybe your countess sister-in-law is no longer coming."

Sempad's heart leaps as he reads: "My dearest brother, I think I'd like to buy a villa near the Farm, or have one built. You and Ohannes could oversee the construction. . . . "

For many years Yerwant will remember those sentences, with secret tears and a slow, slow prayer: "I never built that house in my lost fatherland. . . . Thus I beg of you, Lord God of my fathers, give it to me in the ancient heavenly fatherland. . . . " And in his old age, he will suffer acutely from private, unsharable nostalgia, deprived of loving colloquy with any of his nieces or nephews, his sweet mother tongue constricted within him, as if dying—rich, and guilty for having survived.

. . .

But Sempad is simply happy. He quickly takes his leave from Krikor, runs outside to his gig. He sends Veron to take his place in the pharmacy, too excited not to leave at once to see (though he knows the place like the back of his hand) where Yerwant's villa might be erected. He has already picked the spot. It will be entirely new; there are several old buildings near the Farm, but none seems worthy of his brother.

He's thinking of a piece of land not far away, a small plateau above ancient caves, where old women gather dill and valerian. The plateau breaks off at a certain point and slopes sharply toward the falls. They could build a summer pavilion down below, like the one at Marienbad of which he has seen an illustration—all white wrought iron. And a balcony along the front, covered with thick wisteria, purple and white.

The house will be set farther back, facing the view of the falls with the rear of the house toward the road, in the modern style, a suitable distance from the great plane tree that will shade the lawn.

The Tree of Knights, it's called, because an Armenian prince used to hold summer court in its shade, already vast in those bygone days, and it was there that he received and fed a group of knights-errant, crusaders who had lost their way, for whom hospitable Anatolia, with its small courts rich in flowing water and lovely maidens, proved more pleasing than their gloomy, distant northern lands.

They were smitten with the sun of that blessed land and with the chance to make their fortunes. They forgot their wives and their cold little fiefdoms back in Champagne and Normandy and remained here—their graves are here, and their descendants.

Every so often the women emerge from the caves with a bone or some other object: a stone bauble, a metal stud. Nothing valuable—the tombs have been thoroughly plundered—but Krikor is fond of such relics, and is willing to pay for them. The women who gather herbs and the children who play here have spread the word.

Sempad races along in his gig. He loves horses, and riding transforms him. His face becomes resolute and confident, his shoulders stiffen proudly, evoking earlier days. Seeing him hurtle past over the cobblestones in front of the prefecture, the *kaimakam*, sitting on his balcony and smoking his after-coffee cigar, mutters to himself, "What gall! He acts like he runs this town. But all that will soon come to an end."

ALL THAT IS ALREADY coming to an end. Private conversations are taking place in Constantinople between Talat, Enver, the chief of police, a select group of party faithful, and those in charge of the Special Organization. Not all the members of the Union and Progress Party are in on the plan, and in any case only the most zealous have been invited, among whom are a pair of high-level bureaucrats. Present, too, is Colonel Hauptmann, of the allied German forces.

The disarming of Armenian soldiers has been completed, as has the roundup of Armenian officers. The soldiers have been eliminated, and care has been taken so that the officers will not suspect.

"The internal passport, the *teskere*, has already been revoked for many, but we must proceed with a certain caution," says Selim Effendi, a graduate of the Sorbonne and chief secretary of the Interior Ministry.

"Today"—now Talat is speaking—"today is the day, here in the capital. The Easter celebrations have weakened and distracted them. This evening you'll take them from their houses, from hospitals, from newsrooms. You'll destroy printing presses, demolish the editorial offices of magazines and publishing houses. Every non-Armenian employee must be severely threatened and sent home. If they can keep their mouths shut, they'll get a medal from the government.

"Instead of prisons, use barracks. Allow no visitors, confiscate books, and above all do not reply, ever, to any of their questions.

"Take only the men. Don't touch the women."

Enver, who has been nodding gravely throughout, suddenly lifts his head, surprised. "There will be time for them," Talat adds, smiling thinly. "There are all the women of the Seven Provinces. As for the ones from Constantinople, these libertine giaours who frequent the embassies and even write for the newspapers, for now we must tread lightly. Their men are being arrested for conspiracy against the state, not for being Armenian."

"And Zohrab—what about him?" asks Enver, reserving a note of irony for Talat's famous Armenian friend.

"I'll see him today, in fact, at four: it's our backgammon day. He's always right on time, a real gentleman, with a fine head for politics and poetry. We'll leave him alone—don't lay a finger on him. But if he looks for me, assure him that you will relay his messages, let him write them down. Then throw them away in such a way that he realizes what you're doing."

Now it is Enver who smiles, amazed. He had not thought in such refined terms.

CONSTANTINOPLE, the evening of April 24, 1915. The great roundup begins. In front of his children and his pregnant wife, Maria, the poet Daniel Varoujan puts on a brave face: "It's a security measure. There's a war on. International attention is focused on us, they can no longer repeat the horrors of the Red Sultan years." (But a black wing, in the corner of an eye, troubles his vision, and a deep shudder shakes him.)

Maria throws together a bag for him, stashing a loaf

of bread, a spoon, and a jar of marmalade beneath some clothes. "He won't be needing that," says the officer in charge. "This will take very little time."

Daniel finds the well-mannered voice suddenly jarring, and looking the man in the eye he sees death. He hugs Maria, calmly and coolly, as if it were just another parting, and on the way out grabs a book, a pen, and the notebook with the poem he was working on. "I'll have some spare hours, I'll bet; I'll take 'The Song of Bread' with me. If you see Alexei, tell him about it." (He hopes Maria will gather from these words that she should go to Alexei Semyonovich Burkin—an official in the Imperial Russian Embassy who is also a poet and a contributor to his journal—to seek asylum, if it comes to that. In reality, the two men have recently been arguing, something to do with poetic fashions, though Daniel no longer understands what. It seems a foreign language to him.)

Maria stares at him, annoyed. She's tired, her third pregnancy is suddenly weighing upon her, and she seems to be bearing the burden of it alone. Why is he going off so docilely, she wonders. Then she feels the absence of his body beside her, and just like that he's already gone, and the air is so heavy, and no longer has any fragrance to it. It never will again.

IN THE LITTLE CITY, Djelal is running madly about. He knows, and he wants to save Azniv, whatever the cost.

He'll go back this afternoon, he'll take her away with him, one way or another. But how to persuade her, unless with force? (He doesn't know her thoughts.)

Djelal has no desire to save her family. Only Azniv interests him, and saving her would release him from the horrific task that awaits him. Djelal is not just any officer; he's young, he has enthusiastically embraced Union and Progress Party plans to reinvent Turkey, to get rid of the sultan, to modernize. Implicit in the notion of modernizing Turkey is the axiom "Turkey for the Turks." These inferior peoples, who are always conspiring with the Western enemy and helping to break up the Empire, they must be eliminated. Out with them, out with Armenians, Greeks, Assyrians, Syrians—riffraff. Each country to its own people, as in the European wars for independence. Greece is for the Greeks; why shouldn't Turkey be only for the Turks?

Djelal's head is full of these ideas, and it doesn't occur to him that the Armenians and the others have lived on Anatolian soil for millennia, working it and rendering it fertile, that this is also the homeland of their dreams— they have no other. And being a gentle, daydreaming people, and since it is a large, generous land, they would gladly share it (that was the poet's message, in the poem Yerwant kept in his wallet).

But Azniv, Azniv—she's the woman for him. Djelal happened to see her, as he rode by on his horse, dancing in a fruit orchard at an outdoor festival, and her grace captured him forever. For her, he rediscovered his people's flowery love poetry, defied his friends' gentle mockery, and contented himself for months with dreaming of her and following her. Now he has chosen to confide in his best friend, Dedyaev, to whom he feverishly lays out his desperate plan.

Dedyaev is of Russian origin, the grandson of a Cossack who many years ago left the black soil of the Ukraine, converted to Islam, and made a life for himself here. He is an officer like Djelal, lives a comfortable life, and is tolerant and idealistic by nature. It was he who accompanied Djelal to Hamparzum's funeral, and he has always thought of Djelal's infatuation as a game, only faintly romantic, to stave off boredom in the provinces.

Now he discovers a Djelal who is furious and—how to put it?—impassioned and offended at once, his veneer of respectful courtship crumbling further with each word as his predatory instincts get the upper hand. Just the other day (the memory is vivid in Azniv's mind) he was on his knees; now he wants to carry her away no matter what, by force if need be. The fact that she let him through the door means she has chosen him as well, and thus it would be not violence but persuasion to push aside her scruples. Because there's no time left. And they will have to leave the country: he knows she will never be the sort of wife one can veil and keep hidden; she must be on display, like a precious forbidden fruit.

Dedyaev is amused. Without fully understanding the urgency, he pledges his support, even going so far as to promise his father's carriage and horses. He advises immediate flight, away from the theater of war that is coming perilously near, and a quick embarkation from Smyrna. Dedyaev is not a member of the party and has heard nothing but a few whispers about the Armenian project. (Pan-Turkist theories, as Djelal knows, have no resonance for him.) But he's young and adventurous and likes the idea of saving this girl. And as it happens, he knows someone in Smyrna, a friend of a Greek captain who runs contraband, and for a hefty sum . . . which, no problem, he'll provide himself. Anything to put one over on that lazy, dull-witted *kaimakam*, on one hand, and on Azniv's family, so pious and powerful, on the other. And what about that doctor who's turned Italian, who's coming with a sports car and a piano? (Rumors travel fast—poor Yerwant.) "Another Paris-Peking race," snorts Dedyaev, "this one stopping in the middle of Anatolia, among the village chickens and goats."

But in these very moments the *kaimakam* is acting. Around midday, Nazim the beggar dropped by; Nazim always supplements his income with a little well-paid spying. He knows all the Armenians, and it's thanks to him that their every move is noted and reported. They all speak freely in his presence; he's like a piece of furniture: quiet, obsequious, always there. Ismene is the only one who doesn't like him, because he never does anything for the family. "You take their money, no? But you don't do them any favors in return."

But Sempad says the poor are blessed by God. "And who would we be if in our charity we distinguished between Christians and Muslims? Besides, this is the twentieth century; even religion is modernizing."

Sempad chuckles into his mustache. He enjoys mildly scandalizing the women and doesn't notice Nazim, off to one side, spit in disgust.

"OFFICER DJELAL IS IN LOVE with the pharmacist's sister. He wants to marry her, and convert," Nazim whispers. It's a tasty piece of news, and truly strange: an officer might carry a girl off, might sneak her into his home, might even marry her—but convert! Unheard of. And in these times, no less.

The *kaimakam* nonetheless thinks it prudent to proceed with caution. Nazim is canny and clever, but this is not a case of shaking down the usual Armenians; these men are Turks, army officers, and he doesn't want to act alone on this matter. He'll hand it off to the bellicose Colonel Hikmet, who is champing at the bit here in the middle of nowhere; he'll tell him that Djelal has compromised a Kurdish girl, that her relatives are looking for him, and that Dedyaev helped him. The colonel, who is old-school and has an aversion to the party bosses, will jump at the chance. And Dedyaev, besides, is a pain-in-the-neck atheist.

Djelal and his sidekick Dedyaev receive a dispatch instructing them to be on the road to Damascus within two hours. They're being sent to the front, orders of Djemal Pasha, the third man in the triumvirate of power along with Enver and Talat. And there's no getting out of it, because a group of soldiers commanded by an under-officer has come to keep an eye on them while the colonel is away.

Djelal, stunned, despairs. Dedyaev smiles and bows, already wondering how he'll tell his father, how to play the game. But as it turns out, there's barely time to call his orderly, pack his things, and hug his mother.

The first night they sleep on the road. Djelal seems dazed, and Dedyaev romantically imagines galloping back the way they came, in the night, trying to get the pharmacist to let them in, and deserting along with his friend. What if they all went to America? Perhaps they would find another girl there, for him.

But when they reach their destination, Djelal suddenly flexes his hands, tired from the ride, and says, "I'm hungry—you?" Dedyaev stares at him, speechless, and Djelal adds, "It was a nutty idea anyway, don't you think? They say Damascus is a fine city, full of temptations."

Dedyaev claps Djelal on the shoulder, as though relieved of a burden, and they enter the caravansary together.

AZNIV KNOWS NOTHING of all this. Days pass, and Djelal never reappears. Everyone has noticed that Azniv
spends every evening beneath the pergola, and that she has
become nervous, always listening, as if to a faraway voice.
Veron thinks she's a little envious of her Constantinople
trip; Azniv lets her think that. A feeling of growing
doubt, of dull, nameless anguish, gnaws her from within.

And yet, she's telling herself, it's better this way—
what madness it would have been! And besides, would I
really have run off with a man, me, Azniv? Would I have
deceived and offended Sempad and the rest, my whole
family, the Armenian community, making us all laughing-
stocks? Certainly not. Still, I would have liked to tell him
no in person, weeping, so that he might admire my little
theater. (Or else, or else: What if he really did convert? As
modern people can actually do?)

The month of May peaks, on the second Sunday,
with the spectacular Flowers to the Virgin ceremony. All
the Armenian girls in their Sunday best carry bunches of
roses to the cathedral to deck the altars, and then, with
brimming baskets of plucked petals, they form two lines
and cover the road down which the procession will pass.

But this year there's something new. The colonel of
the regiment stationed in the little city (the man who sent
Djelal away) received a mysterious phone call from his
cousin, an attaché at the Foreign Ministry, informing him

of an urgent personal dispatch (not a telegram, which too many people can read). The cousin explains that something is in the works regarding the Armenians. From one day to the next, their spokesmen, the most important members of their community in Constantinople, their doctors and teachers and journalists, have all disappeared; the newspapers are silent, and the whereabouts of the Armenian delegates are unknown. The patriarch is nowhere to be seen, and many diplomats are cautiously looking into the matter.

"If you know any well-off Armenians you care about, warn them of the danger," the cousin advises. "You can charge a lot for a protection, a safe-conduct." That has always been the custom in this country, when the massacres start.

The colonel, in fact, calls Sempad, warns him. So does the chief of police, to whom Sempad lent a considerable sum so that he could afford lavish, decorous weddings for his two daughters, Zinaida and Zelmira. It's May 10: Sempad has received another letter from Yerwant, fixing their rendezvous in the capital for June 10, at the famous Pera Palas in the Galata District, the new hotel popular with the international beau monde.

And it seems to him that his Italian brother constitutes a powerful defense all by himself; but perhaps, as a show of deference to the police chief and the colonel, it would be wise to promise handsome sums for protection and, perhaps, to call off the procession of the Virgin,

especially as Ohannes has reported some suspicious movements among the Kurdish tribes who live in the mountains beyond the Farm, and it's never a good idea to let
them see your daughters.

Sempad consults with Monsignor Kuyumdjan and
with other community leaders. They are all well aware
that canceling the outdoor procession (the second biggest
spring outing after Easter; many matches are made on
such occasions) will give rise to anxiety and annoyance.
The women and elders will start to whisper, quickly leading to general panic, which hotheads and fools can handle
in a variety of clumsy ways.

For these reasons, in the end, they will hold the procession, and beneath the innocent sun, in the splendid
glow of a perfectly luminous day, those bodies and those
faces will dance harmoniously one last time, those living
corollas will pulse, light with their usual joy and expectation. Toward evening, however, from the direction of the
falls, a torrential downpour will approach: the tears of
their grieving angels.

IN THEIR SUMMERHOUSE IN DOLO, Yerwant has metic-
ulously gathered everything that could be useful for the
trip: maps, binoculars, sunglasses, duster coats that match
the car's exterior, galoshes, torches of all kinds, flasks, a
well-appointed mini-pharmacy (replete with serums and

syringes, boilers, purifiers, and filters), boots, spats . . . He even had two pairs of damask spats made, a folly he has secreted away in the false bottom of his monogrammed medical bag, along with Austrian talers, gold coins bearing Queen Victoria and the kaiser, and some loose gems.

The drivers he has chosen are both experts—one went to Russia (and back) with the Demidoffs. The three men deliberate with great seriousness over spare parts, gasoline, fuel tanks, pumps, cranks, and every other instrument that a mechanic's imagination can devise. But Yerwant is also counting heavily on his own knowledge of the countries and languages, which, along with his good stock of money and sangfroid, ought to be sufficient to avoid serious trouble.

He neither asks advice of nor gives advice to his sons, whom he thinks of as cargo (precious cargo) that can't possibly be of any assistance, delicate little gents in the mold of their mother the countess. There is currently a stalemate: she has mobilized all her relatives to block this pernicious journey; he has told her sharply that in that case he and the boys will go without her. Now she's wringing her hands. She loves them all, truly she does. She loves her exotic, virile husband, she loves her sons . . .

The sons remain silent. Indeed, the truth is that, as staunch interventionists—one because he's a boy and shares the bellicose, patriotic dreams of his teachers and friends; the other out of simple, childish bluster and a contrarian spirit—they don't seriously believe that their father can actually win the race against time that he has unknowingly begun.

The boys believe with every fiber that Italy is about to enter the war, and they monitor with a kind of pity their father's increasing absorption in a return to his roots, to an obscure past of which they remain slightly embarrassed, to that article-free speech that renders him instantly foreign, even to inexpert or benevolent ears. Will Yerwant manage to depart before the borders with Austria-Hungary are closed? How can he possibly think so, wonder the two boys, cross because they, too, are required attend the preparatory sessions. And how can he think of dragging our delicate, sensitive mother through lion country?

Yerwant neither hears nor sees. He writes continually to Sempad but doesn't mention to Teresa or the boys his plan to buy a house. He'll make a down payment there, he decides, then send the rest of the money from Italy.

For the rest of his life, Yerwant will recall those months as the pinnacle of his existence, as absolute happiness: the joy of being able to allow himself a perfect arrangement; the prospect of finally relaxing, unthreatened; the taste of July grapes; the blurred, distant, beautiful face of his mother, Iskuhi. To be able to plunge again into the falls, to purify himself at last, and to reemerge. A rebirth.

His every muscle goes slack, as all his long struggles

dissolve into a newfound peace. He has arrived, and this is his reward. The sleepless nights, the dogged study in Padua and Paris, the months of eating dried apricots and poor man's soup, the cholera victims, the worry over his first patients, the children's clinic in Venice, the consumptives on the Lido . . . Scalpel always in hand: neat, efficient, commanding. All of it swirls in his heart and is finally becalmed.

He suddenly recalls the pergola in the garden, the perfume of dangling roses, and the month of April, and the procession of girls in May. He was thirteen when he left. He wonders what Madame Nevart looks like today, she to whom he owes his flight—and everything that followed from it. He finally feels ready to forgive her.

Things have gone so well. And besides, Iskuhi and Hamparzum have now been reunited—in heaven, thinks Yerwant, who feels religion in a fairly simple way, as a return home, to a place where no one persecutes Armenians, where eight-year-olds don't lose their mothers. And now: the little city, the falls, and Sempad—how will he bear such happiness?

It's SUNDAY AFTERNOON, May 23, at the summerhouse in Dolo. The headlines leave no room for doubt. In the cool billiard room, the table still covered for winter, Yetwart and Khayël consult feverishly. Their father isn't likely to stumble on them here; he has gone out to the Caffè

Commercio, his usual Sunday spot, to field the tributes and requests of the villagers. Weeks have passed since his last visit, and he thought it would be good to stop in prior to his departure.

Italy enters the war, alongside France, England, and Russia, denouncing the Triple Alliance. D'Annunzio and Mussolini work the piazzas, beating their drums in the excited imagination of a country convinced that a few months will suffice (the eternal illusion of an "easy war") to extend its borders to their natural limits, to the Brenner Pass and the Alps. A fever grips the country, with many volunteering.

"What should I say to Dad?" wonders Yetwart, to whom, as the eldest son, the thankless task has fallen. Besides, Khayël is only eleven and could do no more than provide the support of an attentive listener, though a frightened one.

Their mother, who has already heard everything from her brothers (Andrea came by to see her that afternoon), says nothing and prays, on the verge of fainting. Yetwart has no idea how to cushion this news, and he can't bear his father's cold wrath, his way of withdrawing into himself, offended by the world, foreign.

In that moment, they hear the doorbell ring violently, and then the steps of the cook, Letizia, going to open the main entrance. The villa, with its low, wide nineteenth-century construction, faces the street, across from the railway station. Behind it is a vast, ancient park that slopes down to the bend in the river, through the dense shade of century-old trees. The two automobiles, ready for the journey, sit side by side near the well, in front of the stables.

The two boys sense more than hear their father's footsteps. As if on tiptoe, Yerwant passes through the house, bypassing the sitting room, where Teresa waits nervously. The boys hear his breathing beyond the door of the parlor that communicates with the billiard room; they hear that he has paused, and for a long moment they think he's going to come in, that he will find them there in the dark: mute, motionless, scared.

But the footsteps slowly resume, heading for the rear door, which opens onto a flagstone patio and the lawn around the well. On that soft grass the footsteps gradually fade. The boys stand at the window, peering between the green, half-open shutters; they see their father from the back, already far off, walking with his usual reflective gait, though perhaps slightly more tired.

"He knows," Yetwart guesses, breathing a sigh of relief, then repeating himself to his brother: "He knows." A dull relief pervades them both, like the comfort of a familiar scent. And then the cruel elation, which each hides from the other.

They brush past each other without looking and leave the billiard room, Yetwart to his violin to seek refuge in Kreutzer's dull exercises, and Khayël to his mother, who questions him nervously.

None of them will see Yerwant again until the next day. As darkness falls, the house explodes in light. It's dinnertime, and Antonio and Pino—thrown by the news—are hanging around the kitchen; Teresa sends them out: "Find the professor. He may need you."

Their heavy, fearful voices echo through the large gardens. The superb May evening lingers in the air, heavy with the scent of climbing roses, the same kind that grow in the faraway pergola.

In the end, Teresa calls for dinner to be served, and the plates make their grim rounds. Letizia is watching, leaning against the door, wishing with all her heart that nothing had happened. She hates war, detests the enthusiasm of her son, who is twenty and wants to join the army. He is all she has. Her kind employer has helped her raise him, paying her a fair wage, keeping her healthy, and every so often looking at her thoughtfully and asking how things are going. Sometimes, recently, he has talked to her about the trip and that far country.

Letizia has a brother in America, she understands. Understands so well that in this moment her heart could break, and to keep from crying she bites her hand and goes off to wash the dishes.

The silent boys and their mother finish their meal.

"Outside, at night, with this humidity," Teresa sighs, then she falls silent, too. "He's such a strange one," she concludes. The eastward expedition will never be mentioned again in this house.

Yerwant has gone out the back of the park, through the little door in the curve of the high wall that faces the river and the small, silver-colored footbridge that he had built for Teresa. He leans back against the wall beside the door, like a beggar, like a foreigner. The war will not be brief. He and his family are on opposite fronts, the visit is canceled, his lost country recedes and settles back into its distant frame.

"Oh, Sempad, my brother," sobs Yerwant, "at least send me your children." He spends the night like this. Never again will he speak of his journey.

TOWARD EVENING, Sempad cautiously makes his way to the colonel's. They have an appointment at the comfortable flat of Madame Sesostris, the Egyptian palm reader who is widely known to be the high-ranking officer's paramour. No one's sure if she's really Egyptian, or if her readings are accurate; what's certain is that she's a beautiful brunette, on the thin side, with a fiery gaze.

Sempad knows a lot about her, but Sempad (though it doesn't always seem that way) knows when to be silent. She gives consolation and comfort to the poor, to the hopeless, and then she carouses with the colonel, keeping him under her pretty thumb.

Sempad has heard frightened voices, whispers. An Armenian railroad man who works the Constantinople route has brought back news of massacres to the east, near the front. The Russians, it seems, are advancing. The Turkish generals' containment strategy isn't meeting with much success.

Everyone is beginning to recall the massacres of '96. But Abdul Hamid is dead ("clay for pots and vases," Ismene would say), and the new government—as Sempad's pharmacy friends argue, reasonably, between cigars and coffees—has more important things to do than persecute Armenians. And besides, we have delegates in the capital, the patriarch, newspapers . . . And our soldiers bring us honor, we are loyal subjects.

"We just have to stay calm, quiet and calm," says Krikor the doctor. "We ourselves should arrest the members of the opposition parties, whoever meddles in politics, whoever agitates. This is our flag: Pharmacie Hayastane." *Hayastan* is the name Armenians give to their lost homeland: the land of Haik. And Sempad's pharmacy is respected and known by all, an institution. He has introduced countless new medicines into the little city— he was one of the first to obtain aspirin.

"Like a beacon of progress and civilization," intones Levon Toumanian, known as "the botanist" because for years he has been compiling an atlas of Anatolian flora. Everyone laughs, because Levon never speaks, but today he's happy because he has discovered a new flower, a small purple primula, in the meadows above the falls.

Still, Sempad is rather uneasy, and he confides in the colonel, after having slipped an elegantly wrapped book stuffed with banknotes to his intermediary, Madame Sesostris.

The colonel, benevolent and relaxed, tells him what he knows. Some hotheads were arrested in Constantinople; a few soldiers on the Eastern front have deserted to join up with the Russians ("and that, as you well know, is very serious").

Sempad proclaims his full agreement. The colonel thinks to himself that whoever commanded those troops must not have been terribly competent; he wouldn't have had such problems himself. His Armenian soldiers never gave him any trouble, and it was with reluctance that he obeyed the order to disarm them and send them all to the labor battalions on the Eastern front.

The colonel does, however, have suspicions. If he knew how to probe his own thoughts more deeply, he would realize that he knows—more than merely suspects—that the soldiers were sent east in order to be able to eliminate them more easily. But the final truth of the Armenian Project continues to elude him; he is unable to imagine it. And he doesn't know that this is precisely what renders him suspect to the higher-ups in the party and the government, that this is the real reason why he's stuck out here, far from the front.

Madame Sesostris, who grasps much more than the colonel, would like to warn Sempad, but he is looking at her with such tranquil, trusting eyes that she puts it off till later—another day, another time. Later will be too late. But she will never forget those eyes, and many years afterward, in Alexandria, in King Farouk's sleepy Egypt, the beloved and respected wife of an important Copt will make large, anonymous donations each year to the Armenian orphanage in the River Harbor District— and that will be she, in her makeup and nail paint, lying through her teeth to her husband about her supposed gambling losses.

ON MAY 24, Italy enters the war amid a flurry of flags and patriotic anthems. The day before, Yerwant sent his brother a hopeless, helpless telegram. But Sempad, the telegram man, will never receive it, because it is precisely on the evening of May 24 that the *kaimakam* finally receives *his* telegram, the official one. Every party member in the little city is already on alert. The German allies have advised silence until the decisive moment, order and organization.

From house to house a careful web is woven. All the knots are in place, and the Kurdish chiefs have been notified—but with strict orders not to show their faces in the city yet, if they want the right, as promised, to loot and take their pick of the girls later. The *kaimakam,* like a fat spider, stands at the center of the web. He's a man of the old Ottoman regime, a man with no merit and much to atone for in the eyes of his new masters, which is

exactly why his obtuseness is now equaled by his zeal—
he's firmly resolved to seize this opportunity.

On the morning of the 25th, the milkman is running
late. It's the *duduk*-playing shepherd, Hrant Agopian, who
brings the milk every morning to Sempad, his employer,
and to several others on the same road. Each day he fills
Irene Zingarian's saucepan for free, since she's eighty and
has been slightly touched ever since her son stopped writing from America. Each time Sempad receives a letter
from Rupen, Irene somehow finds out and comes to see if
it contains any news of her Boghos.

When the shepherd does arrive, he asks to speak to
his boss. Sempad comes to the courtyard, strangely inhospitable. He doesn't offer bread, he doesn't offer wine. He
is silent, as if dazed by sleep, or by a dream.

The shepherd explains that a Kurdish man of his
acquaintance today refused to buy any milk: " 'Tomorrow
all your animals will be mine,' he said. So I said, 'They don't
belong to me, I take care of them for the pharmacist.' So
he said, 'You mean the poison man, he wants to kill us all
with those medicines of his.'

"I'm going to Van, boss, to visit my brother," the
shepherd says now, calmly but firmly, hat in hand, as if
changing the subject. "Last night I dreamed about him,
and I know he's waiting for me." But he doesn't mention
that in the dream he saw his brother as the archangel from
the apse of the church, sword in hand, surrounded by a

ring of evil fire, which he leaped across before the circle closed (nor that he thinks he can smell, on himself, the odor of singed garments).

Sempad allows him to go. He knows the old man lost his children and wife in '96 and has lived alone ever since, conversing with angels and with his mythical brother, Thoma, whom no one has seen since that time.

"Hrant, you must follow God's path," Sempad tells him. But on that sunny morning, for the first time, he feels a crushing weight bearing down on him, and he wonders (oh, for an instant) whether he'll see again these dawns and these sunsets, and Yerwant.

"WE NEED TO REPLACE old Agopian," Sempad tells Shushanig the next day, at breakfast. But then they lose themselves in a complicated game from which they derive wild amusement: imagining episodes from Yerwant's return. In her utter innocence, Shushanig has felt none of the doubts regarding her sister-in-law that have been nagging at Sempad, fueled each day at the pharmacy; he is grateful to her for this.

In that very moment Leslie emerges from beneath the cupboard—his cupboard. Everyone has long since ceded him that territory, and only occasionally do the women run a broom over it.

He's holding a whistle and a straight razor. He approaches his parents solemnly and smiles. But Leslie is always smiling, with naïve cunning, beneath that important nose of his.

"Of all of you, Leslie has the most exotic name and the most Armenian face," Sempad always tells his children. He always smiles, and he always gathers things. He's nine years old.

Inside two large shoeboxes, which his Aunt Veron lined with cloth for him, he arranges, according to a metaphysical system all his own, buttons and trundles, screws and whistles, scraps of fabric and ribbon, two images of Greek saints that Ismene gave him ("since I don't have a particular saint," the child thinks, "they're all mine, I can pray to them all"), a revolver bullet Krikor gave him, and his reader.

But today Leslie explains himself even less than usual. He hands the whistle to his father, the small rusted razor to his mother: "You call, she kills," he proclaims categorically. Then he turns around and goes back to his cupboard, pushing the two shoeboxes up against its squat little legs, which culminate in powerful lion claws on each side. That's the signal, known and respected by all, that Leslie does not wish to be disturbed. He will emerge when hungry, though certainly no later than lunchtime, a solemn event for which no one is permitted to be late.

Today, however, lunch itself is late. Strangely, the children are all there, standing erect behind their chairs. Sempad is there, at the head of the table, with Madame Nevart at his right. Veron and Azniv are there. The one missing is Shushanig herself, who is in the kitchen, speaking to someone in a low voice.

For Henriette, who is three, the world stops at this moment. The smell of large oval loaves, freshly baked, covered in sesame seeds and crunchy poppy seeds; the tart scent of three brimming bowls of yogurt with sliced cucumber; the intense smell of eggplant and kid meat; the carafes of falls water and of bubbly cider: all of this will coalesce in her memory into a single, enduring feeling of guilt, of offense, of inadequacy. On that distant sunny day in May, she and her family members, small and large, have all been judged—and found guilty of existing. And God has covered his face.

KRIKOR THE DOCTOR appears at the door, agitated. His pocket watch dangling, his collar askew, he runs to Sempad, leans in close, nearly kneeling, and whispers, "They're arresting us all, let's run!"

"Where? How? And what's more, why? They'll always need pharmacists and doctors," replies Sempad thoughtfully.

"Let's go to the Farm."

"And then?"

At this moment, Ismene appears at the kitchen door, wringing her hands, but Shushanig is right behind her, carrying the French tureen in her outstretched arms. In her voluptuous, showy fashion, Shushanig draws rich comfort from the warm feel of the Parisian porcelain, and today she clings to the elaborate handles and sets the dish down almost with regret.

Araxy, the young cook, follows her with silver ladle in hand; for a moment, order is restored and everyone, subdued, sits down to eat the soft semolina.

"The *kaimakam* has ordered all the Armenian heads of household to come to the prefecture today at three. The town crier is making his rounds," Krikor whispers to Sempad after the first course. "I don't like it. If we hurry, we could take that gig of yours. Azniv could hitch the horse and bring it around back, to the alley, and we could leave through the garden door and slip away behind the cathedral—we'll take the long way and stay at the Farm till tomorrow. If we don't know anything, we can't be guilty of anything, and meanwhile Azniv and Veron can find out what's going on."

Sempad is easily convinced. Being modest, he never believes he's indispensable. He thinks the summons could mean only one thing, the usual: another request to pay "special taxes," for making the *kaimakam* look good in the eyes of the soldiers, for "supporting our troops," for any other reason they can conjure up.

Luckily, he thinks, people always need medicine—or French cosmetics, which for several months have been available at a counter in back, entrusted to Veron's judicious little hands.

After the two men leave, the family remains seated, as

if scared to move. Shushanig finishes her meal in silence, and then she and Ismene withdraw again. Ismene's news is fragmentary but frightening. Shushanig has said nothing to Sempad, and it was with a pang in her heart that she let him go.

Now she must act, alone. Her father, David Zacharian, the legendary merchant who had traveled everywhere, had warned her, on her wedding day, "There comes a time, in the life of every Armenian woman, when her family's welfare rests on her shoulders. We would die to prevent this weight from falling to our pearls, our roses of May—indeed we do die."

Shushanig softens for a moment, quickly saying her prayer: "Our Father, and you my father David who are with Him, sitting in Abraham's lap, adorn for us our heavenly homeland, and sweeten for all of us the mysterious path that leads there." (For Shushanig, too, Paradise is a garden, with pomegranate trees.)

She then leads Ismene upstairs, to her bridal room. Opening the French box of perforated cardboard that contains her gloves, she extracts the pair she wore on her wedding day and turns one pinky finger inside out: out falls a tiny key shaped like a hand of Fatima, inset with a little turquoise.

Plunging into the large mirrored wardrobe, inherited from her mother Haiganush, a pallid girl she never knew, the strong Sushanig pulls out a small, flat, metal jewel box, a sort of safe-deposit box in which she keeps her private reserves of gold and gems. With mute tenacity, deaf to the mockery of her progressive husband and their friends, Shushanig refused bonds and banks; she converted every personal annuity, every gift, every bit of income into gold coins and loose gems—and now she and Ismene gaze thoughtfully at her small treasure.

They both make the sign of the cross, and then from another hiding place Shushanig extracts several small sacks of common cloth, and divides her treasure in two.

She entrusts the larger sack to Ismene. "Leave now, Ismene," she says. "Look, listen, observe everything you can. If they're going after us, they may even come for the Greeks. But you're Ismene, no one would dare harm a wailer. If it comes to it, think of the children first. I've lived well."

Like a child being sent away, Ismene weeps, her face resting in Shushanig's hands. Nothing, as far as they know, has actually happened yet. Still, Shushanig wipes her eyes and says, "Old friend, yes you, the one who accompanies the dead. No one ever said this would last forever."

In that moment, a *zaptieh* bangs on the front door, enters, and looks into the dining room. He is embarrassed and aggressive, but says nothing as he waits for his partner and greedily eyes the lunch leftovers. "I'm coming." Shushanig and Ismene no longer know what to do with all the things to say to each other, with all their affectionate thoughts. Each will do her job, like a good soldier.

The little sacks have vanished inside deep pockets. The safe is back in its place, with a little money left inside.

They descend the stairs in ritual order, as mistress and servant, as if performing an ancient women's dance.

"If you're looking for the master of the house, he left this morning," Shushanig tells the two gendarmes, with utter calm. They notify her of the order that her husband report with the others to the prefecture. "I'll tell him as soon as he returns."

The two men look at each other, highly amused, and one says, "It makes no difference; he'll be in time even tomorrow." Then with a slow, precise gesture, he reaches a hand toward the tureen that's still sitting in the middle of the table. For a moment, he seems to caress it, then the motion accelerates and the tureen falls to the floor with a clang. "Oops," he says, smiling again. Then he and his partner leave.

FROM THAT MOMENT, time moves in fits and starts, speeding up and then stretching into deceptive lulls. Ismene slinks out behind the two *zaptiehs*. Following her feline instincts, she hopes to retrace the web in reverse, to find the spider. Her dusty black dress blends in with the street corners. She mutters curses to boost her courage.

Meanwhile, a deathly silence gathers like an evil cloud over the Armenian quarter. Ismene isn't the only one following the two gendarmes: an entire wake of old earth-colored women—servants, beggars, poor widows—lie in wait behind every corner, watching the two men enter, laughing, one house after another, leaving silence behind them each time.

Theirs is a muffled, dense astonishment. A hundred anguished cries are sealed away behind their smiles, a hundred thoughts of death rise up, flutter hesitantly, then weave together in a dark dance. Children fill their pockets with sweets and hide. The acid odor of fear spreads like a miasma.

For the first time in many years, the pharmacy closes. Veron has been warned. Her evening escorts, the same cheeky men who yesterday were amiably courting her, now appear like ghosts one after the other, sneaking along the walls, whispering, "They're rounding us up . . . they're going to loot the stores . . . it'll be like '96 . . . where's Sempad?" Veron tries hard to respond calmly, but they pay her no mind and go back to sneaking around, their eyes glassy and wild. There are no customers. In the deserted space, she can feel the city holding its breath.

Veron knows that Krikor the doctor is with Sempad at the Farm, and she persuades herself that their decision was the right one, and that the most important thing to do now is to join them, with the whole family. "As long as the children haven't run off somewhere," she thinks, nervously. By this time she can no longer bear the swelling silence, the whispers, and so, as she does each evening, she diligently stoppers the bottles on the counter, arranges them neatly on the shelves, in order, pulls down the blinds in front of the poisons room and locks away the opium and the morphine, the laudanum and the hyoscine. She takes the morning proceeds, straightens the cosmetics counter, screws the lid back on the Eau de Coty, the latest perfume from Paris, and makes her way out.

She is trying to remain calm, and she has prepared a reassuring excuse should anyone ask her why she's leaving. But no one's around. The heavy key to the front door suddenly slips from her sweaty hands and falls to the ground with a tinny clink, like a coin.

With a sudden motion, as if remembering something, she hurries back inside. From a small box that is ostensibly hidden (though everyone knows Sempad's secrets), she takes the key for the ultramodern American safe, which Sempad had installed last year by a specialist who came from London. As in a fever dream, she easily manages to unlock the complex mechanism, which she has never before touched, then rapidly pockets nice rolls of gold coins, pouches of silver, banknotes.

She works quickly, like a master thief. When she finishes, she relocks it and replaces the key; then she leaves, heavier than before, not once looking back. She will never see the Pharmacie Hayastane again. Looted, ransacked, it will for years to come host a cluster of poor Turks, who will while away their afternoons beneath its crooked, faded sign, recalling, without needing to speak of it, Sempad's generosity and good cheer. And Veron, every evening in the desert, will remember that falling key. Thanks to that gold, those coins, swallowed time and again against repeated searches and then retrieved, the children will manage to stay alive, to reach Aleppo, to be saved.

AT HOME, all appears calm. Nevart has gone to visit her friend Zabel the cloth merchant, and everyone is relieved not to be subjected to her nerves, her pesky questions. Veron looks first for Azniv, who has also gone out in search of news, and then for Shushanig, whom she finds on the mezzanine, her head in the tall linen wardrobes, counting the sheets after the big spring wash. A row of laundry sacks rests on the table to the left, a pair of scissors and a pile of colored satin ribbons rest on the one to the right.

"I have all the time in the world," says Shushanig's back, curving gently forward. "Here I am in my nice house, counting and putting away my nice sheets." Nubar is playing with a ribbon at her feet.

Foreboding, anxiety, and resignation flood Veron, along with a tremendous regard for that strong back, which suddenly seems to bear the weight of the world. "Ah, Shushanig, dear friend," she gushes, knowing that only her sister-in-law, not her brother, can make sense of what is happening, and especially of what is about to happen, of this throat-gripping fear. (Because nothing has happened yet, or almost nothing; what Armenian youth doesn't know about massacres and threats?) "Shushanig, forgive me, I closed the pharmacy." (She says nothing of what she took from the safe, just as Shushanig says nothing of the small treasure she divided with Ismene; what you don't know can't hurt you.)

"You did well," replies Shushanig, composed. "Now we wait for them to come back from the prefecture. And we prepare, we women, for . . ." Her voice becomes dreamy and distant, as if unsure whether to continue or not, whether to confide. After all, Veron is a young, untested woman. At that moment they hear voices and shuffling coming from near the front door. Several people. Shushanig and Veron rise together and go downstairs, holding hands like sisters.

In the foyer, standing or sitting on the heavy, columned oak chest, Sempad's pride, they find the Sarkissian twins, the carpenters, along with Garo the sexton, who is holding little Garo's hand, and the other sexton, the Catholic one, Vartan Arakelian, with his son, who bears the ambitious Western name James. The inspector-postman is also there, and Isaac the Greek priest (who hasn't been summoned but is nonetheless afraid), and Hagop the house servant with one of his friends, whom everyone calls Lefty. And Nerses the gardener.

All of them turn to Shushanig with hope in their eyes. She'll know what to do. By now, of course, they all know that Sempad is at the Farm, and so, moved by a powerful feudal instinct, they are turning to Shushanig for protection. Every member of this little population has faith in her, and they wait, respectfully patient, their gentle Armenian eyes following her and brightening as she descends.

"*Mayrig*, my friends were looking for you," says little Garo in his squeaky voice. *Mayrig*, mother. Shushanig is startled; Garo is speaking for everyone. But not only is this little population of simple folk depending on her, as if they were her own children. So is Sempad, up at the Farm. An irresistible desire to see him again suddenly sweeps through her like a whirlwind, dimming her serene gaze.

Shushanig forgets the house, the wardrobes, the linen. The angel of death has chosen, and his grave eyes are staring at her—and though she convinces herself that she has (yet again) devised one of her good feminine strategies, this time she will be the instrument of her family's misfortune.

"WE'RE ALL GOING TO the Farm," Shushanig decides. "No one will dare set foot there. We'll meet in the alley behind the house, by the garden door, in one hour. We'll have a picnic this evening, to spite those who wish us ill. We'll eat together in good cheer. The days are long now, the air is warm. Bring your women, too; they can help me."

Vexation and anxiety melt into a stolen joy. Everyone runs to fill baskets; Shushanig's hospitality is proverbial, but one mustn't arrive empty-handed.

Shushanig dresses the children with the help of Araxy the cook and Azniv, who has returned after a fruitless trip through the neighborhood; she didn't have the courage to go farther. On a whim, they dress little Nubar in a frock, with a starched piqué ruffle and one of his sister's little pink bonnets; the rustling of his sisters' clothes thrills him and keeps him happy. Little Garo, always bursting with affection for everyone, is overjoyed: an evening with all his friends, and *Mayrig*, and his aunts, and his daddy . . . At the Farm he can dance and run through the fields beneath the falls. With a happy sigh, Garo promises his angel he'll be very good.

Leslie and Suren, on the other hand, pout. They don't wish to be disturbed—Leslie because he has already been away from his cupboard once today, before lunch, and Suren because he can't help trembling with fear and the desire to take flight, as he feels the vast web tightening. What he really wishes: to be on a horse, brandishing a sword, to be one of the great heroes, David of Sassoun, Vartan Mamikonian . . . He also wishes, deep down, to escape alone, from this little world that understands nothing and is blind to the shadows on the walls.

But Shushanig is a whirlwind this evening. Even Madame Nevart adapts to her pace and climbs quickly into the big carriage with the children, Azniv, and Veron. Shushanig follows in the smaller one with the provisions, Araxy, and all the others. Father Isaac has left his wife, Katerina, at home, not wanting to disturb her. The carpenter brothers, who have finished painting the dome and depart in two days for the United States, serve as drivers. This will be their send-off party; they've brought a bottle of old cognac and musical instruments, for a dance.

In the oppressive silence of the Armenian quarter, the merry band sets off and rides at a steady trot, thinking of the feast, past the prefecture.

The summons doesn't actually apply to any of these passengers; there are no heads of family among them, except for the carpenters, who, however, consider themselves practically foreigners by this point, and Father Isaac, who isn't affected because he's Greek. The soldiers on duty at the prefecture—more of them than usual today—can't believe their eyes. Two of them run to Lieutenant Ismail Kizilgik, an officer freshly arrived from the capital, who is commanding the detachment. The two are locals, recognize the drivers and the carriages, easily guess where the group is heading, and know how to get there.

"The dogs are provoking us!" "They're going to have a party at their country villa!" "Uppity traitors!" The two soldiers work each other up with dubious zeal. The unguarded house with all its loot has flashed through their minds, to say nothing of the smiling eyes of those girls. And yet they wouldn't know how to take the initiative themselves.

But the lieutenant is a fervent Ittihadist, an educated city man, who wants to advance and distinguish himself. The Armenian roundup is in progress, and he knows perfectly well how it must end. Where is this family going? What are they up to? Who are these people? Where are those carriages headed? Excited voices offer explanations. "Skylark Farm? Near the falls?" It's the opportunity he's been waiting for; no need to share the credit with anyone else. A little imagination is called for, a little initiative. In any case, they will all have free rein soon, and those arrogant people are already *res nullius,* no one's and everyone's. To take action in this instance will set an example and provide amusement.

Thus the lieutenant makes his decision. He puts a subordinate in charge of his detachment—a good man, though slightly coarse, who doesn't ask questions—and races off, along with the two soldiers who alerted him, to the barracks, where he asks for another ten volunteers for a good time with a group of rebels, promising compensation. His posse chosen, they arm themselves and get on their horses.

"Come with me," he says brusquely. "We'll have some fun. But keep quiet as we're leaving the city; we don't want to alarm anybody." And so, an hour after the merry passage of the carriages, the same road hosts these thirteen motley riders, silent and lethal.

But Arsine, the withered old ragpicker, is watching. She saw Ismene two hours ago, and they exchanged whispers. Now she's doing business with Hüsnü the stable hand in a corner in the regiment stable. But she watches and listens, and she understands. Besides, Hüsnü, instead of selling her the surplus scraps of cloth that now and then he pilfers from the officers, for the first time has simply given them to her; his whispered "I pity you, too" dies in his thick mustache in the dim light.

Arsine grabs the cloth and limps hurriedly away. She knows where to find Ismene and the others: at the old, abandoned caravansary on the road to Marash.

Meanwhile, the Armenian men are still gathered at the prefecture. They came at three, one after another, waving hasty greetings, denying the fear that hovers like a sour cloud, trying to trace the situation back to some reassuring precedent. "How much will they want?" asks Hagop the haberdasher, excitedly, of Arshag the blacksmith; and "What do you think, Your Excellency?" asks Melkon the ikon painter, humbly and trustingly, of the wealthy Ashod Mendikian.

No one wants to think about anything worse—it's wartime, and we must all make sacrifices. They're all feverishly adding in their heads: this much to this man, that much to that one . . . the colonel, the *kaimakam*, the gendarme on my street . . . A tax is a tax, we'll survive the way we always do, and then, perhaps, the war will end.

Among these philosophical, resigned men, who are already reassuring and consoling themselves with thoughts of the family dinner that will follow this swindle, of their wives and children, of the warmth of their homes— among them, the industrialists visiting from America stand out: the four Fabrikanian brothers, impressive in their double-breasted frock coats, struggling to accept this new instance of what they believe to be the usual slow Eastern haggling.

But behind them, the *zaptieh* and the *kaimakam* close the doors with unusual care, and plant themselves before them. The absence of the pharmacist is noted but doesn't cause alarm: that's how Sempad is, no doubt up at the Farm to oversee the final touches before Yerwant's arrival; no doubt he didn't receive the notice in time. His absent-mindedness with regard to anything that doesn't concern his potions or Shushanig is legendary; he'll arrive late, but no one, as usual, will be angry with him. He's too inno-cent, too carelessly generous, too well liked.

SEMPAD'S SIMPLE HEART IS far removed from such things at the moment; he is happy again. The surprise of Shushanig arriving with their friends, the send-off party for the carpenter brothers, the sisters with their cheeks shining from the ride, all his children together, Nubar's humorous transvestism—all this reassures him. Shushanig is his leafy tree; if she has decided that this is how things should be, he's overjoyed.

His thoughts wander—tomorrow we'll worry about the new tax, we'll see what the *kaimakam* wanted, maybe we'll even receive one last message from Yerwant before our meeting—and he gives himself over to the pleasure of inaugurating the new Farm with a private surprise party, prior to the solemn event planned for Yerwant's arrival.

All that remains to be finished is the tennis court. But a splendid set of croquet mallets arrived last week from England, and the lawn is ready, as are the bow window, the stained glass, the Austrian chairs of bent cane and Vienna straw, with their motif of small red and blue crosses alternating in each panel. The glass sideboards and the kitchen pots shine. They are still waiting for the man with the piano, from Vienna, who left from the capital two days ago. His telegram arrived yesterday.

THEY OPEN THE BASKETS AND arrange the great banquet on the lawn. The afternoon is adazzle with colors and scents. In the kitchen, Shushanig oversees the women's cheerful busyness, ordering, answering, comforting. It's all part of her role, but after the fleeting excitement of the ride, her heart is growing heavy, her fingertips are numbing, a slight pulsing at her temples is making her dizzy. She sits down in a corner of the kitchen, and in that moment she feels, in her deep pocket, the weight of the jewels and coins she placed there a few hours earlier.

"How long has it been, and why?" she wonders absentmindedly. At this point Sempad enters the kitchen looking for her; he sees her and puts a hand lightly on her hair. "Ah, wife of mine, you always know how to cheer me up," he says gaily, and then adds one of their old, long-forgotten private jokes: "If your hair was made of pearls, your hands diamonds, how rich I would be, my love. We could run far away."

All along the dreadful road, Shushanig will turn these words over in her mouth, drawing comfort from them. Evil cannot triumph as long as good exists: if we deny the present, deny that it exists, Sempad's voice will return, within the infinite voice of God.

IN THAT VERY INSTANT the squad of horsemen pulls up in front of the Farm. The gate is standing open. For a moment lights, sounds, and colors stop them, and a sudden uneasiness grips them. "Tomorrow, tomorrow," grouses one of the two soldiers who reported the passage of the carriages, and he rubs his hands on his pants, uncertain and intimidated.

But the officer employs a well-timed fury: "They're rejoicing, the dogs, over our defeats," he exclaims. "They're just waiting for the Russians." Soon, in the gathering dusk, the evening star appears. And then, as the fragrance of red roses and climbing jasmine spreads its intoxicating sadness through the air, Hrant begins tuning his *duduk* on the little bandstand, beneath the three tall plane trees on the edge of the lawn; he sounds one long, sustained, tender note.

But the note breaks off with a muffled gasp. The men have quietly scattered through the garden, and a well-handled knife has slit Hrant's throat from one ear to the other. Levon Yakovlian, the inspector-postman, who is getting his camera ready to take a souvenir photograph, determining the proper distance from the table, meets the same end, and he falls to the ground without a word, his gentle eyes rolled back, white against the grass that is slowly soaking up the blood.

How does a massacre happen? What liquor does blood become, and how does it rise to the brain? How is it that one acquires a thirst for blood? Those who taste it are said never to forget it. In a matter of seconds, the men turn into a predatory pack, and with feline agility they close in on all the doors: the large entry door, the kitchen door in back, the French doors of the sitting room, with the bow window and the new English leaded panes. The house offers itself to guests, defenseless, as innocent as Sempad, its owner.

Sempad and Shushanig are still in the kitchen. She's sitting down, he's standing behind her. In that moment, everyone becomes aware of everything: the soldiers with flashing blades appear at all the doors like too-real demons; the lieutenant comes in behind them, crosses the sitting room, and moves toward the kitchen, looking around with such obvious hatred that everyone feels his gaze like a slap.

"You traitors, dogs, renegades," he barks. "You have disobeyed the *kaimakam*'s orders, but I have found you, and now you will be punished." Sempad looks at him and doesn't understand. Shushanig does: death, slaughter. She tries to get up, to make a gesture of hospitality that might disarm the officer; she doesn't yet know that Hrant and the photographer are already dead, outside.

But Ismail, the officer, doesn't even look at her. He turns to his men and resumes: "Find all the males and bring them into the other room."

Like fish in a net, unable to escape, Sempad and the stunned Krikor (vainly crying, "I'm a doctor, and he's a pharmacist—you can't hurt us") are pushed into the sitting room, with the carpenter twins, Isaac the Greek priest, and the rest. Suren, who was upstairs, depressed, contemplating the sunset, hears the din and comes down, calmly, quietly. He stands beside his father and waits. The other male children—Leslie, Garo, James (son of Vartan the sexton), Rupen (son of Nerses the gardener)—are also led into the sitting room and lined up before the brightly painted wall, its floral designs freshly completed.

The women and girls are brutally shoved up against the opposite wall. Shushanig is motionless, gazing at her loved ones. Her wide eyes show no expression, her hands are in her pockets, holding her little treasure tight. Veron and Azniv are on either side, leaning against her, arms wrapped tightly around the girls, forming a seemingly composed group. No superfluous gestures, no lamentation: you would think the women are trying to disappear into the wall decorations.

Only Nevart, slumped in a corner, apart, is moaning softly, as she clings to Nubar in his dainty pink dress.

And this was how Sempad and his family met their fate. Blades flashed, screams rose, blood everywhere. The red bloom on Shushanig's lap is from her husband's head, severed and tossed there.

Between her skirt and apron (she's absurdly proud of that apron, with its crosses and its Easter motifs) Henriette is hidden. She's been talking in a substantial way for only a few months now, and she chatters incessantly, telling stories to herself and looking for hiding places, like a melodious mouse. Now a jet of warm blood that has squirted from her father's neck soaks her, through the apron, flooding the cozy darkness of her maternal refuge. A overpowering odor erases all other smells, and her open mouth fills with liquid, warmer than her mother, like an awful river blackly encircling her little heart, sweeping it away.

Henriette will never again speak her mother tongue spontaneously, and in every other language, as in every other country in the world, she will always feel herself a foreigner: someone who steals the bread, out of place everywhere, with no family of her own, envying other people's children. Curled up in the dark, she will cry every single night, surviving, until eventually she will seek refuge in a quiet hebetude, a living trunk waiting passively for the return of her lost homeland, of God's light, of the innocent gaze of her father.

Garo lies placidly with his handsome smile, holding his little hands over his open belly. Leslie, scurrying on all fours, tries to hide beneath the sideboard sparkling with crystal, but he's dragged out by his feet and flung against the wall, where his small round head smashes like a ripe coconut, spraying blood and brain across the delicate floral designs. Thus are flowers born from the blood of the Armenian calvary.

Suren, also fatally wounded, concentrates on one thing: covering the shame of his decapitated father, who has been slid up against the wall and is still gushing blood. So much blood in a human body . . . The pharmacist's diligent little hands, absurdly white, lie palm up, as in a deposition, in vain beseeching mercy, mercy for having existed. The boy eventually manages to reach his father and drape himself across him to die, covering the headless torso with his body, as if seeking his forgiveness.

Krikor the doctor, who protested, is to be left for last. Executioners have their ways. So it is that he manages to add, pointing at Isaac, "He's not a part of this. He's not Armenian." (Everyone by now realizes that this is no band of marauders, that things won't go any better for those gathered at the prefecture, that it is specifically for the Armenians that God is hiding his face and the blood-red clouds are galloping across the sky.)

And indeed the lieutenant, who in the midst of the carnage has continued giving orders and pointing out the next victims with the tip of his sword, pulls Isaac out of the corner he has been chased into and sends him away with a kick, unscathed. Each day of his life Isaac will ask forgiveness for not having shared the fate of his Armenian friends, for not having at least stopped to bless them, as was his duty. And these prayers will rise up to God's throne each day, until in 1922, in the Smyrna fire, he will meet his destiny as a Greek, with honor, together with Ismene.

Krikor is stripped and his testicles are cut off, to great amusement. "Was he your lover?" sneers the lieutenant when Shushanig and the other women scream. Krikor's own shriek of agony is interrupted when they stuff his testicles into his mouth. His eyes, once so ironic and judicious, now widen alarmingly, and Shushanig in her focused agony wishes for a hatpin so she could kill him mercifully.

But Krikor—still alive—is dragged outside with the corpses and thrown into the pit excavated for the tennis lawn, fresh and redolent of newly turned earth. The women, too, are shoved outside, chaotically, to watch.

The smiling lieutenant says, "Invite the lady of the house to take a seat, and remove that head from her lap." (She has in the meantime closed Sempad's wide, innocent eyes.) "We're not savages, we have liberated you. Now, as soon as we dispose of these bodies, we can dine. The males of your infamous race are guilty and need to be eliminated because if even one survived, he would later want revenge. But you are women."

Below, Sempad lies with his head placed awkwardly near his body, face pressed into the ground. On top of him, their eyes glazed with death's chill, the two carpenter twins lie one on top of the other; they will never see the America of their dreams, and their father, for years, will write to many, many survivors, remaining hopeful and patient, since none of them saw the brothers die. Big Garo, his eyes closed, lies wrapped around little Garo, whom he was unable to protect; he squeezes him in a desperate vise with his powerful, useless arms, which death has not unsealed. Vartan the sexton is thrown into the pit on top of them, and with him his son, whose chest is ripped open, whose exotic name—like a pitiful charm—has failed to save him.

The stacking of cadavers proceeds at a feverish, though orderly, pace. As they work, one soldier, voicing an impression shared by all, including the lieutenant, remarks, "They sure treat themselves well, these infidels!" His companion, laughing hard, replies, "*Treated*, thanks to us. And now their perfumed women are all ours."

The group is looking forward to the violence that will follow, ogling the women, the adolescents, and the young girls alike. There are enough to go around, they think, and they can throw them away when they're done. But the night is long. For now, they begin by shattering the bow window's stained glass and the crystal ware.

The stained-glass knight and his lady radiate their exotic beauty in vain: they are eyed with hatred, slashed and stoned. And the delicate English flowers of the side panels are pierced with swords, systematically, or else shot with pistols, in a sudden contest that breaks out amid a rowdy jubilation of noise.

But back in the city, far from the contaminated villa, Arsine, Ismene, and the other women busy themselves like worker ants. Ismene has learned from Arsine about the expedition to the Farm, and she understands that the villa has become a deadly trap. She would like to run there, with the others, summon insults and curses against the aggressors, frighten them, cowards that they are. (It's axiomatic for Ismene that men, in general, taken individually, are poorly endowed with courage.)

But then she reflects that the lieutenant would probably play the unbeliever, the tough guy, in order to maintain his authority. She doesn't underestimate the group's eagerness, its easy cruelty toward the weak, and she guesses its true purpose: to display anti-Armenian zeal and personal initiative, with an eye toward the powerful triumvirate ruling in the capital.

She sends all the others—the wailers, the widows,

the old cemetery women—to the house to make a ruckus. The idea, a desperate one, is for them to arrive en masse, to disconcert, to disrupt, to witness. She herself runs to the colonel, who knows her, as everyone does. She takes him aside with a whisper, slipping a nice gem into his hand, a lapis lazuli from Shushanig's little treasure, and warns him that a subordinate—a lieutenant named Ismail, an outsider—has abandoned his post at the prefecture and run off with a group of volunteers to Skylark Farm, to visit the colonel's friend, Sempad the pharmacist.

"He's a rich one, he is, effendi," whispers Ismene. "It would be a real shame . . ."

That's all it takes to enrage the colonel, who was just thinking of sending for Sempad, in order to build on the lucrative conversation begun a few days earlier. "My cousin's message was a timely one," the colonel thinks. "Now Sempad will be truly frightened, and thus easier to milk."

By this time he has learned that a massacre of Armenians is under way. But he's an old-fashioned man, who thinks as he did in the days of the Red Sultan; he hasn't grasped the implications or the dimensions, and he still believes that, among the flock of poor Armenian Christians being rounded up and eliminated, who matter not at all to anybody, one can choose to save a few nice fat chickens—a sort of private life insurance. The extent of Armenian fortunes doesn't escape his sharp eye, which is assisted by his well-paid spies, like Nazim the gimp. He knows, then, where and how much he can sponge.

But what if this zealous cretin Ismail has taken Sempad? The colonel gives an order and gets on his horse. He is followed by a sizable squad of riders, all men he trusts. These are dangerous times—we must watch our backs.

And thus it was that, at the height of their raging ecstasy, Ismail and his twelve followers were surprised by a terse order, uttered by the colonel in a fearsome, icy voice, barely louder than his usual voice, but punctuated by a massive fusillade.

In the same doorways in which the assassins first appeared, the colonel's men now stand, guns in hand, no more reassuring in appearance and yet infinitely welcome. The colonel makes Ismail and his band disarm. "I'll accuse them of insubordination," he thinks, "and send them all to Damascus, to keep that other skirt-chasing fool of a lieutenant company. I'm still in charge here."

"And where are the other fool Armenians?" He looks around, doesn't see any of them. But he smells the blood. When he goes out the back door, he finds Shushanig sitting rigidly on one of the elegant new Vienna-straw chairs; around her, the other women of the family, only women, looking at him with blank eyes. It's a portrait of tragic, helpless feminine composure that makes instantly clear to the officer what has happened: "The men are not here, so they've already been killed."

His first reaction is pure annoyance. Then his gaze lights upon the tennis court excavation, on the unseemly confusion of bodies, and he detects a sweetish stench. On top, his face disfigured from a blow, a hole where his nose should be, the gentle, exceedingly polite Levon Toumanian, who has on many occasions explained to the colonel his discoveries of Anatolian flora, stares at the sky with open arms, his shirt untucked. His eyeglasses, absurdly intact, have slipped into his hair and reflect the light of dusk.

The colonel is a reasonably honest, reasonably humane, moderately corrupt man. His trade is war, but he has no love for massacres. He's quite greedy, and thus is no fanatic: the fanatic kills for pleasure, or because he worships some idea, and blood leads him to further blood.

Furthermore, the colonel is embarrassed about having to face Madame Sesostris, who was fond of Sempad, and who will certainly accuse him of ineptitude. *Your own troops, behind your back* . . . At bottom—and he's also ashamed of this, as if it were a military inefficiency—the colonel knows the advantages of tolerance, understands that the darkest day for a country is the one when, in order to feel united, it feels the need to eliminate a defenseless segment of its population.

And finally, the stupefied Shushanig, surrounded by her daughters, her sisters-in-law, old Nevart, and Araxy the cook, brings out his sense of manly honor, a gentleman in the presence of a lady, as well as his contempt for the coarse lieutenant with his "modernizing" ideas. He feels like a man of the old regime, of the old Empire, and he knows that, for his career, this is the horrifying end of the line, and also that his heart will never be the same, and he accepts these things. He accepts them to the point of taking a stand, a risk, in order that all not be lost, in order that his people need not be ashamed of all their leaders.

And thus, in a gesture of ancient nobility, he puts an arm around Shushanig and gently helps her to her feet. With an imperious wave, he has their carriages brought up, and then whispers paternally to her to go back to the city; he will send an escort. Then, respectfully, he says, "Trust me. I'll see to the burial, I'll call a priest, I'll take care of it personally. But you should all go back home, these are calamitous times."

Shushanig, broken, follows him to her carriage. Only now does she cry, looking back; after this day ends, she'll never cry again. During the deportation, she'll be as tough as a lioness.

After they have gone, the colonel, pistol in hand, approaches Ismail the lieutenant and forces him and his men to personally remove the bodies from the pit, to lay them out in a row beside it, and to close their eyes. When he notices Krikor, the skeptic, everyone's loyal friend, and sees that he's still moving, his anger turns to leaden sadness, to heavy obligation. With a steady hand, he cuts the bootlace gagging his mouth, closes his eyes with his left hand, and whispers, "Old friend, forgive me," before shooting him in the temple.

And he says to Ismene, who has arrived with the other women, "Weep for them, you who know how. And God have mercy on us."

SECOND PART

Shushanig

As soon as they leave the Farm, the carriages are surrounded by the women Ismene has sent ahead, who don't know quite what to do, other than their jobs: compassion in a time of mourning.

The black aura around Sempad's women hasn't frightened them yet: they offer screams, laments, shoulders on which to cry. Tattered, avoided by everyone, the old cemetery women hang back a little, clustering in a rough circle, in respectful silence. Their moment will come, followed, they think, by the obligatory funeral banquets—a chance to fill their bellies properly. Such is the limited horizon of the poor.

Everyone is looking at Shushanig, but Shushanig sees no one; she is crying like Niobe, rigid, not moving even her face: frozen, relentless. It is Azniv who stirs now, Azniv who has grown up in an hour, who counts the survivors to make sure they haven't left anyone inside the villa. Behind Henriette (sobbing, caked hideously with blood), she discovers the small, stunned face of the cross-dressed Nubar in his rustling silk frock; this charming little girl is the only surviving male. Azniv promises herself to make certain he survives; she will succeed, with that energy she now feels thrumming within her, rising unbending and indomitable.

Taking the reins of her colt, she looks around. In that moment she sees Ismene approaching in the gig belonging to her nephew, Giorgios, who has accompanied her. "Get in the carriage. Comfort Shushanig," Azniv orders her. Ismene, who understands at once, responds respectfully, "Right away. But first let me send the women in. Your poor dears will have a Christian burial, or my name isn't Ismene."

Thankful to have something to do, the old cemetery women and the wailers begin their lugubrious dirge, setting off single file toward the gate. As dusk darkens with the colors of night, they light their ancient lanterns and make their way, chanting impartially for all members of the mysterious human race.

One group of lights surrounds Hrant the musician, stretched out on the grass; another, Levon the inspector-postman. Their bodies are composed, their eyes shut. Then, efficiently and with brusque familiarity, they are carried inside to be cleaned and then lined up with the others along the edge of tennis-lawn pit.

There the women, each with her lamp, surround the victims, take them by the hand, and solemnly begin their inviolable ritual. This time, too, Sempad's family will have Christian burials. As for the rest of the Armenians

who will lose their lives during those baleful months—
slaughtered, tortured, dead of thirst and hunger along the
roads of Anatolia, and laughed at all the while—even
funeral rites will be denied them. Or rather, there will be
no need for them. A single dead man was once a breathing
being, was once alive, and what's left of him is a corpse
that can be honored; a hundred thousand dead are a heap
of rotting flesh, a pile of manure, more nothing than
nothing, a foul, negative reality of which to rid oneself.

Approaching the house, Ismene glimpses, from the
corner of her eye, a shadow skulking in the dark corners of the terrace, and without hesitation she addresses
him bluntly, "Come out, Father Isaac. How is it that you
survived?"

Glaring at her, Isaac replies, "Krikor the doctor
saved me. He said I wasn't Armenian." Then the shame
brings him to his knees.

Ismene has no time for his anxieties. "You're alive,
you're a priest," she exclaims. "What are you waiting for?"
Then she looks into his eyes, which are full of misery and
submission, and takes him by the hand, helping him to his
feet. "Go to them, Isaac. God sees everything. But you're a
priest, you have to bless them. At least they can be buried
in peace, and their souls can bless us. The colonel's waiting for you."

Consoled, Isaac joins the wailers, and his fine voice
soon rises, strong and sure, intoning the liturgy of the
dead: "May they be blessed who return to You with

cleansed souls, through the red veil of martyrdom. . . .
They whom You created with immaculate hands . . . O
taste and see that the Lord is good. . . . Bless the Lord in
heaven, you who see Him now, you whom He created
with immaculate hands. . . ."

The women's countermelody fills the night with
screams and piercing shrieks, which gradually subside
before the rhythmic, hypnotic melody of Isaac's voice,
until at last they harmonize in that powerful, cadenced
murmur that has long alerted the inhabitants of the city
to the approach of the wailers' cortege.

But here only the night listens, and the mournful
creatures huddled together in the carriages, a mass of
trembling flesh giving and receiving its paltry heat in an
effort to stay alive. At its center, walled in by the warm
bodies around her, Shushanig continues to weep without moving, exuding chill. In the corner, Henriette lies
forgotten—and forgetting. Her little blood-drenched
heart has been lost in the darkness.

Now Ismene arrives. The colonel has gladly put her
in charge of the funeral duties, leaving behind two soldiers to bury the dead, as soon as possible, in the freshly
excavated tennis pit, which seems made to order. Father
Isaac, who is Greek and not Armenian, but no less Christian for that, shows up just in time, and hurriedly decides
that he himself can bless the land, transforming it into
sacred ground, and care for the bodies.

Because everyone is in a hurry to leave. The colonel wants to use his authority, while he still has it, to have the lieutenant tried, or at least sent away. But what should he do with the crew that accompanied the lieutenant? They are his men—it wouldn't be wise to go after them. He'll have to pardon them and leave it at that. To hang them, as they deserve, is out of the question.

Ismene wants to save what's left of the family. She is feverishly making and unmaking chimerical plans, ever more aware that the bell for Christians in Turkey—not just for Armenians—has tolled. Meanwhile, she climbs onto the larger carriage and takes the reins, Azniv climbs onto the smaller one, and they slowly return to the city.

IN THE ARMENIAN QUARTER, whispers and more whispers. The men have not yet returned. A few of the old women said they saw them, lined up, accompanied by soldiers with raised bayonets, in front of the Salt Warehouse, an old building that has stood empty for many years. The return of the carriages does not arouse particular curiosity, but someone soon comes looking for Shushanig, to ask advice, and so the news comes out. The net of whispers and horror tightens, rocking the entire quarter. But no one really knows what to do.

Without their men, with the elderly and the children

to worry about, the women tend toward panic, but they are eager to believe any reassuring voice, and above all to deny the desperate truth—if it even occurs to them.

Thus the plan is able to proceed unhindered, without significant rebellion on the part of this passively foolish people. Later that night, the usual guards appear, accompanied by a crier proclaiming that Armenian families have thirty-six hours to leave the city and their possessions behind—every family member must go, no exceptions. "The government is moving you in order to better protect you. Your houses and your stores will be entrusted to the army."

"And our men? Where are our men?" shouts a group of anxious women (already regretting their threatening tone). "Ladies, ladies—they'll meet you outside the city, because if you were together, crafty as you Armenians are, you might try to trick us, to hide your money instead of entrusting it to the man who is a father to us all, the *kaimakam.*"

This is precisely what every family begins trying to do. Money might be salvation; it is always salvation. In every house, in every kitchen, from tins, from old wallets, from secret pockets, banknotes come to light, gold and silver coins, Maria Theresa talers and Queen Victoria sovereigns, even ancient florins and rare, circular Venetian sequins. Precious stones of all colors come to light, shiny pebbles that give off heat, that illuminate the weary feminine hands that hold them.

During the frenetic course of that night, the astonished children—who for the first time are seeing adults lost, confused, agitated, to such an extent that they discuss important matters without sending the children away—contemplate the shimmer of the stones, of the gold and silver, and they understand, in a flash, as a muffled fear grips their hearts. They wish they could speak to their fathers.

But their fathers are not coming back. It's the middle of the night by now, and no one considers sleeping. Against their will, children are put to bed, but except for the youngest they get right back up again, quietly, not crying, to stay close to their mothers, their grandmothers, whose dismay and desperation they can sense. Quick feminine hands sew secret pockets, mysterious pouches, into which the shiny stones and the gold sequins fall. Other hands knead, select, and assemble food and bread, round apples and dried pears, figs and cookies. But there is no joy in this bustle, and the children don't deceive themselves—they can smell the fear, the menace, the death.

Azniv takes charge. This family isn't waiting for anyone—its men are already gone. Shushanig and Veron, arm in arm, sit motionless in front of the fire, staring at the faces of their loved ones in the flames, seeking repose for their desperate minds.

Azniv laughs at herself and at Lieutenant Djelal, who loved her, who disappeared so suddenly. She finally understands his words, his mania for taking her far away. Now, provident and defiant, she makes arrangements for the small group of her surviving family. There's no one but Araxy the cook to help her; Madame Nevart is whimpering softly in a corner. Flames dance in her heart, which grows stronger with the passing minutes, feeding on the weakness of the others. She feels herself to be the daughter of Armenia, the heroine of the legends. She will save them—she has the strength and the courage to do so.

And you, young Azniv, you will let your bones dance in the wind of the dead to save these children and Shushanig; you will offer yourself to the soldier, and to the Kurdish horseman; you will laugh maniacally, wrapped in the piece of red silk with velvet roses and solid gold thread, the one Zareh sent you for Easter. Heroic, generous creature, you will allow yourself to die, contaminated, at Aleppo, your heavy living braid hanging down your back, your mission accomplished.

THE NIGHT IS OVER, and no trace of the men. None of these families will see them again. Many years later, with the Armenian passion and the world war both at an end, in a Turkey undone by defeat, the fate of the men will be discovered: forced in the night to leave the Salt Warehouse, where a few women had ventured to bring bread and then had returned home, calmed, they were killed one after the other in Falls Valley, where their unburied corpses were left staring at the sky, their eye sockets empty, naked and stripped of everything, even the majesty of death.

So it was that the next morning the Salt Warehouse was empty, as Ismene confirmed, having run there at dawn after scouring the entire quarter and sending her women everywhere. The only thing left, stuck on a wooden peg that had once served for coupling salt carts, was a small sheet of letterhead paper—*Andonian Frères. Robinetteries et Pompes*—fluttering in the breeze, and Ismene wouldn't have even noticed it but for a gust that lifted it gently and deposited it right at her feet. There, hurriedly scrawled in pencil, a message: "They're coming for us now. It's pitch-dark. They'll take us to our deaths. Whoever finds this paper, in the name of merciful God, notify our families and pray for our souls."

But Ismene couldn't read Armenian; she slipped the page into her pocket to show Azniv, and then forgot it. Ismene wasn't a woman of the written word. And yet she knew at once, without reading anything, that all the men were dead. She decided not to speak of it to anyone, to go back to Shushanig. In the warehouse, the air was livid and had the acid odor of deathly fear.

DAWN HAS ARRIVED like a blood-red bruise, and a torpid apathy seems for a while to have taken over in the houses of the Armenian quarter. Coins and jewels have disappeared during the night, hidden in a thousand ingenious, pathetic ways: sewn as buttons onto clothes, divided and subdivided such that the discovery of one part of the nest egg will not mean losing it all, tucked into the hems of the children's little outfits or in tiny sacks hidden in the thick braids of the girls.

Meanwhile, boys and girls are sleeping wherever they happened to fall; the adults rest briefly, then gather for coffee and a glass of spoon sweets, exchanging opinions and trying to fight panic as they ready the caravans. They listen closely to the old men and women who must accompany them ("no exceptions," the crier said) and who can offer testimony about the massacres of 1894–96, help keep memories alive, minimize the frightening void that engulfs the future, give advice, suggest rules . . . They all still think that the traditional Ottoman deference to the wisdom of elders will save them, that perhaps their pleas on behalf of the women and children for respect and comfort will be heeded, will hold them until they rejoin their men, farther on, near Aleppo. A goal.

Tasks are divvied up, resources inventoried. The day passes quickly as they prepare to leave at dawn the coming morning. An antlike frenzy: they count and round up all the means of transport, arrange mattresses and blankets in the carriages, furnishings, food, clothes . . . They mustn't forget anything: disinfectant, medicines . . . There are no doctors left, though old Serpuhi the midwife is doing what she can.

Hearing Serpuhi talking with Azniv in the kitchen, Shushanig suddenly sits up. She gently frees herself from Veron's soft embrace, straightens her hair, then stands, making the sign of the cross, and says, "Here I am. Let's get to work. Where's Ismene? Give the children some breakfast. What time do we have to leave? In any case, I'm going to go change clothes."

She takes Henriette by the hand, the little girl who shared her terrible bath in Sempad's blood, and gently changes her clothes, touching her to reassure her. Henriette lets her do it, inert as a doll. Shushanig sighs, kisses her forehead, then makes a pile of their clothes and takes it downstairs to throw into the large stove, which burns slowly and evenly. A pungent, sickly sweet odor spreads, lugubrious, through the whole house.

They all smell it, understand, cross themselves hastily. This is Sempad's send-off, the house he loved saying goodbye to his simple heart: a strand of dense smoke in the air, straight as a finger pointing to the ancient, lost homeland, an inescapable stench that sticks to the walls and makes breathing odious, a reminder to get moving in order to survive.

APPEARING AT THAT MOMENT at the door, which now stands open, unguarded, violated: Nazim the gimp, the *kaimakam*'s beggar-spy, who has just been recruited by Ismene as a double agent. It's hard to know his thoughts.

"Knowing when to speak is a talent possessed by beggars and kings," he loves to say, sententiously, taking snuff from the worn leather box that Sempad gave him long ago.

"It was nearly new then," Nazim suddenly recalls, feeling his world wobble as it occurs to him that Sempad is no longer in it. And his old, obsessive mind feels (along with the warmth in the bottom of his pocket from the shiny colored stone Ismene gave him, promising him others) the dull fear of having lost some of his most attentive protectors, and of no longer being free as a bird, with this Armenian secret weighing him down, with this clingy odor everywhere.

Ismene speaks to him in time. Following his own lights, Nazim, before going to the colonel and looking around on the way, has come to see Shushanig, the mistress of the house, whom he finds in the kitchen, giving orders. Everyone in the house responds to her imperious voice.

"Nazim, may God be with you, here's some bread," says Shushanig as soon as she sees him, and Nazim's withered heart gives a sudden leap; it seems to him that God is truly nearby in that moment. He takes her cold hand and touches it to his forehead, his lips, his heart, and chants slowly, "From now on, I am your servant, *Valide Hanum.* I am the dust on the road, but I hope to be on the road that you must travel, and to make it smoother."

Nazim knows everything about the extermination plan; it isn't easy to tell when he's listening. But in this moment he feels like one of Harun al-Rashid's knights, loyal combatant beneath the walls of Jerusalem. He stands tall and smiles a broad, toothless smile.

Ah, Shushanig, dear kinswoman, if only you had asked him to lend you his hut! (Thus was how Nishan, the youngest Tachdjian boy, was saved.) Ah, Veron, golden girl in the funny bonnet, if only you had hid among his wives! (Nazim had two wives—fat, dirty, and lazy—and one hut.) Azniv, dark-haired beauty, if only you had run off with Djelal. (But Djelal is at Djemal Pasha's general headquarters, in Aleppo, and he's having a fine time.)

MEANWHILE, Nazim is rummaging in one of his pockets, and he draws forth a yellow envelope, with many stamps. "Here's a letter, my lady, from the city. The postman's no longer around." And here he gets tongue-tied, unable to say that it is addressed to Sempad. Yerwant's telegram.

Shushanig takes the envelope, looking at it without understanding. She opens it with care, with her grandfather's fancy letter opener, which is always near the front door. Yerwant's words dance incomprehensibly before her tired eyes: Italy is entering the war, Yerwant isn't coming—all for nothing, all for nothing. Then she remembers the game she was playing with Sempad just yesterday, and her chest heaves painfully. Her horizon is narrowing sharply, as if her bright soul were burning in from the margins, gradually sinking into a shadowy, black abyss.

With insidious sleepiness lying in wait for her, burning her eyes, Shushanig begins to dream of abandoning herself to that coolness, those shadows. It doesn't seem to her that she has much left to do. She no longer has to worry about what clothes and what trunk Suren will take to Europe, about the packages for Rupen to give the carpenter twins on their way to America, about Garo's American school, about new clothes for Leslie: all lost, all of them, in her soul's flaming margins, which are too hot to touch.

Now she must dress the girls, prepare for the journey. Shushanig's exhausted mind looks at Nazim without seeing him. She slips the telegram into an apron pocket, then thinks better of it and hands it to Madame Nevart: "In the end," she says, "you were the only one who knew him." And then, "If only it had been us visiting them. We must try to warn Zareh."

Azniv, who has been discreetly keeping an eye on Shushanig, rushes over and takes the telegram from Nevart's hands, reads it, and says, "I'll hold on to this." (A kind of talisman, she thinks, something sacred from the West, proving that Armenians do exist elsewhere, and are free, and can even send messages—a light beyond the dark horror that surrounds her.)

Lost and scared, the other women of the quarter show up at Shushanig's door. The fate that has befallen her has impressed a seal of painful authority upon her face: the gay smile is fled; the heavy, earthly features of her face now stand out.

But she is *Mayrig*, the mother, as sweet Garo was saying only yesterday (centuries ago). Whom else to ask if everything has been done properly, whom else to seek approval from? And Shushanig, lovingly escorted by the vigilant Azniv, who stays a step behind her, manages. She checks the carriages, counts the people, distributes the elderly, the goats, the children, the stores of water, the sugar, the blankets, even the little cages with their little birds.

It's her idea to raid the pharmacy and the Viennese confectionery. Bonbons, perfumed cartons of Western sweets, tins of English biscuits, Swiss chocolate, fondants, and pastries—all are counted and distributed.

For all the children, it's a feast of fresh sweets. For them and their mothers, and for her own surviving daughters, Shushanig puts on a kind smile, claps her hands, sets the table ("no need to wash dishes anymore," she thinks), and briskly opens the large sideboard, taking out the finest china (gold-rimmed porcelain from Paris), the English silver, the Sheffield teapot.

"Let the children have this memory," she thinks. Azniv understands at once. She opens a drawer and shakes out the great tablecloth of Flanders linen, embroidered by the lovely Iskuhi as a gift for her beloved Hamparzum: Anatolian vines and grapes in green and burgundy, with tendrils of gold around a large, benevolent central sun that sends out perfectly symmetrical, pointed rays, all of it stitched with silk and gold thread and bordered with a thick, wide strip of shot moiré taffeta—the lively imagination of a happy young woman passed down as a family legacy.

The colorful treasure glitters, the clean dishes, the cups, the aromatic desserts all sparkle, the children are wildly happy, the May sun winks benevolently through the windows and is echoed in the center of the table. "What feast day is it, *Mayrig*?" asks the little, lame Sarkis, son of the widow Andonian.

"It's your feast day, children," replies Shushanig, "to prepare you for the exciting journey ahead of us, when we go to meet your fathers. The war is coming, and we're going to travel like the pioneers in America."

This is an notion everyone understands, and it raises their spirits. Even Ismene has come, and for the umpteenth time she tells the story of how she met the Indian chief whom she later married, and then she sings her Cherokee song. But she eats nothing, and *Mayrig* eats nothing. Only Azniv displays her usual robust appetite. Her white teeth flash, sinking into a cream puff. And she sings *"Ov sirun sirun,"* her song.

On this night, everyone sleeps, worn out from their preparations, hoping, in their subdued docility, to have distanced themselves from their destiny. They all dream of their overseas relatives (they all have some) opening their arms to welcome the refugees. "I'll work, I'll do any-thing," the grown-ups think. "I'll grow up in America," the children think.

These gentle, hardworking people have already given themselves over to the rise and fall of the ocean waves. None of them genuinely believe that they will return to their homes; they already feel, around them, the greed of the others, their compatriots, those who have not been marked by destiny, who are of the proper race and religion, who will take possession of their worldly goods—their fields and houses, their shops, their lush fruit orchards. Yet they will manage to escape the accursed circle, of that they are certain. And their sturdy arms, strengthened by their courageous spirits, will rebuild elsewhere.

No one in this little city, except the women of Sempad's family, suspects that something else is happening: a massive trick, a deadly trap, a move toward that nothingness that will be their journey's true destination. None of them know that the men have already been wiped out.

THE CARRIAGES LINE UP in the quarter before dawn. Most are driven by boys, the males who were not sum-moned. Serpuhi the midwife drives her own, which shel-ters a woman in labor who failed to push the baby out during the night. Arsine, the fair-skinned, strong-armed washerwoman, drives the first of three artisan carriages, in which are crammed the most essential tools of several trades: nails, hammers, screwdrivers, horseshoes, a small portable forge (the one that during the summer was installed in the cavern beneath the falls), saws, files, shovels of various sizes, washboards, soap, lye—everything they might need. Arsine is proud of the set of aluminum pots that her eldest son, a carpenter in Marseilles, sent her from France, and she has packed them all, along with their lids and the shiny copper ladle, even if they do take up a bit too much space. On the carriage floors ride the children, her own and those of the blacksmith and the farrier, whose sensible wives watch over them. The children are sleepy and whiny, but the angry voices of the *zaptiehs*, outside, quickly silence them.

Finding the carriages ready and the people intent on peaceably closing their houses and securing the shutters, the gendarmes don't know whom to be angry with: they ride balefully around, rattling their sabers and muttering vague threats. They peer into the carriages, grimly pleased but taking no hostile action; indeed they seem more sober and calm than usual. The fact is that they know, they have been informed.

The news of the massacre at Skylark Farm spread in a flash. The colonel immediately sent Ismail packing, into the war zone, but he has no idea that the lieutenant, enraged, has already sent a factious report about him to the all-powerful minister of war, Enver Pasha, principal organizer of the Armenian roundups and deportations that, throughout eastern Anatolia, are progressing according to a strict timetable that is monitored daily by the most zealous Ittihadists and the fearsome Special Organization, which was established specifically for this purpose.

Though the lieutenant has been sent away, the soldiers who were his accomplices have merely been scolded paternally by the colonel and forgiven. This may have been a mistake. Times have changed. Their lust for those recently glimpsed Armenian possessions, combined with a certain uneasiness regarding their own excessive actions, is causing them to shout more loudly, to silence every interior voice. Why didn't the colonel punish them? No doubt because they were in the right. And they talk, they talk with their fellow gendarmes, the *zaptiehs*, recounting the villa's marvels, imagining riches hidden inside every Armenian house.

The *zaptiehs*, mouths watering, are eager to get started: with killing, with enjoying the lovely Armenian virgins, with rummaging around in search of legendary hidden treasures. The men are dead, anything goes. There's no one to stand in their way.

But they have precise orders. The operation is to be carried out in a very modern fashion, with surgical precision. They must avoid frightening or involving, through piteous spectacles, the Armenians' neighbors, their Turkish friends, the American missionaries, the Jews, and of course the Greeks, of whom there are many. The departures must take place with cold regularity and should remind no one of the unseemly manhunts of the sultan's day, when Armenian corpses were stacked triumphantly along the streets of Erzerum and Constantinople, when more than one man was immortalized by Western reporters leaning on his rifle beside such stacks.

We are not venting personal resentments, the Ittihadists have explained, but rather lancing a boil, in order to heal the sick body of our nation, to cleanse it. And for those who operate successfully, much will be forgiven, and they will be allowed to freely enjoy whatever they can squeeze out of this impure subrace of priests and peddlers.

All they must do is proceed methodically, move on the appointed days, refrain from causing too much of a stir in the cities. Once out of the cities, the exodus must, above all, proceed unbendingly, in Prussian fashion.

"We will be admired by our allies for the impeccable precision with which we handle the Armenian Question," thinks Enver, who with every telegram reporting the departure of another caravan feels a sharp satisfaction grow within him. In his office, trimmed with Bulgarian leather, he follows them, drawing long lines with colored pencils and affixing little red emblems over the blues and greens of his personal map of the Empire, until the many lines, thinning, merge into one, which finally becomes lost—imperceptible—in the Syrian desert.

To party ideologues, the idea of a deportation through the desert thus seems a kind of purification ritual, a propitiatory sacrifice of slaughtered animals for the honor and glory of a secular, impassive, jealous God. And so, this time, even the *zaptiehs* manage to dissemble; the trusting blindness of the Armenian women, alone now, does the rest. Thus it is that they depart in peace.

THE COLONEL, poor man, understands nothing of these modern concepts. He prays regularly but is no fanatic; his God is the true God, and he pities those who have not yet been enlightened. But he feels deeply the echo of the tolerant master's ancient pride in treating his servants well. That's what Christians are: inferior but useful. People who do the housework for the sultan's proud warriors, helpful people, who deserve benevolent protection—though any who (God forbid!) get mixed up in politics must be isolated and eliminated.

The spectacle he witnessed has filled him with horror. The pious, just man who was his father (buried now but still alive within him) and he himself, the man who is at ease with Madame Sesostris, both recoil in disgust and embarrassment that only increase, in the hours following the massacre, as the colonel thinks of that group of women—those seven pairs of dark, unmoving eyes that stared into his—and of the intolerable fate of Krikor the doctor.

The words he uttered then are binding. He feels noble, on the side of right. And so he goes to spend the night with Madame Sesostris, who helps him devise a rescue plan—well remunerated, to be sure—for Shushanig and her daughters and relatives.

"They'll all pay a visit to my Egyptian relatives, my Coptic cousins in Alexandria," Madame Sesostris says excitedly, "and even if no one saw them arrive, I'm sure that with a few shiny pieces of silver, properly invested, they'll all recall them arriving, say, ten days ago. And now they're afraid of the war, so you can have them escorted from there to Aleppo by a squad of troops."

In the end, however, this doesn't strike them as a good idea. "Someone might double-cross us, we'll have to share the windfall," the colonel reflects. Better to hide them away at home until the storm has passed. The prospect intrigues the palm reader, who already foresees a tidy profit and a fruitful friendship that will provide the social connections she has always desired. And besides, well, Sempad's eyes haunt her, too.

The massacres will pass, they always have. And an alliance with that family, an aura of affectionate respectability for her newfound affluence, earning precious praise and at the same time doing good—it's an attractive opportunity.

Perhaps they could withdraw to the country together. (To the Farm, she was about to think, before the horror struck her: Shushanig will, of course, never go back there. Perhaps she'll sell it? On the cheap, to a friend?)

Her thoughts race, and her exquisite hopes, too. And

Madame Sesostris (whose real name is the mundane Gabrielle) is already trying to imagine the layout of the rooms. Then she falls asleep, happy, beside the colonel, who is leaning against the silk pillows of the large odalisque bed he likes so much, calmly smoking his English pipe, his heart at peace, his mind full of well-conceived plans. Reassured, he'll sleep late the next morning.

But the hours have sped by too quickly, and destiny mocks him. The colonel has been intentionally left in the dark with regard to the actual scale of the deportations. He stays in the barracks, but his soldiers know more than he does. He was already suspect, and now his actions have confirmed him as a man of the old regime: having the bodies buried at the Farm, having the women escorted . . .

No one told him that a detachment of the Special Organization, commanded by a group of zealous Ittihadist officers, arrived three days ago, and has conferred at length with the *kaimakam*. He hasn't seen the telegrams, the exact orders. He knows only about the roundup of the men (for one of the usual warnings, he thinks). He has no specific knowledge of the deportations.

And so, the next day, when he summons a group of his most trusted soldiers, led by the devoted sergeant, Hakim, and orders them to go collect Shushanig and the other women of the family, pile them into a carriage, and take them to Madame Sesostris, keeping the whole thing quiet, and promises a nice sum for each of them in return, they exchange furtive, silent glances. Then Hakim speaks, for all of them.

"We speak to you as sons to a father, effendi," he begins, hesitant. "We'll go, if you want. You're the man in charge. But there are ugly rumors going around the city, and ugly things are happening."

Then, seeing the colonel's knitted brow, he plunges forward: "The Armenian men have all been killed, like your friend Sempad, the pharmacist. And the women, and everyone else, left this morning, at dawn. They've been told they're being moved for military reasons, but everyone knows, right?" He looks around the circle; the men lower their heads, silent. "We all know they're going to die. We've been told that no one, effendi, no one is allowed to help an Armenian. Not the women, not the children, not the old men. Penalty of death for helping an Armenian."

He continues, nervous, headlong: "Their *vartabed*, you know, the old priest Hovhannes, left with the gold cross from the cathedral, dressed all in gold and silver and wearing the slippers from mass, walking at the head of the caravan, and as he passed everyone knelt down, and a woman yelled, 'It's not our fault. Bless us, father,' but the soldiers made her shut up. Then the priest got into Madame Shushanig's carriage."

The colonel is stunned and has trouble finding his voice: "Even the old priest? But where are they going?

And which soldiers are escorting them if I don't know anything about it?"

He's gauging, as he speaks, the extent of his loss of power, but he still doesn't understand.

"Not our soldiers, effendi. They're from the Special Organization, and they take their orders directly from the *kaimakam*. They say we're good for making war on men. But this, they say, is a special kind of hunt, no quarter, for the shrewdest of animals, and there's much to be gained."

"But their houses, who'll take care of their houses?" the colonel asks, as if frightened to his heart's core.

"They're on their way, sir, coming down from the mountains," the sergeant replies. "The Kurdish bandits are on their way—fortune has smiled on them this time: they've been promised the Armenian houses. Whoever takes possession first has the house to himself." (The sergeant is rather annoyed: he too could have been comfortable in one of those nice Armenian houses, and he doesn't have the highest regard for the Kurds.) "And we don't know where the Armenians are going. Some say to Aleppo, but caravans of deportees are leaving from every *vilayet*, and how can they all fit in Aleppo?"

The sergeant's broad face, now that he has spoken, brightens. If the Armenians have been sent away, by government orders, what harm would there be in pocketing some of what was theirs? And he looks—the whole group looks—hopefully at the colonel. They realize he didn't know any of this, which means that his status is no longer what it once was. (Shouldn't he be the one, in time of war, deciding everything in the city?) And yet he is still an important man, and they are his soldiers, his sons . . .

But now Colonel Hikmet has truly understood.

Without replying, he turns and straightens his shoulders. He goes into his office, carefully closes the door, pulls out his English pipe and looks at it, meditating, waiting. Not much patience is required. Ten minutes later, a *zaptieh* rushes in with a sealed message. The colonel opens it and reads without surprise that he has been relieved of his command of the local garrison and ordered to the Russian front, along with his battalion. He is accused of aiding and abetting suspected enemies (poor decapitated Sempad . . .). The order takes effect immediately—just enough time to retrieve his handsome Chinese silk robe from Madame Sesostris and to quickly tell her what had happened.

"I won't ask you to follow me," he concludes, downcast. But in the depths of his simple heart, he isn't completely unhappy; it seems to him that by leaving this place, he is making up for so much unavoidable dirty work, for so much cowardly baseness, for his overly comfortable life—and escaping the Armenian curse.

He'll be a real soldier, as brave as he used to be. He'll be back on a horse, as proud as the time he went hunting in the mountains with Sempad and his friend from the Laz country. And he will kill like a true Ottoman warrior, face-to-face, in battle.

And in that moment, as he and Madame Sesostris, that odd couple, are parting, each has a vision: the colonel sees his father, a just man, nodding gravely and showing him a white desert of bones; she sees her mother, the Italian adventuress, the lover of the governor of Alexandria, calling her to return to Egypt.

"And I haven't asked you to leave this godforsaken country and come away with me," she replies, relieved. And because she is good, she gives him a passionate farewell kiss and the lovely leather-bound book that Sempad had stuffed with banknotes, which she had been keeping beneath a pillow. She really is good: she took only half.

IN AN ITALY decked with flags, a somber, grieving, forlorn Yerwant for the first time no longer feels in control of his own destiny. For the first time, he is an avid reader of newspapers, and he snorts perceptibly at the triumphal tones of the first reports from the front. Everyone agrees: the war—now that Italy, with a mighty about-face, has joined the Entente Powers, opening a new front—will be brief.

"Austria will fall at once," the journalists shamelessly declare, convinced forty years after the fact that Italians made the difference in the 1866 victory, and intoxicated over having snatched Libya and the Dodecanese, three years ago, from an Ottoman Empire that could now be legitimately torn to pieces.

"France, England, and Russia need our help to win, and we'll get back Trento and Trieste"—thus sing the boys in the streets, thus preach inflamed lecturers to the ladies who throng the irredentist societies. Many a young man volunteers, dreaming of the new flying machines, the aeroplanes, of heroism in the skies, of beautiful war, of the new guns and the self-propelled vehicles, of the Big Bertha—all rather confusedly.

War, after fifty years of peace, is a fatal infatuation. Yetwart and Khayël read, too, become enthusiasts, find it quite tiresome to continue going to school in a world suddenly so youthful, so full of life and loud colors and violent events. The journey to Anatolia, their aunts and uncles down there, even the new automobile that had excited them so, all disappear from their attention, like a dissolving nightmare.

Yetwart, at sixteen, is old enough to begin driving, but he refuses to learn how. He will never drive: for the rest of his life, his small, rotund figure and legendary hat will come into view beside a driver (and often a new one, as Yetwart is fickle and quick-tempered).

Khayël, on the other hand, one boring July day, will rediscover the car and fall in love with it. The journey toward the distant family will become a fairy-tale adventure, ripe for the imagining, in which he, not his father, plays the hero—and tames the powerful red Isotta Fraschini, now motionless in the barn, which he imagines as a crouching beast. Soon he'll steal the keys and learn to start its engine; for the rest of his life, he will be a careful but daring and rather inconsiderate driver, drunk on speed and on the challenges that his nimble, sure hands succeed in mastering.

Yerwant, during that splendid tail end of May, seems blind to his sons, his wife, and her relatives. He moves them all, for the summer, to their villa in Dolo, and every morning, after his coffee and bread, he leaves in a rush, as Letizia silently watches him like a nurse. He takes the short train ride into the city, to the hospital, works himself into a stupor, and then goes looking hungrily for news he doesn't find.

Virtually nothing is heard from the Eastern front. The Russians advancing, Enver saved by Armenian troops from an ambush—that's old news. An immense silence now stretches over all of Anatolia, and Sempad hasn't even replied to Yerwant's telegram of May 23. This is without doubt the most disturbing symptom.

Sempad has never missed the chance to send a telegram. Even if the little city had suddenly become a war zone—though it's quite far from the front and hasn't been mentioned in any dispatches—it would still be easy enough for Sempad to "make the loop," to have the message relayed through the Constantinople offices of one of the German pharmaceutical firms that supplied his pharmacy.

Mad with anxiety, Yerwant feels personally threatened without knowing why. Shapeless nightmares resurface in his worried brain, vague visions of blood, of which his almost exclusively Western life experience has given him no real understanding. Thus he isn't sure whether these clouds that gather each day around him are genuine or imaginary—wild fantasies provoked by a mysterious sense of guilt (and perhaps unrealized desire?), or real perceptions of an immense evil, crouching with its tentacles of shadow at the edges of his consciousness.

At this point he sends another telegram, asking for news, to Zareh in Aleppo, but Zareh doesn't respond, either. And Rupen in Boston can do nothing but echo Yerwant's question and share his apprehension.

Thus pass two weeks, the weeks during which Sempad's fate is sealed. Then, in one "briefly noted" article among many, the first news arrives, via an American newspaper—imprecise news, but charged with a truth that Armenian ears, even Westernized ones, recognize as a death knell: "In the city of ————, the famous American College has been closed indefinitely. The building has been expropriated, the children sent home or enlisted in work battalions. The college president and the American consul raised objections and were declared personae non gratae. Ambassador Morgenthau made formal protests to the Turkish government, to Enver Pasha personally. But he obtained no satisfaction."

From that day on, the fragments of information begin piling up, random and isolated at first among all the agency dispatches regarding the European war, then gradually becoming more prominent, until they form a picture that cannot be ignored. In those dark beginnings of the summer of 1915, Yerwant reads not the war news but rather, bit by bit, the slightest details leaking out about the Armenian massacres—a few lines that speak to him with terrible eloquence.

The newspapers publish them in support of the many articles on the treachery and wickedness of the Austro-Germans; after all, the Ottoman Empire is allied with the Central Powers. But Yerwant comes to realize that the events are not merely random massacres or by-products of wartime disarray. He begins bitterly to sense the dark design, the net of death in which Sempad has no doubt (since he hasn't written) been snared. And he soon reaches the profound, absolute certainty that that world to which he had deluded himself he could return is gone, swallowed whole, and he looks back nostalgically on himself as he was a year ago, when old Hamparzum died, and he wrote with relief the letter renouncing his birthright and began thinking again of the Lost Country.

But Sempad was there then. For Yerwant, Sempad has always been there: Sempad and his simple heart, Sempad and his telegrams, his pharmacy, his backgammon, his children, the ones who sit on Yerwant's desk in the portrait, polite and composed, of the whole family around old Hamparzum, stretched out on his bier, with rich floral swirls, retouched with silver, surrounding the central image.

Sempad, his brother, he who kept the keys. Yerwant's heart shuts tight, sealed forever. Weighed down by an infinite sense of guilt—guilt for being Armenian, for surviving, for succeeding—Yerwant will never again willingly contemplate the roots of his belonging, the musical, colorful memories of the Lost Country, never, that is, until he recounts them to his granddaughter as fairy tales, distant, perhaps inaccessible, perhaps dreamed.

He will, of course, look after the children who reach Aleppo: he'll have them brought to Italy, pay for their voyage, raise them. But then he will separate them again, cruelly, sending two to America to live with Rupen in Boston, while Nubar and Henriette remain with him, in Italy. Except for Henriette, he will allow them to grow up as Armenians. For his sons, however, the old fatherland will forever be forbidden, confined to vague memories of things that cannot be denied: a few photos, a few names. And in 1924, he will petition the Italian government to allow him to legally remove from his surname that embarrassing three-letter suffix, *-ian*, that exposes so plainly his Armenian origin. His new, truncated name could even be Turkish.

His two cars will tour the Veneto region. As for the gifts, forgotten in a chest of drawers beneath the billiard table, one of his wife's clever nephews will later sell them off for a tidy sum.

Yerwant keeps one part of his life to himself, never discussing it with anyone: his periodic trips to visit his

Zurich friends, a group of wealthy cigarette merchants with whom he spends several days at a time, days that pass in long smoking sessions, fierce games of backgammon or cards, the occasional cup of coffee, the occasional pensive remark.

One of these friends, Masraff, supplies Yerwant with Egyptian cigarettes, which are delivered to the house twice a year in splendid wooden crates, perforated so the tobacco can breathe.

When Yerwant decides to quit smoking, shortly before the outbreak of World War II, he'll leave the last crate, sealed, in a corner of the wardrobe as souvenir and charm. The crate, dusty and alluring, with its Eastern labels, will be discovered there by his granddaughter in December 1945.

As they leave the city, the old priest Hovhannes climbs into Shushanig's carriage.

"Cool off with a sip of *tan*," Azniv quickly offers. She's wearing a bonnet, like Veron, against the burning sun, and now she smells the heat and sweat coming off the old man. Suddenly she wonders, "How will we wash?" And the menacing implications of their journey begin to crowd her mind. There are no hotels to the south, only endless dusty roads, barren land, and villages. The other abrupt question is "Where will they make us stop?"

Azniv deliberates intensely, then looks at Shushanig,

whose eyes, gone dark again, seem to see nothing, and she decides to hold her tongue for the moment.

The old priest, exhausted, falls asleep. His majestic beard sprawls fluidly around his broad, worry-lined face, which relaxes into slumber.

"Sleep, dear father, sleep," whispers Azniv, as her heart, joyous by nature, can't help but brighten a little. The sun is so pleasant, the air so gentle in this tail end of May. Maybe Sempad's assassins were a group of outlaws, the terrible *Hamidie* Kurdish regiments about which she had so often heard; Armenian women know how to survive—they have to. Strangely, the memories of the Red Sultan's massacres calm her. Her family has paid so dearly that, perhaps, the debt they owe for existing has once more been settled, and they can again begin thinking of the future. The names of Zareh in Syria and of Rupen in Boston swell in Azniv's mind, hour by hour, like beacons in the fog; already she's wondering how to let them know. If Ismene, as promised, reaches them . . .

The countryside around them appears so inviting that Azniv and Veron, sitting side by side in front of the carriage, driving the horses slowly, with skill and care, soon decide that it's nearly time for a snack, something to restore everyone and return smiles to the long line of funereal faces that stretches down the road.

There's a meadow shaded by a great plane tree, beside which a centuries-old spring burbles up into an oval basin of Greek marble, decorated with charming designs, worn down by the use of generations. A place for children to bathe, huge oxen to dip their snouts, stars to reflect. Beneath that spout of perpetual water, barely visible to those who look for it, is a small cross, etched there long ago, by someone. All the Armenians and Greeks know this, and for this reason they call it the Hermit's Fountain. It's said that Saint Irenaeus, or else Saint Athanasius, caused the fountain to flow when he withdrew to live in the overhanging rocks, in a cave so small a child could barely fit inside. Today, in that cave, there's still a candle, awaiting the wayfarer.

The carriages stop along the road. The children are already running back and forth between them, and the women are deliberating. The men are gone, the strong spirits who took superstitions with a grain of salt and knew what needed to be done. The women, restless, consult the elders. Someone goes up to the cave and lights the sacred candle.

The *zaptiehs* that had accompanied the caravan to the edge of the city have since disappeared. The women gradually realize this, and rather than being happy about it, they are troubled. In the last carriage, Serpuhi the midwife has put a woman on lookout duty and is tending to the girl in labor, a newly married seventeen-year-old, whose husband is in the capital on business.

"He's thinking of you, sweetheart," whispers Serpuhi, mopping the girl's lips with a piece of bread dipped in vinegar, "and you are strong, you're young—this is nothing. The little bull doesn't want to come out, he's too warm and cozy in there. But we've stopped now, we've stopped, and this is the moment—right, sweetheart?"

The girl closes her eyes, ashen, and gathers herself.

"Too much pain, too much," she thinks, feeling something like a ball of fire between her legs, a terrible scalding in her pelvis, followed by a hoarse cry.

"Good girl, Hripsime; your saint has blessed you," says Serpuhi, caressing her hot cheek. "Now, you must bless this baby boy, in the name of his absent father, and say his name."

"His name is Vartan," whispers the girl, abandoning herself with infinite relief to Serpuhi's expert hands.

Eventually the others arrive, all those unable to ride in the carriages—the oldest of the old, the loners, the beggars—and they're all cheered at the prospect of rest, of good water from the fountain, of the blessing from the Hermit who protects those who drink that water, and they have food on their minds, bread. They're already tired, and they give themselves over to the wisdom of the ones leading them.

But the fact is that, because Shushanig still seems so distant, so absent, the ones leading them are a group of girls. Older girls, the most liberated, the ones who have attended school and know some French, some history, some geography—the young ladies. They are busily conferring. Not about the route, which is a given: there is only one road that goes through the hills and gradually descends into the plain. About, rather, what comes after, and also about how to organize the journey, share the resources, govern this little traveling community.

The elders are more or less useless, given to moaning, prophets of doom. Women with children have their minds on the children, and they can help prepare the food.

But Azniv, Veron, Haiganush (the teacher's daughter), Vartuhi (the postal clerk), and the young lady who works for the railway are all convinced they can make it; deep in their hearts they feel the faint but exciting goad of pride: they, always so sheltered, will demonstrate that women, too, have minds; they'll be able to handle this emergency. And for starters, in the grip of egalitarian ideas, they promise solemnly that on this journey everyone will truly be equal, that resources will be shared equally, just as Kevork, the teacher, always preaches. It will be as though we were in the United States already, Veron suggests, as it is in my church. And they all nod, convinced.

So it is that they all sit in the wide meadow—the old men, the women, the children, the beggars—as the old priest Hovhannes intones *Orhnyal eh Der* (Blessed be the Lord) and, taking a seat beside Shushanig, who is still wrapped in her cloud, whispers words of peace in her ear.

And in that precise moment, with the sun sparkling overhead, they see them, cresting the hills on all sides and then hurtling down on their swift horses: the Kurds who live in the mountains above the falls, who have been promised the Armenian spoils. In a matter of moments, fierce shrieks fill the air, swords and carbines gleam in the sun, and with the innate scenographic talent of warriors on horseback, they pass several times through the encampment, barely injuring the people there but trampling the bread, overturning the jugs, breaking the dishes. The chief grabs the priest by the beard and drags him through the dust behind him.

After the first arrivals more follow, amid war cries, and together they quickly and skillfully surround the carriages. The Armenians—motionless, petrified—hold their breath. For an infinite moment, their passion is suspended, and deep in the heavens a solitary voice moans high, imploring, inside God's time.

Then everything happens. The shining grass and the sacred spring quickly absorb blood from the throats of babes, slit as examples to their mothers. The priest is stripped, his eyes dug out. He cries softly, like a child. Then he dangles, naked, hung from the lowest branch of the plane tree.

A warrior mounts each carriage and urges the horses on, trying to get them to run, holding the reins firmly in one hand and shaking a rifle in the other. But there is no resistance. Quickly, chaotically, the carriages begin to move, and with them go the food, the dishes, the medicine—all hope of survival. An old man tries to stand firm inside one of the carriages and is run through with a sword and flung out. The blonde, Vartuhi, who has Persian blood in her veins and a Greek fiancé who has promised to join her this evening, catches the eye of the Kurdish chief, who rides up to her to take her away. She screams, staring at the man looming over her, and her scream finally penetrates the torpor of Shushanig, who has been sitting in a daze and who now jumps to her feet. "No," she says, and in a flash she puts her hand in a deep pocket, takes out a stone, and extends it toward the Kurd.

The stone glints, red. It's a splendid Burmese ruby, one Shushanig intended for the marriage of her eldest daughter. Red and hypnotic, it flickers in her steady hand. The Kurdish chief calms his horse, dismounts, and bows; this barbaric offering has charmed him. He takes the jewel, raises it to the sun, which floods it with light, and shouts with joy.

Then, as in an ancient contract, he bows again and makes a sweeping gesture with his hand, giving the girl to Shushanig. He doesn't try to milk further riches from her, but instead remounts his horse and shouts to his men to hurry up, it's time to leave. They disappear down the road, the men and some of the carriages.

Shushanig's gesture has saved Vartuhi, and also the carriages belonging to the artisans and Serpuhi, which were farther back than the others. They were to be attacked last, but at the chief's shout, all the horsemen moved at once, dropping everything, drawing up around the carriages that were already in motion and spurring their horses. Now the Armenians watch their resources disappear.

"Quick, quick," says Shushanig, "we'll take the priest

down and bury him here, it's consecrated land." Arsine the washerwoman and her daughters, together with the old man Aram, lame but still strong, dig and pray. The whole meadow quivers with prayer; all the women now feel orphaned and alone—an irreparable solitude. Mothers weep, placing the small bodies of children in the old priest's arms and his worn cross, retrieved along with its snapped leather cord from the foot of the plane tree, between his joined hands. They've lowered his eyelids, straightened his beard, put him back in his old cassock. Now Shushanig tells Veron and Azniv to gather the blue and purple flowers that grow thick around the basin of water, which continues to flow with its calm, soft noise, and to scatter them over the old man and the children in his arms, after having dipped them in the blessed water. And on top of the cross she places the candle from the little cave, which she blows out with a decisive breath. "We won't need that anymore," she explains curtly, adding, "No cross on this grave—they'd rip it out. God knows who his servants are."

The *zaptiehs* have reappeared, sneering. They have split the contents of the carriages, as agreed, with the Kurds. As for the precious stone, they know nothing— the Kurdish chief certainly didn't tell them—and so Shushanig's little treasure remains safe, for now.

.   .   .

THE LONG MARCH begins in earnest, the road of no return. They are far enough away from the city now; the caravan, what's left of it, is at the utter mercy of the gendarmes and their whims. Survival becomes an accident, a clever ruse, a test of strength, a mocking game of dice with death at stake.

"The old and the children," orders Shushanig, "will ride in the remaining carriages, for as long as we manage to keep them." Spurred on by *zaptiehs* on horseback, the caravan stretches out along the road. They were not able to bring much water with them—there are but few containers left—and the sun is beating down. The arid and implacable plains of central Anatolia open wide before them.

When they are first allowed to pause, that evening, they take stock. The night is cold. They pitch a few tents, distribute some milk. Bless you, Arsine of the strong arms, for the foresight with which your packed your carriages! She even brought three fine goats, each now tethered behind a carriage. But if it were not for the elderly and the children, the women might at this point simply sit down and give up. Escape is impossible: there are sentinels around the camp, and beyond them, Kurds. And besides, where would they go? The region they are entering is, as they all know, inhospitable for hundreds of kilometers. The few miserable villages could offer no shelter even if they wanted to. (And a new law—the women don't know this—prohibits giving refuge to Armenians, on penalty of death.) Talat, in a telegram, has written, "No mercy for women, old men, or children. If even one Armenian were to survive, he would later want revenge."

And so, in the uncertain light of four small fires, over which a little food is warming, they take stock, and all those simple hearts ask themselves and their saints for the courage to continue existing.

Aram, the lame old man, pitiable in appearance and fluent in Turkish, a baker and sometime grocer, is elected spokesman (though Shushanig and Azniv will be right behind him, to make suggestions). Adolescent boys and young girls will be kept out of sight; the group must appear decimated and miserable. The old women will go up front—they always elicit a little fear from the Turks, and also a little respect—and they'll carry the smallest babes, in the hope of softening their enemies. The Turks are more likely to respond to the cautious humility of an elderly woman, one who resembles their own mother, than to any direct request. The small, pathetic stratagems of survival . . .

"Each of us," suggests Azniv, "should tie on a blanket and some pans, some supplies. If they also take the last carriages, at least we won't be completely empty-handed." The proposal seems sound, and in the deepening night, like diligent ants, the women busy themselves with portioning out and bundling the contents of the four remaining carriages, packed so well two days before.

The few remaining sacks of coffee are each tied to the back of a child, with countless instructions. They weigh little but signify much.

AND SO, hour after hour, day after day, the Armenian curse was carried out for the women, the elders, and the children of the little city. Each day brought its quotidian horror, and each day the pain grew for the survivors, who dragged themselves along step by step, ever more wretched, ever more emaciated, as each day they confronted their quotidian deaths.

The Kurdish tribes descended often to plunder; the third time they took away the pretty washerwomen together with their carriages. When old Serpuhi cursed them, a *zaptieh* shut her up by sitting on her and smashing her head with a stone. That was the eighth day.

This was sufficient time for the young bride Hripsime to recover from her delivery and to see her baby die, skewered on a bayonet and held aloft like a monument to the contempt of masters for their subjects. But Hripsime closes her eyes and sees the joyous soul of her little Vartan hesitantly trying out his new wings. Then she prays to him to protect her, as he looks down from the vast meadows of heaven, where neither hunger nor pain exists, onto the leprous, desolate earth.

And Hripsime will survive, by thinking of her husband. And they will find each other again many years later, and will have other children. (*This is one of only two stories with truly happy endings that the granddaughter recalls; the other is the epic adventure of Musa Dagh, which she read in a single sitting in her fourteenth summer.*)*

The *zaptiehs* stormed in more and more often, searching everyone, hunting for hidden money or jewels (people in Anatolia still speak of the mythic "Armenian gold," shepherds tell stories of hidden treasures). They seized the coffee, then the money, then the jewels; they found the hiding places: in the braids, under the skirts, among the rags.

They killed male children, raped women, carried off girls of all ages for their distant harems. The elderly died a few at a time, of consumption, of hunger, of heartbreak. They took everything, day after day: saucepans and blankets, the poor goats that no longer gave milk, and Veron's English biscuits, tent canvas, and hats.

Every so often, a piece of bread was thrown the Armenians' way as if they were dogs, from on high. Every so often, a spring, a little water. They always had to drink after the horses of the *zaptiehs*, and on all fours like ani-

* The reference is to Franz Werfel's 1933 novel *Die vierzig Tage des Musa Dagh* (*The Forty Days of Musa Dagh*), the story of the survival of seven villages perched on the slopes of Musa Dagh ("mount Moses"), north of the bay of Antioch, that managed to organize and resist on the mountain until they were saved by a French cruiser. Werfel, an Austrian Jew, told the story of the Armenian slaughter even as Hitler was planning the slaughter of Jews.

mals, sometimes amid grotesque scenes of the troops
entertaining themselves—shooting someone in the neck,
perhaps, just to see the water redden.

Half naked, dirty, sick, starving, sun-blind, their
filthy braids held somehow together, their clothes in rags
and rags on their heads, the Armenian mothers walked,
from town to town, like lepers, like plague victims. Kept
out of the cities they passed, they laid themselves down
on the ground not knowing whether they would have the
strength to get up again, in that grim tomorrow with no
hope and no end, bewitched by misfortune—walking,
forward, no longer knowing why, yet feeling some pri-
mitive animal need to lie down, at night, beside their
children.

DURING THE MARCH, Shushanig thinks constantly,
feverishly—a circular obsession of survival thoughts, limited to the horizon of each day (and her rough, swollen
hands slip repeatedly down to the little sack of gems,
fingering it manically). Her thoughts are obsessive and
few, and then they always begin over again: must count
and recount her little population; must keep the children
between Azniv and Veron and Araxy the cook; must keep
an eye on Madame Nevart, who drags herself along in
a mute stupor, as if accusing everyone of this unforeseen, unbelievable event. Nevart, the sensible, provident
wife who gave Hamparzum no fewer than nine children,

who has earned the right to die in bed, respected, and to have an important funeral, almost as important as her husband's.

Nevart, with vicious, helpless irony, carries on an endless internal dialogue regarding the majestic funeral she longs for. She no longer seems to recognize anyone. Though she eats virtually nothing, an indomitable, spiteful, grim energy propels her fat body, which is collapsing around her. Only Veron can approach her, at night, with a damp handkerchief to tend to her a little.

Her white hair, always so well groomed, tumbles, frightfully wild, down her back, tangled with leaves, dust, and bugs; her teeth gnash against scant saliva and garbled words. Like an Erinys, like a miserable, wasted Fury, Nevart, a good woman—a little foolish, a little spiteful— with a happy little brain, a woman who used to make marmalade and cookies, proceeds tireless and bent, eyes half closed and alarming, fixed on the horizon, carrying with her all the dust from the road, all the destiny of the Armenian women, unwitting symbol of debased fear.

Even the *zaptiehs*, superstitiously, refuse to touch her. She's bad luck, they whisper. Nevart will disappear one night, unnoticed, called by a mysterious wind, by a dazzling mirage, a warm kitchen that appears to her atop the bare hill at the foot of which the group is huddled, on a night like any other in that endless June.

Only Henriette sees her go. But Henriette doesn't speak. And besides, she, too, has seen the light beyond the hill. Nevart walks, and her small, poor heart is cleansed with every step. Her feet are bleeding beneath their crust of filth, and they leave a clearly visible trail, which is of no interest to anyone.

But with every step her heart opens, and thus in the end it is to Nevart, that woman without qualities, that the immense strength of an entire dying population, along with the tears of God that accompany them, is entrusted. She can redeem herself as an offering for the children, for her daughters, for the admired and envied Shushanig. She will not see her sons, Rupen and Zareh, again, or her pretty daughters-in-law, or distant lands. She will never again embrace Yerwant, the son of Iskuhi, who left rather than accept her as his mother.

Now, however, God has forgiven her, and Nevart walks in light. She hopes to find Hamparzum again, but at this point a humble seat in the second row would suffice; his true wife, as she well knows, is the radiant Iskuhi.

"How can I compete with a nineteen-year-old?" she wonders, reasonably. "I'm old, and so dirty, and so tired." Then she falls, like a felled tree, across the path.

A mule driver from the nearby village will find her at dawn. He is a pious man, and since no one is there to see, he quickly overcomes his disgust at the large, already wasted body, and he buries her beside a stream, murmuring a prayer to the living God, who is holy for everyone.

· · ·

OVER THE COURSE of the march, all the old men and women are lost, one by one, like Nevart. They drop away simply by stopping. No one looks for them, no one asks them to go on. Sometimes a merciful *zaptieh* runs them through on the spot; other times they are simply abandoned, by everyone, and no one looks back. They squat beside the road, wretched, motionless figures, like the guardians of eternity, and behind each of them, invisible, stands the angel with his unsheathed sword. In the dead of night, in the wretched huts of every village in Anatolia, men and women stir. They see them, the glowering angels, and they fear their wrath, and so it is that they approach the little rag heaps that line the road and bury them, covertly, with their feet pointing east, so that they can hear the trumpets at the Resurrection of the Dead, the mysterious *anastasis ton nekron* of the Last Judgment. The Turk cannot help the living Armenians, not even with the wayfarer's bread and water, and so he buries the dead ones, trusting them to redeem the obscure guilt that oppresses him. And then he returns to his usual labors.

THE NIGHT FOLLOWING Nevart's disappearance, Shushanig, Azniv, and Veron hold council with Araxy the cook. Each has a secret in her heart; Shushanig's is her unyielding desire for death, which deepens during her inner dialogue with Sempad, with whom she speaks day after day, and she feels that he comforts her, is near her. "It won't be

long, dear," she pleads, and, "Why don't I hear the children? Why can't I speak with them?"

Shushanig now understands, thoroughly, the mystery
of the force that unites forever the man and the woman
who have chosen each other. "Wherever you are, I'm
there, too." No one can truly interrupt the colloquy of
two loving spouses, nor separate their vitals, which are
intertwined.

Veron is thinking that if she manages to reach
Aleppo, she might be able to warn the Methodist minister there, Herbert Lewis, who came to baptize her when
she converted. She imagines herself prostrate at his feet,
not a lost sheep but a very dirty, very hungry one, and sees
him—tall, sober, with sunken iron-gray eyes and a well-
trimmed beard—lean down to her, lift her up, give her a
cup of thick, milked coffee and lots of bread . . . Veron's
imagination doesn't dare go further than the taste of the
coffee. Each time she reaches this point, her eyes moisten
and her throat tightens.

Azniv, on the other hand, thinks of nothing but the
people around her and of making it to the end of the day.
On the fifth day of the march, wearing a mad smile and
Zareh's sheet of red silk, she offered herself to a *zaptieh*
who approached their little group. He was stirred by the
idea of a woman who, for a change, didn't have to be
forced, and a little flattered by the special smile she gave
him, by the submissive tenderness with which she welcomed him into her.

It satisfies his masculine pride. These Armenian women who would rather die than yield (the gendarmes have all heard the story of the convoy from Van, the one where all the women, together, singing, threw themselves into the Euphrates with their daughters), these haughty infidels who know how to write and how to scheme—well, he has one all to himself, and she seems happy, and she makes love well. Naturally he'll give her a little of his bread. Azniv doesn't ask for anything, she just smiles. And in that hopeless universe of death, amid life's hard labors, her smile seems to the soldier the only joy, his recompense.

He has one wife in town, but Azniv has told him that she'll convert and marry him, at the end of the journey. (Though he doesn't know that she isn't eating the bread he gives her; she passes it to Shushanig, Veron, and the children. And he doesn't realize that her rosy cheeks are glowing only with fever.)

The others lower their eyes before Azniv, but they greedily take her bread. The truth is they have nothing left to eat. Araxy the cook is still carrying a ladle and a pot strapped to her back, and a can of muddy water balances on her hip. But each evening she cooks only grass, and the children cry. She wishes she should could cut off a hand and give it to them, that her braid were food, and she stares impotently at her sturdy, uselessly skilled hands.

Her last resource is a small bag of pistachios, which two nights ago she managed to untie from the saddle of a *zaptieh* who had taken her for the night. She yelled a little, for form's sake, then prayed fervently, and while the man was grunting above her, she looked around and spotted the bag. It didn't matter what was in it: it was food, and that was enough. Thus far, and she's proud of this, Nubar seems healthy and is still fairly lively, the girls are not ill, and no one has taken them for pleasure—they're too small, with the exception of Arussiag, who is eleven, but luckily is quiet and rather ugly.

No fire is lit, and no one is really sleeping. Each, huddled around her poor possessions, lies curled in the dark. Some sigh, some groan, some try to soothe their tortured feet. Furtive shadows pass through the camp: the *zaptiehs,* looking for women and the legendary gold. Every now and then a flashing knife, a cry.

Shushanig and the others whisper softly, stretched out over the little bodies of the children. How can they make use of their little treasure, without having it snatched away in an instant—and maybe even getting killed for having hidden it through all the searches? How can they use it to buy food? They have to be able to reach a village, and then succeed in speaking with the frightened farmers, and negotiate, letting them see the stones and the coins one at a time. And all this must be done before dawn.

But who has the strength to do it? They can't show up like beggars, their hands trembling, the cold sweat of mortal hunger upon them. The poor farmers of that desolate territory have a boundless fear of Armenian ghosts, and they keep their distance from the ranks of mendicants who, like an endless river, drag themselves along the road.

Then Araxy stiffens, straightens her hair with a bit of saliva, and says, "I'll go. The cook should logically be the one to search for food; it's no job for a lady." And she laughs, baring her remaining teeth, stark white against her thin face. So Shushanig pulls out, with a thousand precautions, the famous little pouch, extracts three gold coins, then adds another two, and says, "Go, Araxy, and may God be with you. But listen: if you see only one way out, one way of escaping our fate, take it, don't turn back, save yourself. Only, don't forget us. We've shared everything, including our fate: Araxy, dear girl, if you find a hole in the net that's killing us, go. You have my blessings. Follow the path of our forefathers."

Shushanig knows her to be agile, strong, and loyal. She knows that, if she can, Araxy will come back with food. But it's a desperate mission: even if she manages to get beyond the circle of *zaptiehs* that hems them in, she'll have to get the farmers to listen to her, and then return— all before dawn. And so, after she has crept out, if she manages to get her bearings in the fields, maybe, alone, she can save herself. Araxy withdraws the bag of pistachios from between her breasts, takes a handful and slips it into her pocket, and then she hands the bag solemnly to Shushanig, makes the sign of the cross, and slips away quietly, like a furtive little eel in a canebrake.

No one in the family will ever see her again. But for

the good reader, there's this: Araxy, nimble and quick to smile, will spend her life, content, in a brothel in Alexandria. That night none of the farmers around the camp opened a door to her whispers. A few dogs bayed, mournfully. The stars loomed overhead, like punctures.

The girl pressed on, getting lost in the vast dark, full of hostile, stealthy life. But in an abandoned barn she found a cat that had just given birth, and like a terrorized animal, but too hungry to stop herself, she fought with the cat, took two of the kittens, killed them with her pathetic knife, then skinned and ate them while they were still warm, drinking their blood. Sated, she fell asleep wrapped in a sackcloth, in a corner, and slept, exhausted, for the rest of the night—and for the entire day and night that followed.

Then, feeling better physically but lonelier than ever before, and like a traitor, a perjurer, she wandered night after night, from one provisional shelter to another, drinking from the troughs of animals, rummaging through straw in search of seeds or rinds, light and nimble as an animal, blazingly quick when it came to escaping and hiding.

She gave a coin once, to a woman, in exchange for some hot lamb-intestine soup. Like her, other fugitives roamed the nocturnal paths: boys, mainly, and small children whom desperate mothers, taking advantage of a lapse in the gendarme's attention or the cover of night or a softhearted farmer, had shooed away from the caravan of death: little demons, hungry and knowing, heading east toward the advancing Russian army, or else west, toward the sea, guided by the infallible compass of instinct.

Sometimes dogs barked in the night. Sometimes Araxy killed them, to take their food. The farmers, locked in their houses, dared not go out at night during that summer of horror; they didn't want to see, to hear. Every so often they took a corpse and stripped it, looking for gold and jewels. Others, out of kindness, set out pieces of bread or buckets of water at crossroads.

In the end, Araxy reached the sea, at Smyrna. No one had spotted her, no one had noticed her. At dawn one August day, she slipped unobserved into the big city, among the harbor's ragged derelicts, and offered herself as a cook in a Greek tavern. The proprietress, a fat woman named Elefteria, looked at her and laughed. Araxy smiled, too, and said, "Clean me up, ma'am. I was the cook for a great family. I can make everything, even French soufflés." Elefteria realized she was Armenian and said tersely, "We'll see. The tub's over there. But first, girl, take this plate." And she served her a ladleful of mutton stew. Araxy fell to her knees before the brimming dish and wept.

The Armenians were not being deported from Smyrna. General Liman von Sanders, the German commander of the city, did not allow any of them to be touched. Smyrna's fate would be decided later.

But by that time, Araxy would be gone. She fell in

love with Stavros Anastasiopoulos, Elefteria's brother, a
talented harbor-district pimp with a thin mustache and a
quick smile. She happily followed him to Alexandria, to
Madame Louloudaki's brothel, of which he owned a
share—she would have followed him to the ends of the
earth. Stavros became her father, her lover, her master, her
warm refuge, filling all the empty spaces in her docile
heart. A docile whore with a kind heart, who didn't
know—or want to learn—how to say no to anyone.

Every now and then, however, she made Stavros write
a letter for her, always the same letter, to Yerwant, the doctor in Italy. Stavros wrote them out carefully but never
sent them, and Araxy, in the dead of night, when she
wasn't working, would cry and put away money for a trip
to Italy, so she could see him in person. "So many things
I must tell him, so many things he needs to know," she
would sob—biting her pillow as she did, because Stavros,
otherwise so good to her, couldn't bear her tears. "And I
must pay back the money Madame Shushanig gave me.
And I must know what happened to Nubar."

Araxy remembers vividly the circumstances of old Hamparzum's death, and she's convinced that, as the omens
predicted, Nubar survived.

When Shushanig saw that Araxy had not returned,
she found herself briefly at a total loss: *It's true, then, there's
really no hope left.* The bag of pistachios is the last food she

has; she gives three to each of the children and puts one in her mouth. When these run out, we'll all die together, she hopes. And she sets off wearily in the gray of dawn.

A few hours later, she is approached by one of the surviving old women, Berdjuhi, who in better times was the tidy janitor at the American College. Berdjuhi always chews tobacco and still has, in her pocket, a few crumbs left, which she mixes with herbs, randomly. "It's disgusting in any case" is her refrain, which always gives way to endless chatter in which past and present are bizarrely intermixed—the gossip of happier days, the caravan's wretched little resentments.

"Hang on, Shushanig," she whispers instead this time. "Don't give up. Look, we're approaching Konya— Konya, the holy city, city of dervishes."

And indeed the *zaptiehs* seem nervous: usually the smell keeps them at a distance, but today they're sticking close to the deportees, prodding the stragglers forward, the column of them so much thinner now than when they left. A month ago, the little city, happiness . . . But the refugees don't allow themselves to think back, even for an instant. Bent toward the earth, the surviving members of various families huddle together, each cluster silently hostile to the others, and utterly uncurious about anything that isn't food, the remnants of food, or at least vaguely edible. The children pick through horse manure for undigested seeds; they catch lizards and devour worms. Their gaze is opaque, pointed, obsessive.

But today even the children forget, for a moment, the hunger that burns them from within. The caravan's road is growing lively: a few carriages, a few real houses appear; a few green oases, a few trees.

For a moment, they all nurture a faint hope: "Someone will see us, someone will realize what's happening." But instead the people along the road seem barely to notice them; they cross their path with blank eyes, or sidestep them with visible disgust. Nothing but distance between them.

Up ahead, the *zaptiehs* caracole menacingly, screaming and waving their weapons, as they lead the little convoy down into a small, secluded valley at the foot of the city walls. It's a slope with patches of dry grass, two scrubby trees, and a trickling spring.

"Don't move," calls the chief gendarme, ordering them to stop even though it isn't yet evening. "You can rest here. We'll bring you some bread before long."

They clearly want to avoid contact with the people of the city, as well as the curiosity of the few foreigners who live there. Though they prefer to bypass inhabited areas, there is no way to bypass this particular stretch of road, and so the chief has decided that it's better to give them a little bread and stop the convoy near a spring, letting them drink, undisturbed, for a change.

The bread is requisitioned without much trouble from the humble houses of the farmers who live on the outskirts of the city, and soon a line of women approaches the miserable group, setting a few large loaves on the ground for them.

On seeing them, the Armenians start screaming— they scream like madwomen, raising the smallest children high above them on emaciated arms, they scream so loudly that all the air fills with echoes. The *zaptiehs* hit them with their rifle stocks, but the women scream and scream. And miraculously the city inhabitants begin appearing at the ancient walls to look, first a few boys, then men, the older ones draped in commanding robes; the imams, the spiritual leaders of that ancient city; men wearing the turbans of the ulema; and then the veiled women, and the German consul, Herr Walter Müller, and the shopkeepers, the artisans, even the blacksmith and the farrier with his pincers on his shoulder.

Surrounded by a night of moaning, the Armenian women scream, their children cry with rediscovered voices, the few surviving elders moan softly. And the inhabitants of Konya understand everything, including the fate in store for their own Armenians, deported only a few days earlier.

And suddenly the great leader of the dervishes raises his cane into the air and shouts, loudly, "This is not the will of the Prophet, blessed be his name. Feed and lodge these people, because his voice is coming down to us again from the heavens of the Almighty, and it brings curses."

Thus it was that, for an instant, the fate of the surviving Armenians from the little city was suspended, and Ismene found Shushanig again.

ISMENE, FATHER ISAAC, and his wife Katerina, assisted by the wailers and Nazim the gimp, had put their ears to the ground everywhere in the days following the departure of the Armenian convoy. And what they heard chilled their blood. All the news was of death. The ugly thugs of the Special Organization had taken up residence in the Armenian houses—not the Kurds, who after a rapid but systematic looting had returned to their mountains laden with embroidered sheets, with carpets, with drapes, with lavish and fanciful furnishings. Twenty years later, in Diyarbekir, the diploma (with its Art Nouveau swirls) of Kevork Mendilian, chemist, stood out among other prized possessions in a Kurdish chief's tent, its elaborate frame intact.

In Armenian orchards, ripe apricots were splitting open on the ground, while tall nettles and couch grass were already covering the well-tended walkways of our family garden.

In the ample sitting room, the gutted sofas yawned at the broken frames, the shattered crystal. But Ismene and her group were listening and watching, and one moonless night quick shadows materialized in the empty house, gathering blankets and photographs, rummaging under the furniture with a thin broom, finding Leslie's boxes, and a silver Viennese box in the shape of a coiled serpent with sapphire eyes, an exquisite little trinket that Shushanig adored, a gift from Sempad.

Everything light and precious wound up in Ismene's capacious pockets or Nazim's grimy haversack: Nevart's linen handkerchiefs, the monogrammed *N* and *A* pleasingly intertwined; the Swiss doll that belonged to Anahid, the youngest of the cousins, still in its tissue paper in its lilac carton; the little boxwood box one of Veron's aunts had brought her back from Italy, graced with a wreath of forget-me-nots carved around the words *Ricordo di Pompeii* and the slightly dazed-looking face of the Virgin.

Ismene also found, in the false bottom of a cabinet, coupons from the Empire's big bond issue, to which Sempad, as a loyal subject, had subscribed. ("It's a kind of tax, sweetheart," Ismene suddenly recalls Sempad explaining to Shushanig. "We have to be able to show we bought them.")

Ismene stuffs the titles in her pocket, then lingers a moment, recalling the sitting room inhabited: Madame Nevart sorting out skeins of silk embroidery thread in her favorite corner, in her favorite chair; Veron playing a Mozart tune on the piano, an Erard upright; Shushanig settling accounts; and Sempad blissfully puffing bluish clouds of smoke, with Nubar on his lap.

Veron abruptly stops playing, because Sempad has

stood up and turned the crank on the brand-new phonograph, which he received recently along with a stack of
Western records. Caruso's voice fills the room, weirdly
nasal and yet miraculous, and Sempad rubs his hands,
thoroughly pleased.

Ismene gathers up these memories and places them
carefully alongside those of her Red Indian husband and
other snapshots from her many-colored memory. She also
dutifully gathers up the broken phonograph itself (there's
a boot print on it). It will meet its end along with the
other relics of her past, along with Ismene herself, who
will die trying to defend them in the Smyrna fire.

But now Ismene's energies turn entirely to reaching
the convoy. She knows about the law that forbids aiding
the Armenians, and so she must act on the sly, and she
feels hampered by the fact that everyone in the little city
knows about her friendship with the family.

People know very little, on the other hand, about
Nazim, and nothing about his meeting with Shushanig.
Thus everyone, above all the *kaimakam*, believes him to
be a faithful spy, one who has rendered many services;
Nazim, however, is clinging to the image of Shushanig
and her lost world, one he now mourns as his own.

Thus one day, eavesdropping on the somewhat
breathless arrival of two *zaptiehs* on horseback, he hears
several quick phrases from the mustachioed mouth of Ali
Suleyman, the *kaimakam's* rotund secretary: "Still two hundred left, damn them. They're approaching Konya, and

we don't know——" But here the officer lowers his voice, and Nazim flattens himself against the wall and closes his eyes.

The two men pass nearby and, as usual, they don't even look at him. But the secretary, his chest puffed out, hisses, "Out of my way, beggar." Nazim takes no offense at this, since he is in fact a beggar. But Ali isn't, of course, and yet he never gives Nazim alms, his duty as a believer.

Nazim slips away, leaving his bowl with his son (business is business), who is truly gifted as a mendicant, and rushes off to Ismene, whom he finds whispering in the market.

"We have to rent a carriage and disappear without arousing suspicion," Nazim says.

"Impossible——you and I in a carriage together? Like rich folks? And what will our story be? And where will we go? We don't even have a *teskere*, and it's wartime," replies Ismene, frantically, feeling a deadly clock booming in her heart.

Then she has an idea: Father Isaac. He really could rent a carriage, and might have reason to go to another city. And so Isaac quickly invents a cousin who is a bishop, and for his wife some garish relatives who arrive with the bishop. The real bishop is informed and, despite some reluctance, agrees to cooperate, lending them the church carriage, which they cram with food. This all happens at night, with everything carried in beneath the ample overcoats of the wailers and the cemetery women.

Isaac takes out the two bottles of arak that he had set aside at the birth of his son, and at the memory of his death and of Sempad's concern he falls to his knees and prostrates himself on the ground, praying fervently to the Theotokos, the Mother of God, to watch over their expedition.

Near dawn, with a bearded monk in the coach box—actually an expert driver, disguised and well paid—the carriage, bearing the bishop's ancient coat of arms on the doors, leaves the city. Isaac has assumed a very authoritative air and put on a clean robe. Ismene is squeezed into a corner inside, next to Nazim, while Katerina, also dressed in her finest, is looking out the window with a calm, cool air.

The most dangerous part of the journey will be when they deviate from their declared itinerary in order to climb the steep slopes of the Taurus Mountains and reach Konya by the shortest route.

Along the road, horror assaults them. In one valley, where the driver said they could refresh themselves at a perennial spring by a small lake, they find the ground completely covered with thousands of rotting corpses, the spring polluted. In their anguish, they brave the hideous stench to look, but the dead belong to another caravan; they recognize no one, though all are clearly Armenian. They lie, stripped of everything, awaiting the trumpets of Resurrection, no one having prayed for them.

Isaac would like to stop, but Ismene says, "Crazy priest! The bandits may still be around. Cross yourself and let's get out of here."

And indeed, a lone carriage is anything but safe, and the days pass in ever-growing torment, as abandoned corpses, already decomposing, become more numerous. The only calm one is Nazim, who is praying to the Prophet and feeling like one of Harun al-Rashid's paladins. He knows that they will find Shushanig, and that her salvation has been entrusted to him, a pledge of the Paradise that awaits him.

Moving by night, they quickly traverse the final stretch of road, reaching Konya near dawn. They've covered the coats of arms on the carriage doors, because they've passed into Kurdish territory and the Kurds are not ones to make fine distinctions. They have come to a stop in a quiet spot; there isn't actually any Greek bishop in Konya, which means that now they are in Nazim's hands.

Nazim gets out and disappears at a quick hop. The Brotherhood of Beggars has members everywhere, and Nazim questions a baker, who gives him a crisp loaf for love of God. He then hurries toward the city. The three in the carriage wait anxiously, reaching often for the bottle of arak.

The sun is now high. Ismene decides to display the priest. Konya is a very religious city, and Greek priests travel often, and are decent businessmen, too. Isaac sits on the ground in his priestly robes, leaning against the carriage as if asleep (but his wary eyes are keeping watch). He's an unusual spectacle, but still he's a man of God, and the carriage's coats of arms, which have reappeared, protect him in the eyes of the tranquil villagers who are going about their business. The smell of fresh bread tempts his nostrils, but Isaac, not known for his initiative, doesn't dare move and remains quietly seated.

Three hours pass. Isaac and Ismene are whispering impatiently, about to drive off, when they hear a soft whisper from a slowly approaching hay cart, pulled by two splendid crescent-horned oxen. The cart stops quietly nearby. The farmer driving it stares straight ahead, impassive. Nazim emerges from the hay, along with an accomplice filthier and fouler than he, a one-eyed man wearing many-colored rags.

"The Armenians are real close," says the man. "They'll be here in a few hours. They're bad off, worse than a louse in a beggar's beard. And helping them's forbidden."

"We know, we know," replies Ismene, "but some of my relatives are among them, and if I find them"—here she takes out two gold sequins and lets them shine for a moment—"everyone will benefit."

The one-eyed man, named Tarik, raises his hands in a languid, polite motion. "To let you get close to them, I'd have to talk with one of the *zaptiehs* on guard duty. And in these times nobody talks for free."

Ismene makes an oddly vigorous gesture. Like a conjurer, she draws from her pocket two or three of her famous colored handkerchiefs, and in the corner of one, voilà, a gold coin.

"You can make twenty of those *zaptiehs* happy with this," she says, "and still have something left over for yourself. And I'll pay more, much more, when the job's done."

Four more ragged characters now emerge from the cart and quickly unload the hay, held tightly together by sliding ropes, revealing four solid crates underneath, arranged back to back to form a large cube, with many small drawers facing out. Confronted with this tour de force of the smuggler's art, the Greeks look on in silent admiration, and Tarik, bursting with pride, demonstrates: he opens the capacious drawers, each of which is designed to hold a different kind of merchandise.

"A man's got to live," he sighs, "especially in wartime. With this, we can load and unload quickly, and besides no one looks our way when we're working. The gendarmes are paid off. The cart is slow but safe; once we get to where we're going, we unload the drawers and find others ready to take their place."

The group empties the carriage in a flash. Katerina quietly wraps herself in her shawl and slips out, since much of the cargo is hidden under the seats. The food for the Armenians fills several drawers; utensils, blankets, and pots fill the rest. Then everything is hurriedly covered again, the bales of hay put back in their places. Only a couple of ropes remain visible. The four helpers disappear again into spaces hollowed out of the hay for them, and the cart moves farther on and comes to a stop beneath a large plane tree, from which a thin stream of water seems to flow.

The farmer unyokes the oxen and leads them to drink, and then lets them graze nearby, as if he didn't have a care in the world. He takes out a stubby little pipe, sits down beneath the plane tree, and immerses himself in clouds of foul-smelling blue smoke. It looks like a picturesque genre painting: on this side, the Greek bishop's black carriage (with its coats of arms); the priest with his large pectoral cross, his conspicuous hat, and his short, neatly tied pigtail; his small wife wrapped in her black shawl; Ismene with her majestic gypsy earrings and her immense eyes and sharp nose; the lame beggar humbly posed—all of them eating fresh bread with feta and olives, the arak passing slowly from one to another. On the other side: the hay cart with the peaceful farmer, who is also eating now, calmly, with Tarik, and drinking the cool, glinting water from the small fountain.

Beneath the surface, everything simmers; behind every brow squirm thoughts and schemes of fear and glory, of greed and death. Beneath the hay, the other men, as silent as wild beasts lying in wait.

. . .

As they quench their thirst and Isaac grooms his beard, a gendarme approaches on a small donkey. It's Ismail Muzaffer, chief of the ulema's guard and a friend of a friend of Nazim's. "They're coming," he says, "and they'll be made to stop in the Valley of Swallows, which is near the city but enclosed on all sides by sloping meadows, with a single road going through it. It's a place with plenty of water. They don't want any trouble here— they'll give them bread, keep them calm. Then they'll make them leave again at dawn." Smiling bleakly, whistling a little between his sparse teeth, he adds, "It's a long way still to Aleppo."

They quickly pull the carriage up behind the cart, then unharness the horses and hobble them near the plane tree.

The farmer, climbing back into the coach box, pushes a hidden lever beneath his seat, and some of the hay slides backward, covering the top part of the carriage, which now looks like just another cart. The four beggars hidden beneath the hay jump out and deftly fine-tune the disguise and adjust the cart's remaining hay. Their movements are synchronized and quick, and after a few minutes everything is set.

Katerina will remain with the farmer beneath the plane tree, pretending to be his wife. The carriage driver, who hasn't been paid for this part, also stretches out beneath the tree, to nap in the welcome shade. Isaac is in shirtsleeves; he has removed his cassock and his hat, tossing them into the carriage, and now he conceals his pigtail beneath a low cap. Nazim slips his filthy vest off and drapes it ceremoniously over Isaac's shoulders. Ismene has no need for disguises: any person, of any stripe, can see that she's a wailer, and none would dare bar her way.

Thus Nazim climbs into the driver's seat, and the big oxen begin their slow approach. Too slow for the eager, impatient rescuers, but God's mill grinds finely, and as they make their way around the city walls, the little valley comes into view just as the wretched procession appears from the north, amid the dust and shouts of the *zaptiehs* on horseback.

The cart, which looks like a hundred others, stops abruptly behind a thicket of thorny bushes. But the view from there is excellent.

Isaac, Ismene, and Nazim climb down to watch. They watch the wretched spectacle of women approaching, shuffling their feet, naked in the ubiquitous dust, their faces tilted toward the earth, their backs curved. They watch the skeletal children, also staring down at the road, and they grasp at once that these few ragged creatures scanning the ground for nonexistent food are all that remains of the thousands who departed a month ago, in their grand carriages, from the little city.

Isaac, Ismene, and Nazim quietly watch and weep. They recognize no one. But they know immediately that an evil larger than themselves is at work in this place, one they struggle to comprehend, and with the instinctive

wisdom of simple people, they know that they must proceed shrewdly and very, very carefully.

Mute, barely breathing, they witness the orders to
halt, they see the infinite weariness of the Armenian
women as they slump to the ground and the mad faces of
the children throwing themselves down to drink. Then
they see the Turkish women bringing bread, and they
hear the powerful screams of that tiny population
stretched to its breaking point, and the intervention of
the ulema.

Ismene at once realizes that this is the chance they've
been waiting for. But how can they bring the cart down,
and how unload the food? In that moment, she sees
Nubar, recognizing him more with her heart than her
eyes: the funny little fellow who sang with her at Hamparzum's funeral, a thousand years ago.

Nubar doesn't look sick. His little face is still round,
but his eyes have grown immense, wild. If he's there, other
members of the family will be there, too—Isaac and
Ismene whisper this at the same time. Then they whisper
something to Nazim, who has already taken out a few tins
of meat and cans of powdered milk.

But now, spurred by the voice of the man of God,
the inhabitants of Konya are entering the little valley, carrying bowls of milk, salves, wine. The enraged *zaptiehs*,
who have been peacefully but firmly pushed aside, stand
together, conferring. At last one breaks off, gets on his
horse, and gallops away, no doubt to ask for orders.

At this point, Ismene, Isaac, and Nazim, with the utmost care (no one there knows them), merge with the locals and begin looking into the faces of women and children and trying to reach Nubar. But at the arrival of food, every family group has instinctively banded together, and thus it is that Nazim is the first to spot, in the distance, the head of Shushanig.

He flies toward her. She is slumped beneath a tree and is gnawing, almost unwillingly, on a piece of bread. He kneels before her and says in a whisper: *"Valide Hanum,* I'm here. It's me. Worry no more." Then he kisses enthusiastically her sweaty, swollen hands.

Shushanig looks at him, stunned, and says nothing. Around her, Veron, Azniv, the girls, and Nubar all remain silent. Finally Shushanig stiffens a little, and with her inimitable gesture of welcome, which comes to the surface like a reflection on clear water, she replies, "Nazim. Allow me to welcome you. We can no longer receive you as once we did."

Now Ismene has arrived, too, and with a clean handkerchief soaked in water she wipes Shushanig's brow, her face, her sweat-encrusted eyes. She whispers, "We have food. We're here. Isaac, too." Then she zealously devotes herself to making Shushanig drink some water, giving her some food, tending to her skinned, swollen feet. Shushanig sinks into a benign torpor, and for the first time in a month, she truly sleeps.

Then Ismene confers with Veron and Azniv, after

having comforted them, too. Isaac and Nazim come and go, bringing food, wine, clothes, slipping carefully through the confusion of the camp. The little girls and Nubar have eaten—not too much, warned Shushanig, who knows there's nothing worse after a long fast—and now they're asleep, exhausted, a pitiful bunch curled up together. (By now they know to always sleep this way, a mutual-defense reflex.)

"Much of what I've brought can't be carried by people traveling on foot," thinks Ismene. The shoes, the clothes, those can be worn—but as one must never attract the gendarmes' attention, it's best to wear them under their stinking rags, which can't be thrown away.

"They're our last defense," thinks Azniv, with a bitter smile.

"And dragging a suitcase behind them would be impossible for people so weakened," thinks Ismene to herself, "not to mention that it would get taken away tomorrow."

A thousand absurd hypothetical rescues blur together in her mind, but none seems plausible. And meanwhile time is passing, evening is falling. The deportees lie here and there like broken dolls, inert, worn-out.

The inhabitants of Konya have now gone home. They have obeyed the ulema, and will return tomorrow. Now the German consul, Herr Müller, arrives, with bandages and medicines, accompanied by a spotless Red Cross nurse. He's a rigid, precise man, but not inhumane:

he's horrified by the Armenian deportation, yet he can't manage to think in terms of any personal initiative. He was happy to follow the ulema's orders and thought, rightly, that these poor people must also need medical treatment.

But treating two hundred people with a few bandages and a little iodine doesn't amount to much. These people have passed through every horror, they've drunk polluted water, they've scavenged amid horses' dung, and their own. Azniv laughs, wildly, at this incongruous sight, and hisses: "Coming to see the stockyard? Careful, we're contagious."

Herr Müller kneels decorously beside an old woman with a festering sore on her knee and quickly cleans and bandages the wound. Then he takes out a flask and brings it to her bluish lips; she greedily takes a sip and falls back, lifeless. It was poor Berdjuhi, who ate her fill after so long. After eating, she lay down, and the sore didn't hurt anymore. Then she felt a great warmth and in the trembling of late afternoon saw her son Davit, dead for years, offering her a drink. It's really Müller, but Berdjuhi sees him as an angel, gives herself over to him, trusting, and dies in peace.

Isaac, arriving at that moment, closes her eyes. He sees her tender soul testing its wings, and he forgives himself at last.

.   .   .

MÜLLER'S ARRIVAL has offered Ismene and her little group a useful diversion. The deportees were beginning to notice her incongruous presence, which she didn't want. But their reduced capacity for attention instantly shifted to Müller, and now Ismene knows she must soon leave. The *zaptiehs* are already approaching again, menacing, and only Müller—an ally, a German—commands their respect. Fortunately, the German is a precise man, and nothing will stop him before he has finished with his medicines and bandages.

But his nurse has guessed something, and she quietly approaches Ismene. Slipping a card into her hand, she whispers, "This evening after ten come find me here." Then she hurries away.

Ismene would like to say goodbye to Shushanig, but Shushanig is fast sleep, and her weary features seem in great need of rest. So she sighs, hugs Veron (Azniv quickly moves away) and Nubar, who is also sleeping peacefully. Everything seems so calm. The evening star shines in the twilight, and the ancient walls of the city loom protectively.

Ismene has given Veron and Azniv sacks of food to hide under their clothes, two saddlebags full of water, some money, and a packet containing the precious family photographs she recovered, along with Shushanig's little box with sapphire eyes.

"That's all, my little doves," she sighs. She adds a promise: "They say you're being taken to Aleppo; I'll be waiting for you there, with Dr. Zareh. We'll find a way to get you out of the camp."

She stifles a dry sob and hurries unhappily away, pushing Isaac ahead of her. She doesn't see Nazim, but she doesn't worry—he can take care of himself.

And indeed Nazim has entered into a fruitful discussion with one of the *zaptiehs,* whom he recognized as an old comrade, sent to jail a few years earlier only to emerge gloriously in time for the struggle against the Armenians. He's connected with the Special Organization, an enforcer who has shown a talent for torture and rape. But Nazim has vivid memories of his extreme greed. That can't have disappeared.

And so he pretends to be what he is—an avid, shrewd beggar—and he explains that he's been sent by a great gentleman, an aga of unlimited means, to save a family whom he owes a debt of honor. But not wanting to reveal himself, the gentleman has sent Nazim.

The *zaptieh*'s eyes glint. He can't squeeze anything more out of these wretches, except the pleasure of seeing them die; why not make a little extra cash if he can? Besides, if he can manage to get the money in advance, perhaps they can still be killed, at the last moment: just when they think themselves saved, he'll report them to the lieutenant.

But Nazim wasn't born yesterday; having been a spy all his life, he easily follows the man's tortuous thoughts. He smiles but doesn't let on.

"Which ones are you protecting?" the man asks, falsely solicitous.

"You'll know when the time comes," Nazim replies evasively. "There's a heap of money at stake, old comrade, which the two of us can split. You try not to kill anyone; I keep my lips sealed, for the moment. But I'll be following the caravan closely. In the meantime, here." And he hands him a shiny Queen Victoria sovereign. The man swallows and says nothing. These Armenians are truly diabolical if they bring this much, even in this condition.

Back at the carriage, Ismene and Isaac finally look each other in the eye, discouraged, dejected. What can they do with the leftover supplies? How else can they help Shushanig and what remains of her family? They'll have to go back, return the carriage to the bishop, and then what? In a matter of days the caravan will no longer exist, those poor people will be finished. None seem capable of surviving the grueling final leg of the journey. Their expert eyes did not fail to notice the state of extreme physical prostration and mental confusion to which the deportees had been reduced. And Azniv's wild eyes haunted them. As the unfamiliar darkness falls, Ismene and Isaac weep bitterly.

But a rustling and the sound of footsteps alert them to Nazim's arrival. Ismene shudders. She still can't bring herself to fully trust him—and she doesn't even know what he did that May evening after seeing Azniv's suitor, a dark secret Nazim dresses each day in ragged thoughts and buries inside himself. In the faint light, Nazim sees the two Greeks sitting together, weeping disconsolately, and he suddenly thinks, "I'm sharper than they are. I'm going to save the *Valide Hanum.* I'm not a worthless man." And equally suddenly he feels true human piety, the great piety that makes us all brothers; he kneels beside them, with difficulty, folding his bad leg, and embraces them. Just the three of them, so alone, against Great Evil.

Nazim quickly tells them what happened and adds, "I'm not going back. My son can take care of his mother and my other wife. I've seen my destiny. I'm going to save her, and then I'll either beg in Aleppo or drag myself to Mecca to die."

But first they have to take the cart back and retrieve the carriage and Katerina. Oddly, no one has worried about Katerina, alone these many hours. She lives in a world apart, in endless colloquy with her dead son, Dimitraki. And indeed they find her still leaning against the tree, in the same position they left her in. Isaac approaches her, gently placing a hand on her cheek, to rouse her, the way he usually does, delicately. But Katerina doesn't react; she topples over: cold, dead.

Saying nothing, Isaac closes her eyes with his warm fingers, lays her out on the ground, and clasps her hands over her chest. Then he takes off his cross, which he had hidden under his shirt, and puts it around her neck.

"Poor, anxious, fearful wife, companion of so many years," thinks Isaac. He guesses that she, out of timidity, said nothing but secretly followed them and decided, when she saw from behind them the convoy of dying Armenians, that the world was truly too hard a place and that she didn't want to remain in it any longer. So she retraced her steps, sat down again beneath the tree, sent a pathetic little goodbye smile to her dear Isaac, and allowed her heart to break, rejoining her lost son.

Isaac feels her little soul hovering around him, bidding him farewell. "Don't worry, you haven't betrayed me, my dear Katerina," says Isaac solemnly. "I'm entrusting you to Saint George, fighter of dragons, and may he lead you to our little one, among the roses in God's garden. Have faith and wait for me there, and pray for me, both of you. I have to stay here a little while longer, because of my sins, my foolish blunders. But if the two of you help me, I'll redeem myself soon."

Now Isaac, too, has no one, and Ismene is as free as the air. The plan quickly takes shape, and Isaac puts it into words:

"We'll bury Katerina under the tree, this very night. I'll bless her, and you, Ismene, will say a brief lamentation—that's what Katerina would want. She was a woman of few words, and besides she's happy now. Then we'll sell what's left in the carriage to Nazim's friends, who have helped us, and we'll make it look like we were assaulted on the way back from Konya, in open country. Those good friends will do that for us, too—take the carriage down the road, turn it over, and steal the horses.

"The three of us will disappear. We'll hire a couple of donkeys and make our way slowly to Aleppo, an old Greek couple and a lame beggar, chance companions, heading toward the big city.

"We'll divvy up what treasure Ismene still has, so that if one of us is intercepted the others may continue."

Ismene grimaces, but she knows the plan is a fair one. What's more, Shushanig just gave her almost everything she had left in her pockets, the better to defend her from the outside, to watch over her. The hay opens again, the crates are emptied, and the contents laid out on the ground, beneath Nazim's vigilant eye. Then the empty cart makes its way slowly off, the driver impassive, his pipe flaring. Ismene crouches over Katerina's hastily dug grave, whispers womanly words to her, and sings her a lullaby. The water from the nearby fountain gurgles softly as it disappears into the grass—and Ismene forgets her appointment with the Red Cross nurse. Many years later, they will meet again in Smyrna, where so many destinies crossed. But that's another story.

Nazim and Isaac have much to do, and now it is Nazim who is in charge. Isaac, who has cast off his priestly rank along with his vestments, makes the ultimate sacrifice: he runs to Ismene and has her sever his giveaway pigtail. He can be more useful this way, as a beggar's humble assistant.

. . .

AND THUS THE NIGHT PASSES. Shadows come and go. Amid murmurs and whispers, the Brotherhood of Beggars takes care of business. One tall, agile fellow grabs the reins of the carriage, throws Isaac's vestments haphazardly inside, and takes it away. Another man goes with him, for the horses.

Nazim, in a darkness only dimly illuminated by two covered lanterns, conducts an improvised auction of everything that can't be carried on the two donkeys, which have already arrived and are waiting patiently beneath the big plane tree.

Tins of powdered milk, sausages, blankets, sacks of dried apples—they quickly pass from hand to hand. A portion is set aside for the guards who during the day saw the smugglers' legendary hay cart stop beneath the plane tree and knew to stay out of their way until the next morning.

Nazim slips the money he receives into the ample sash around his waist without needing to count it—the merest touch suffices. His fingertips are as sensitive as those of a pianist, and as well practiced. Besides, no one would cheat him here; his comrades do not take issue with the choice he has made, and more than one of them feels a kind of coarse sympathy for the Armenians, who have now become more wretched than themselves, and who are being persecuted by the godless new government. They understand, the beggars do, that in a godless world their task becomes more difficult, and charity rare. And more-

over, it's wartime: Isn't it better to fight the foreign enemies than to create enemies at home? The age-old wisdom
of mendicants and merchants, in the East, has always lain
in the difficult ability to meet people halfway.

In the underworld Courts of Miracles, which flour-
ish everywhere and are the reverse side of the fabric of all
organized societies, things have a logic of their own, however topsy-turvy. Greed has a place there, along with cruelty, cunning, flight from hunger—but fanaticism doesn't.
Why eliminate all the Armenians, who generate riches
and are charitable? (In the Ottoman Empire, as in every
religious society, charity guarantees wealth, and justifies it.)

"You shear the sheep, you don't kill it," the beggars grumble among themselves. The savage assault on
Armenian possessions has yielded them nothing but
crumbs, and meanwhile they're no longer receiving their
usual generous alms outside churches and houses and during the major Christian holidays.

None of them would turn Nazim in, even if they
weren't having such a profitable night. Their chief, Hassan
Mustafa, makes an appearance only when it's over. He is a
big, tall man, who wears his many-colored rags, the mark
of his profession, with innate dignity.

"You and your friends be careful, Nazim, and may
Allah be with you. Take these animals," he added, handing
him a staff and a rope, behind which trotted two fleshy
goats. "It looks better this way, plus you'll have milk."

At the first glimmer of dawn, Nazim mounts one

donkey, Ismene the other, veiling her face. Isaac follows with the two goats, gripping the staff and the rope. And thus in the growing brightness, just ahead of the convoy of Armenians, they make their way south, with no plan, with their hearts in turmoil and their souls at peace.

IN THOSE HOT, late-June days, Yerwant finally receives a letter from Zareh, from Aleppo. The letter, strangely, is in French. Zareh says that the war is going well for the Empire, but that the good old days are gone, the consulates are closing, and the long afternoons of tea and bridge are now rare. He asks for news, gossips a little about the family, and then three lines are crossed out— only an *S* can be glimpsed. Maybe Sempad's initial, thinks Yerwant. The closing seems casual though affectionate:

"My dear brother, I hope to hear from you or to see you again soon, in part because I'd like you to tell me about the latest advances in ear surgery. I have patients who could benefit from them."

Yerwant ponders the ominously censored letter, feverishly trying to make out what was written there, first with the aid of a powerful lamp, then by scratching and worrying the page until finally he wears a hole in it. And he has understood nothing.

Since when has Zareh been a surgeon? He's a general practitioner—at most he might lance a boil. What could he mean by such a specific closing? And why write in

French? What was Zareh really trying to say? The letter's apparent lightness and discursive tone are not his; they're off-key, they sound false; some kind of distress shows through every line.

Yerwant understands that, even defaced, the letter conveys a message; he closes himself in his study, frantically reading and rereading those few lines from his brother. Did he receive his telegram? Why doesn't he mention it? And where is Sempad? What has become of him and his jovial Shushanig? And their children, their sisters, their cousins?

For days Yerwant, on falling asleep, has been hearing footsteps echoing in his brain. They are always the same, shuffling, endless. As soon as he opens his eyes, the footsteps stop. He has tried a little laudanum, drunk some old cognac, gone to visit a welcoming woman who always has time for him, and whose spirit and flesh are willing—but nothing helps.

Furious, he makes a decision. He grabs the letter, rings the bell. A servant appears, quickly helps him into his white linen jacket, and hands him his cane and hat. "Professor, will you be back for dinner?" the servant asks meekly. He knows perfectly well that he won't get a definite answer, but Teresa wants him to ask.

"I don't know. Tell the countess not to wait for me," Yerwant replies brusquely, as he so often has before, and then leaves the house quickly.

Yerwant has decided to pay another visit to his lady

friend, the only person who has known his mind, who has seen him bewildered and upset. He has told her things. Maria Ferronato is a smart widow who rounds out her meager income with a few well-chosen friendships, and she's very good at listening. She has had no advance notice of Yerwant's visit, but she understands at once and receives him anyway, discreetly instructing her cook, Ester, to cancel another appointment. She and the professor put their heads together beneath her colorful beaded lamp, and they read.

"I don't understand, I just don't understand," erupts Yerwant, bitter tears suddenly streaming down his cheeks. "What should I do?"

She clutches him to her like a child. No one has ever seen him like this, afraid and exposed in his anxiety, which descends from generations of distant fears, of exterminations, of manhunts. His austere white jacket grows damp with tears.

Maria takes his hands, pulls him to her chest, rocks him in the gentle light of the beaded lampshade. As she does, she takes the letter from his hands, carefully spreads it flat, and reads Zareh's flowing French.

She feels as though she has entered a novel; there must be some hidden meaning. Bridge, no, but the consulates . . . Yes, that's it. And the last part suggests the means.

Maria feels like a lioness, and a smart one at that. "If

it weren't for us Venetians, these Orientals wouldn't understand a thing," she whispers in dialect to the trusted cook, who is already back and peeping out of the kitchen, before ordering her to prepare two strong coffees and a tall glass of water with a spoonful of orange marmalade in it, the way the professor likes it.

"Okay, I'll explain," she tells him after they drink their coffee. "I think I understand. The reference to the consulate is of key significance; your brother is the French consul's physician, right? So I suggest you write to him there, not to his home address. And if possible, I think you should do so via diplomatic channels. Don't you know an ambassador?"

Yerwant looks confused but relieved. What he needs is to be doing something.

"On top of that," Maria continues, "I think it might be best for the message to be hidden. Send him something unsuspicious, a medical book, and replace some pages. You could have it done in a print shop or with one of those new writing machines."

Yerwant, always at the forefront of the new and modern, indeed owns a typewriter, a splendid Remington from England. And he has no trouble taking the newly arrived issue of *Revue de Otorhinolaryngologie*, cutting out two inside pages, and substituting them with a letter in French, typed in beautiful charactery.

He wastes no time, and in two days the manipulated magazine is ready, full of nervous, urgent questions. (Deep down, however, Yerwant already knows many of the answers.)

The sweet Maria receives a bouquet of marvelous gardenias—a flower Yerwant adores. And among them, in plain view, is a gold box containing an exquisite medallion, engraved and enameled with an alpine landscape. Yerwant knows she loves Switzerland; he once took her with him to Zurich.

Count Giusto degli Adimari, former ambassador to Berlin, whose son Yerwant saved with a successful operation after the boy had, because of a suppurating mastoiditis, been given up for dead, receives an urgent telephone call and hastens to assist his illustrious friend. So it is that the magazine departs for Aleppo in less than a week.

The count then, as a favor to his surgeon friend, looks into the situation discreetly on his own—and what he learns appalls him. The Italian consul at Trebizond, Giacomo Gorrini, has been sending letter after letter back to the ministry, recounting horrific events, with the anguish of an eyewitness who is powerless to help. Though his own safety is in danger, he nevertheless harbors Armenian children in the consulate.

All the Armenian men in Trebizond, Gorrini writes, have been eliminated, drowned in the Black Sea. He saw the boats full of chained men pushed out to sea and then sunk by gendarmes shooting from shore; he saw the wretched processions of the exiles—the women, the old men, the children—pass below the closed, garrisoned windows of the Italian Consulate, crying out for mercy. And at night, despite grave personal risk, he raced out of the city, defying the curfew, to try to help in some way.

All that he was able to do was to accept custody of a few children from their desperate mothers. But in the following days the consulate was searched and all the children were taken away, except for two of the smallest, whom his wife clasped tightly in her arms, declaring them her own. The officer in charge of the search winked at him and left. After all, what do two matter out of so many thousands? And in any case, the officer reasoned, they'll grow up Italian; the desired effect will still be achieved.

Giusto degli Adimari acts quickly. He bombards the ministry with telegrams, and soon he is able to give Yerwant more precise—if horrible—news. He tactfully writes him a generic note arranging a meeting in a room in the Caffè Pedrocchi. There, holding Yerwant's hands in his, he talks.

Throughout Armenian Anatolia, convoys are on the move. From every inhabited place, cities and villages alike, endless columns of Armenians are in motion, heading south, across the harsh Taurus Mountains, toward Aleppo.

The Syrian city is under siege. Foreign consuls, bombarded by ominous rumors, are requesting instructions from their ministries—but nobody really knows what to do. The Southern Army is quartered in Aleppo, on the orders of Djemal Pasha, whose intentions aren't completely clear to anyone. His rivalry with the other two members of the triumvirate, Enver and Talat, the Constantinople Dioscuri, is no secret, but he has yet to take an explicit stand on the Armenian question—perhaps a stratagem to give himself room to maneuver in an Arab city that is already, on its own account, chafing under Turkish occupation, and that furthermore contains many Christians.

The little city, as a despairing Adimari explains, is one of the crossroads of the deportations. He knows nothing specific about Yerwant's family, of course, but the city has been emptied of Armenians. The Italian consul at Aleppo will be asked to kindly remain on alert. Yerwant listens, frozen. A cold sweat descends from his neck down his back, and soon he is covered in sweat, as if his whole body were weeping for the brother whom—by now he's certain—he'll never see again.

He thanks his friend and takes his leave, shoulders erect, wrapped in his solitude.

AT THIS POINT, there are three related roads, three paths. Ismene's road and Shushanig's road are running parallel. The life road has caught up with the death road, but the outcome remains uncertain; the possible ambushes are many, and many mysteries obscure visibility.

The third road, remote and solitary, is Yerwant's road. This impatient man, this fearsome surgeon, must relearn the Eastern way of waiting, must rely on the incoming news, impotent, passive. Nothing to do but wait and watch his pride die little by little. If he returned, he would be a pariah, cursed like the others. Wounded by the empty-headed arrogance of the warmongers, Yerwant in that mortal summer tastes the dregs of his inner difference, and he ceases to love himself.

Shushanig, the children, and the girls travel the Via Dolorosa. The Taurus Mountains rise up before them, a chilling sight. The comforts miraculously delivered by the people of Konya and by Ismene are hoarded to the last crumb, allowing them to survive a while longer, but more than that they have revived hope. Faint but tenacious: to make it to Aleppo. "Our angels are waiting for us there, we can eat there," Shushanig whispers to the children; the solemn Nubar sticks his thumb in his mouth, gravely. "I'm not hungry," he always says, and he never asks questions, never asks for anything, never whines.

In the great plain at the foot of the first spurs of the Taurus, the tattered remains of the caravans converge. So many, many bones bleaching now beside the paths; so many bloated corpses swept away by the Euphrates; so many children, so many girls gone. The tiny group of survivors from the little city gathers laboriously beneath two scrawny trees, as a high falcon wheels in the cloudless sky.

It's July, probably. No one keeps track of the days anymore.

Where are the castles of Cilicia, where the crusader kingdom of the Lusignans? Milling in the haze, in the blinding heat, among the wretched remains of that proud people, are the ghosts of invincible Bagratid archers, of knights bearing wind-whipped oriflammes. And a gentle death wind blows on these hot faces, on their parched cheeks, bringing a coolness, a forgotten inertia, consolation; Shushanig can see the beautiful, strong warrior angels coming for her, Sempad with them on horseback, as handsome as when he went hunting with his friend from the Laz country.

But a firm hand shakes her, preventing her from leaving. It's Nazim, who has kept his promise not to abandon his *Valide Hanum*. A wretch among wretches, he has crept, at dawn, into the camp of the desperate, and now he feeds Shushanig, nursing her with fresh goat milk, and wraps her bleeding feet. Then he cradles her head in his arms, murmuring the praises of the Merciful One.

The *zaptieh* he has bribed pretends to look elsewhere, while the children are given something to eat, small amounts and in great secrecy, so that those around them don't notice—the terrible selection from among the desperate. But the destination is oblivion; all these people will surely die, sooner or later, either here or at Aintab, either at Aleppo or at Dayr az Zawr, which is rumored to be the final destination . . . What does it matter where? Indeed it's cruel, thinks the *zaptieh*, to prolong their lives. He's tempted to denounce this peculiar gimpy beggar who has returned to help this woman and her family. Just then Nazim appears and slyly flashes another coin. "This one and ten more if they make it to Aleppo," he whispers, and the man is appeased.

Because Nazim knows that during the hard ascent of the Taurus Mountains, Shushanig will be alone again. He's lame, and he doesn't dare expose Isaac and Ismene. And so the threesome moves along, taking the most direct route, and not without difficulties: one moonlit night, Ismene tried to seduce Isaac and was rebuffed. Half-heartedly, but rebuffed. This created some friction. "Impotent priest," Ismene hissed, but it never even occurs to her to try Nazim. All the same, the three become very fond of each other—they're heroes for once, protagonists in a great and terrible story; they're the ones pulling the strings. A spirit of adventure suffuses them, and they do look rather dubious—indeed, they nearly get arrested in an Arab village for waking every inhabitant with some rather unorthodox songs. They have to make a quick getaway, but in the end no one pursues them; these are calamitous times.

Too many unburied corpses are giving rise to epidemics, and the war is not going well. "The Armenians' revenge," Djemal thinks to himself, ensconced there in

Aleppo, furious because the great plan concocted by Enver and Talat means that he gets swamped with the flood of deportees, the skeletal multitudes who are dragging themselves toward his city and surrounding it on all sides.

Aleppo's own Armenians, shut inside their fine houses, are restless and whispering. All the foreigners are whispering, too: the European consuls, the missionaries, everyone staying at the Hotel Baron. To Djemal, it seems as though he personally has been surrounded; he feels liverish and wakes with a heaviness on his stomach and paste on his tongue.

The immaculate nurses of the ———— Hospital are hiding Armenians. The diplomatic missions are hiding Armenians. The Bedouins in the desert are coming to take their pick of the deported Armenian women ("wash them and feed them and they're yours")—never in their wildest dreams had they imagined this. The proprietors of brothels, too, are coming to take their pick, and mothers are offering up their own daughters, who in any case are no longer intact. In the souk, in the shadow of the Citadel, all manner of business is transacted.

Nazim, Ismene, and Isaac reach the city at dusk, seeking lodging for themselves and their animals. They find a reasonably comfortable stable. They want to avoid notice, especially by the Greeks, who are loose-lipped and agitated, afraid for their own safety and inclined to double-dealing, and moreover an injunction is posted at every intersection requiring that any local Armenian who tries to aid the deportees be turned in.

Nazim immediately makes contact with his Brotherhood. He hears of the city's great turmoil and great fear. There's the problem of the war, which is not all that remote, and there's the Armenian problem, which is close at hand. The city is under pressure. With the deportees camped just outside the city wall, the hygiene situation is alarming. No one can come and go from the camps, in theory; in practice, some can, when necessary.

"People say they've got the plague, they've got typhus," whispers the leader of the beggars to Nazim. "But in a few days everything will be all right again. The Armenians will be forcibly removed along the railway lines, out into the desert, all the way to Dayr az Zawr or Ras el-Ain. From which point," he adds, "none will be allowed to return."

"And you, Turk, what are you doing here? And why so many questions?" the man then asks, and not affably, as if regretting his words. "Still have a few more Armenians to fleece?"

"I'm here because of a vow," Nazim replies solemnly. "The Armenians are none of my business. But they shouldn't have killed them all."

"It's a disaster for us," agrees the other, sighing. "Though we're doing good business at the moment. The local Armenians are supposed to be sent away right after this, but I don't believe it," he sneers through his mustache. "The front's not far, and Arabs . . ." Then he looks at Nazim and falls silent. The Brotherhood is the Brotherhood, true, but Turks are Turks and Arabs are Arabs.

Nazim understands the man's hesitation, and he remains quiet, too. Then, in a casual tone, he asks, "Is there still an Armenian doctor by the name of Zareh Arslanian here in Aleppo? His family was from my town, and he'll no doubt pay me well for fresh news."

"I'll ask around," the man replies tersely. "I don't know him. But people don't pay very well for death notices," he remarks, from experience.

"He worked in a consulate," Nazim adds. And that, in fact, is all he knows.

Nazim quickly takes his leave. He's afraid that Ismene and Isaac won't be able to manage by themselves; he's afraid that Shushanig will have already arrived, or is dying along some road somewhere and will never arrive. He's afraid that this time his poor beggarly tricks will not be enough, and he feels naked and guilty before the Almighty. How nice it would be to hide somewhere, to disappear . . . But not to go back, never that.

Just then, the intense aroma of bread reaches him from a narrow alleyway around the corner. He follows it. The walls of the Citadel rise at the end of the street, and a faint light halfway down signals the bakery.

At that moment the door opens, a bell rings softly, and framed in the entryway stands the man whose love for

Azniv occasioned Nazim's treachery, Lieutenant Djelal, biting hungrily into a roll. Nazim sees it as a sign. God has answered him.

He approaches, obliquely but quickly, and stages a recognition ritual that includes cheerful amazement, a request for assistance, and generic memories. He glories in his profession like a bird of paradise in an aviary of golden plovers, tracing in the air a fine network of flattery and deceit.

Djelal, raised to respect mendicants as God's poor ("this one must even be on a pilgrimage to Mecca," he thinks), is charmed; he accepts the encounter, settles into it, reminisces. Then he offers a generous donation and turns to leave. But Nazim darts around him and, facing him again, magically conjures forth the pretty girl that Djelal had pursued so hotly, the joyful Azniv. The lieutenant at once sees her smile again, the geranium at her temple, her quick motions. Whatever became of Azniv?

Between his memory and the present stretches an ocean of horror, such things as Djelal sees every day: the growing nervousness of Djemal Pasha, his commander; the encampment of deportees; the stench of the dead, their corpses strewn along the roads; the edicts; the telegrams from the capital; and the war that, by some evil twist of fate, is not going well for the Empire. Every day Djelal sees the skeletal children who wander all around, no longer even asking for bread, just wandering and staring at other people, at all those who have the right to live. Such things by now are facts of life in Aleppo.

Never has he really associated any of it with Azniv. Indeed, he has remained a little put out with her for having turned him down. Now, in one fell swoop, the horror floods him, implicates him, and he finds himself in the desert with her—he has truly lost her forever.

Nazim reads his thoughts as if they were written out on a blackboard; he throws in a few words about Sempad's death, the anguish of the women of the family, the methods of deportation.

"I wonder," he concludes, "whether any of them might have survived and made it to Aleppo. The ones who haven't already died are almost all here."

At this point their gazes finally meet, and the two men understand each other. It's God's will that caused them to cross paths, each with his sacred mission. Djelal doesn't ask, and Nazim doesn't explain, saying only, "Where do you live? I'll be there tomorrow evening at ten."

NOW HE NEEDS TO FIND Zareh, if Zareh is still in the city. Many of Aleppo's Armenians are fleeing while they can—entire families, people who have lived here forever. But could Zareh walk away from his family? What might he know? How does he get around? Nazim realizes that at this point he needs Ismene. She's not instantly suspicious in Armenian eyes, and she knows Zareh, the brother who sent the girls pieces of Damascus silk.

At the inn, Nazim finds Isaac and Ismene crouching beside the beasts, scowling at each other. "You're a beast, too, you impotent priest," Ismene grumbles, but without malice. "Don't tell me you're still in mourning for poor Katerina; after all, we'll be joining her in a few days."

But meanwhile they're getting ready. Ismene is an illusionist, too—the children of the family knew this well and adored her legerdemain with her many-colored hand-kerchiefs. She has no trouble making herself look like a gypsy: out of one pocket come the circular earrings given her by her husband in America, out of another shiny bracelets. At last a flask of brilliantine appears, adding gloss to her hair, which is nicely gathered into a long braid ending in a red bow.

Ismene seems older and uglier now, even despair-ing, as if she had donned a tragic mask. But the people wandering about Aleppo in the evening are nowadays eas-ily impressed, and as for Nazim, well, his jaw drops in admiration.

"You've never seen American women, have you, you mangy dog," Ismene laughs, preparing to leave. Nazim, not at all offended, laughs, too, and instructs her, "Try to find Zareh, try to talk to him. And be sure to come back before dawn." He knows that Ismene is a noctur-nal woman, nothing will happen to her at night; it's daytime—the patrols, the soldiers—that he worries about. Isaac and Ismene are there without documents, and they are not protected by the Brotherhood of Beggars.

Ismene wanders off into the night, praying for a miracle. She wonders where Zareh could be—holed up at home, no doubt, but where might he live, in this big city? Ismene prays fervently, hurling obscure threats at the veiled God who seems not to be listening to her: "It's too much, too much. Too much evil heaped on them. Don't you think it's enough?" she grumbles, crossing herself three times. "At least listen to Isaac, one of your priests. You can hear him praying, too." But Isaac, lonely and worn out, has fallen asleep, while Nazim smokes quietly by the door, gnawing a piece of bread.

And Ismene walks through the night, going from one café to another, peeking inside without much hope. Everywhere she sees men playing backgammon, smoking and talking calmly. None of them look Armenian, of course—Armenians wouldn't be out at night, in these times.

Yet there's something mesmerizing about watching these men play. A memory flits in and out, an echo of something Azniv said that Ismene can't quite recall. Something to do with that game, she's sure, but what?

At the foot of the Citadel, in an alley brighter than the others, Ismene decides to enter a tavern that looks as if it might be Greek. She's not wrong: the owner is from

Methoni; he shows her a seat in the corner and brings her a plate of mutton with a thick sauce. As she eats, Ismene hears brief phrases coming from people behind her, and regular thwaps. She turns, sees four men playing cards, maybe Russians, maybe Italians. Suddenly it comes to her, and she murmurs a blessing to Saint Paraskevi, the last saint she invoked.

Zareh plays cards—he plays bridge, that modern English game—and Azniv used to say, a thousand years ago, that she wanted to go visit her brother in Aleppo in order to learn such a sophisticated game and make her friends green with envy.

"I must look for the French," thinks Ismene, rightly. She asks the innkeeper where the French gather.

From that moment, everything becomes easier. There aren't many places where the French gather; legation receptions are now being canceled, to protest the Armenian situation. But these days all the foreigners (and as long as they're allowed, the Armenians, too) can be found at the new hotel opened by the Mazloumians: Baron Hotel, the newest, most opulent hotel in Aleppo. Djemal Pasha himself holds his receptions there.

"Go on over, it's not far, and stop in at the kitchens. My cousin Yorgos will help you out—he's a scullion there," whispers the innkeeper.

Ismene kisses his hand, thanks him for the food, and hurries toward the door. As she steps outside, she hears a strange music flood the alley, a lively Western tune. She follows it, turns one corner, then another, and there, in all its Baroque glory, with its resplendent staircase and liveried doorman, there stands the grand Occidental-style hotel famous through all the Orient. Ismene, dazzled, gazes up at it. "So beautiful," she thinks. "Paradise must be like that." She is very careful to remain in the shadows.

Just then an automobile pulls up; the chauffeur stops and opens the door with a bow. An officer gets out and extends his hand to a pretty lady, her dainty rhinestone shoes sparkling, her arms bare. She floats out on clouds of silk and perfume. They climb the stairs slowly, offering themselves for admiration. "That's the German general," says a voice near Ismene. "No use asking him for alms, believe me. He never gives anybody anything." The unknown beggar settles back down on the bottom step.

Ismene is seduced, as always, by the gleam and the glitter, and for a moment she wants nothing more than to follow this apparition. Instead, though, she follows the automobile, which, she guesses, will be taken back to the stables. She slips quietly among the noble horses and the carriages. The uniformed chauffeur greets the stable hands and the coachmen, who are sitting in a circle smoking, and then promptly throws a blanket over the motor, as over a sweaty horse after a hard ride.

This automobile is legendary in Aleppo, and people gather around to admire it. The boy cares for it as if it were a living creature. It's almost dark in the stables, and

Ismene timidly places her hand on the automobile's shiny body.

"How dare you, you old gypsy," shouts the chauffeur when he sees her. Ismene withdraws her hand as if scalded.

"I wasn't hurting anything," she replies, her native pride surging fiercely back. She takes a step forward: "And be careful; I know curses from all over the world." Her tragic mask then appears in full light, and the men there sense that this woman carries with her the seal of pure evil, of the world's horror. And they understand.

"You're not Armenian," says the head groom, "but you've seen the Armenians. What do you want from us?"

Ismene makes up her mind in a flash. She must trust them. And she tells them part of the truth:

"I'm looking for an Armenian from Aleppo, a doctor who's related to my lady. His name is Zareh. Before the war, he often spent time with the French. I've been told he might be here, at the hotel." (She pronounces the word *hotel* with a voluptuous drawn-out final *l*, like someone thinking of forbidden Western pleasures, when in fact nothing could be farther from poor Ismene's feelings in that moment.)

"For whoever finds him, there's a nice reward. I don't have anyone left. I have to tell him about his family, about how they died, and pass on some photographs to him. And maybe then he'll take me into service himself. I'm not young, but there's nothing I can't do."

"I'm sure, nothing at all," the groom says. He laughs. "You're not exactly fresh meat! But I want to help you. You're Greek, right? From where?" Ismene is burning with impatience, feverishly aware of the weary, plodding steps of Shushanig, the girls, and the children as they get closer and closer, and terribly afraid that she has arrived too late, that they will be sent immediately on, beyond Aleppo, where no one will be able to reach them. She forces herself yet again to smile, to put on her little show, to evoke her Indian husband and his songs, his incantations, his passion. And she enchants them all, as always—but her voice is raw, her tears real.

The head groom narrows his eyes, convinced, and then issues a brief order: "Manuk, go up and check. Ask the porter about this Zareh." And to Ismene, "Give me a coin. I'll do your bidding for the love of God and for your lovely story, but the porter doesn't fear any gods or saints, and he likes to be paid up front."

Ismene hands a coin to Manuk. Manuk opens the communicating door at the top of a small stairway that leads to the manager's office. A wave of music and light floods the stables. Closing the door softly behind him, he slips away.

"Now all you can do is wait," the man says. "And pray, if you can, or cast one of your spells."

Ismene thanks him and closes her eyes, exhausted. Dozing off momentarily, she sees Sempad, smiling, holding Shushanig's hand. But Sempad's head has been poorly reattached to his neck, and Ismene, chilled to the marrow, watches it slowly loll to one side, as if about to topple— yet Shushanig doesn't notice and continues chatting flightily. In the dream, Ismene, Isaac, and Katerina are chasing after them, shouting, but no words are actually coming out, and they fail to reach them.

"A brief nightmare, boding ill," thinks Ismene. It feels to her as though an eternity has passed. She looks around: the men are talking softly, but the chauffeur is gone. To denounce her? Ismene regrets having been sharp with him, and then regrets regretting it. Mumbling something, she makes as if to stand—her head feels heavy and there's a sharp pain in her left arm. "Maybe I'm about to die," she thinks. And in that moment, the door opens and an irritated, anxious man appears, peering down from the top of the stairs.

Ismene recognizes the man at once. It's Zareh himself: that large, unmistakable family head, Sempad's nose and his delicate white hands with their round fingers. At last, he'll know what to do; at last, her long anguish begins to subside. He, then, is still free.

The men look around, greedily curious, eager to recount, later, this mysterious meeting. "Who is it that's sick and needs me so urgently?" Zareh asks, nervous. "A woman, I'm told."

Ismene, who has meanwhile dashed up the stairs toward him, says loudly, "It's me, doctor, Ismene. I come with news of your brother Sempad, and of your family.

I'm alone, and worn out, sir—would you for the love of God give me something to eat?"

She hopes that Zareh will understand and not ask questions. In contrast with her humble words, she stares boldly into his eyes, trying to reassure him, so he won't think it's a trap. He has brought with him the good scent of clean clothes, expensive cologne, and good cigars, and Ismene's heart aches, remembering. Zareh is remembering, too, and he's afraid. (Yesterday he received the magazine Yerwant sent, and he is torn with anguish, like his brother.) He takes Ismene by the wrist and whispers, "I don't recognize you, but if you bring news, you're a welcome guest. I must take leave of my friends. Wait for me at the main entrance, beneath the staircase, and stay out of sight."

Then he looks around, at the curious faces watching from below, and with a strained face says, as he tosses down a coin, "Here's something so you can drink to my health."

He grimaces and adds, "It's worth celebrating; I might be the only surviving member of my family. And if you need anything, if you're ever sick, remind me of this moment. I'm in your debt." And he disappears. Ismene disappears, too, as quickly as she can, though not without handing another coin to the head groom. She's still distressed by the chauffeur's disappearance, and so she says, "Keep quiet about this, all of you. And where did the automobile fellow go?" The groom puts a quick finger to his mouth and whispers so that only she can hear, "I'll take care of him myself. Don't worry, and may God be with you."

Ismene quickly walks back to the foot of the dazzling staircase to wait for Zareh. No one pays her any mind, one old gypsy among Aleppo's countless vagrants. But she avoids the beggar she saw earlier, so as not to have to chat with him. Everything now frightens her, and she prays fervently to all the saints she knows, even to Allah—it can't hurt. Ismene is profoundly convinced of the world's evil, but she believes with equal conviction in a Higher World, where all roads meet and the gods smile.

How many times, in her occupation as a wailer, had it seemed to her that she could see the majestic doors opening slightly, how many times had she felt the sudden urge to walk toward that timeless space brimming with surprises? She imagines it flooded with sunlight, with dust, and with rest. The sun high and the waters shimmering, the song of skylarks and a nice juicy thigh of lamb. And stamped forever in that sky of enamel and glass, the august faces of Christ and his patient mother.

Thus comforted anew, Ismene waits, and again she dozes off. Again she dreams of Shushanig together with Sempad, but now they are in that Paradise she was imagining when still awake, and when Zareh comes and rouses her, she realizes, with the immediacy of solemn moments, that this was a truthful dream and that Shushanig will soon be joining Sempad. But in the same instant she also realizes that she's alive now and has reached Aleppo.

ISMENE EXCITEDLY COMMUNICATES all this and much more to Zareh. She talks and talks, weeps and gesticulates in her relief at having found him, at no longer bearing alone the responsibility for what remains of the family. But first, Zareh takes her speedily to his house, via alleys and deserted backstreets, and brings her inside through a small rear entry. Although the Armenians of Aleppo have not yet been touched, there still exists an absolute prohibition against taking in foreigners, even relatives, and against showing any awareness of the human flood slowly surrounding the city.

Not even his status as a doctor truly protects Zareh—a whim, a random command, and he could find himself among those wretches. And so Ismene speaks to him in his kitchen, devouring the leftovers Zareh has taken out. Ismene is always hungry. In the calm light of the acetylene lamp, the horrors she relates assume an almost physical presence, and the pitiable ghosts of his brother, their friends, and the entire population of the little city crowd in on them, each trying to tell his or her story.

Then Ismene also tells about Nazim and Isaac, waiting back at the stable. It would be dangerous for Zareh to go to them; they must stay in touch through Ismene, who is asking for orders and looking at the doctor with that faithful-dog stare that she had previously reserved for Shushanig alone. How will they enter the camp? And how, most crucially, will they find their people and get them out—them and not others—beneath the noses of the guards?

Soon Zareh is giving Ismene some money and setting up a meeting for the next day, same time as this evening, same place, beneath the main stairs at the hotel. He must go there for his usual game, so as not to arouse suspicion.

Zareh has never been a complicated man. He has always taken life with a certain superficial cheer. But now he suddenly realizes that he has become the head of the family. The responsibility—and honor—of providing, with Sempad now dead and Yerwant absent, fall to him. He feels energized, determined, capable; he sleeps a little and early the next morning goes to the French Consulate, to consult a dear friend, Madame Marie-Joséphine, the consul's wife.

Marie-Joséphine is indeed a dear, blond friend, one who has given her heart completely to the young Armenian doctor. She has even offered him refuge in the consulate, and Zareh, as the family physician, could accept. But up to now, as he waited for news of his family, he hasn't wanted to. And besides, his Eastern pride won't permit him, not yet.

But he immediately runs to her for advice and explains everything. Ismene's trio needs to locate the survivors and bring them some comfort, tasks that might even be done indirectly. But how can they enter the camp, and then how leave it? Zareh and Marie-Joséphine spend the entire morning madly entertaining themselves by concocting plans worthy of the Count of Monte Cristo: hiring a few Kurds to enter the camp shooting wildly, seducing (this would fall to Marie-Joséphine) Djemal Pasha and getting him to provide a safe-conduct, persuading a tribe of desert Bedouins with offers of gold . . .

The only point they agree on is how to enter the camp: they must use the consulate's blue, red, and gold carriage, the French coat of arms clearly visible on both doors, and the Parisian driver who never speaks a word that isn't French but is ready, bright, and utterly loyal. And has two pistols. For him, Arabs, Kurds, and Turks are all the same, and saving monsieur's sisters and nieces will, he says, be a special pleasure.

Meanwhile, the stable has become a headquarters. Nazim and Ismene are making plans, too; Isaac is on guard duty. First of all, they must locate their people among the many Armenians who are still arriving in Aleppo, small depleted bands consisting of lost children, a few women, and a few enraged old men who haven't allowed themselves to die. They bring Isaac some bread and a flask of water, and he remains on guard; the two donkeys are valuable assets, and they still have a fair quantity of supplies.

Nazim and Ismene leave together, at dawn. They head in opposite directions, to make their way around the city walls and meet up again. Their pockets are full, of money and food, but their appearance is as humble as that of their peers.

The smell of death and putrefaction hangs like fetid breath around the entire city. It's July, and lethal miasmas seem to rise from those abandoned corpses, from those hands that will never again reach toward the sky. Indifferent guards keep watch from a distance, trying not to get too close. Ragged children wander about, dazed. Ismene passes quietly from group to group, listening, handing out a few pieces of bread, hearing the same stories everywhere: hunger, thirst, rapes, violence. The faces that look back at her are amazed to still be alive.

Nazim, on the other hand, approaches the guards, asks them for alms. He then inquires, casually, where this or that group has come from. His pilgrimage is slow and fruitless. "What do you want from us, old man?" one *zaptieh* asks. "Try asking them for money. Those damned people are always hiding it somewhere."

At that moment a naked, skeletal old man pulls himself slowly to standing against the wall he had been leaning on and shouts, in perfect Turkish, "Come, come, blessed of God. The banquet is served, but God is dead."

His cavernous, blood-caked mouth unleashes a squeaky, mocking, unrecognizable laugh; he seems to see the dogs of Acheron.

Nazim approaches, spurred by some wordless intuition. And beneath the wild beard he recognizes the devastated face of Setrak the baker, a harmless, simpleminded chatterbox. The ruthless law of survival has transformed him into a plaything for the soldiers, who have let him live for the fun of it, someone to kick or yank a tooth out of now and again, who can also perform certain lowly tasks involving the deportees. An assistant guard as it were, a capo of sorts. There's nothing human about him anymore; he just shouts occasionally, like now . . .

But for Nazim it's a sign that the survivors from the little city are not far off. And indeed beyond the old man he now sees, on the ground, a head of wild hair beneath a pile of rags, and above the rags the round eyes of Nubar, which still retain a hint of curiosity. Nazim quickly calms him with a crust of bread. Then he gently touches the tangled mass of hair and lifts the head beneath it, wincing, but the head lolls this way and that, oddly. It's Veron, dead. No one will sing *"Veron, Veron, vrai pompon"* to her again, and her bonnet lies in tatters in the Taurus Mountains. Everything has been bartered or sold, even Azniv's famous piece of red damask.

Veron has died of hunger. The inside of her mouth is still green from the grass that was her only food in her final days; her expression is twisted by pain, her fingers contracted. Veron never saw her Protestant pastor again. Now the universal pastor is leading her toward green pastures, toward that slow love that takes its time. Nazim moves her gently away, freeing Nubar's hands, which are caught up in her hair, and then closes her eyes and lays her out on the ground. Now he begins looking around the camp for the children and their mother and Azniv. At last he finds them at the far end of the camp, arguing with other women in a casual, vacant way over a potato lying on the ground. "It's mine, we can all eat with that," shouts a frightening, counterfeit Shushanig, shivering uncontrollably. Her daughters crowd around her, silent and frantic.

Nazim intervenes with a whisper: "*Valide Hanum,* I'm here, your work is done. Now we're going to save you."

He doesn't know exactly how yet, but the important thing for the time being is to take her aside, give her some food, and begin to prepare her for their escape. "I don't see my *zaptieh* friend around, only faces I don't trust, treacherous faces," Nazim hisses. After all, the reward for turning in anyone who tries to save an Armenian is a tempting one.

Nazim wishes he were accompanied by Ismene's quiet efficiency, but he's forced to fend for himself. So much to do, so little time. The smell in the camp is terrible, and everyone clearly has lice. First he hands out some bread, and then after looking around he whips the canteen out of one of his immense pockets and makes Shushanig and the girls drink. Covering them as best he can, he orders them to stay together, calm and quiet, and to keep Nubar among them.

Azniv has been away looking for her soldier, but at that moment she returns, miserable, her face swollen from blows. The soldier from Marash has tired of her. Though he still takes her every night, he beats her now, and doesn't even give her bread anymore, just fear. Azniv's eyes are bulging and her breathing is labored. Nazim touches her gently, helps her sit down, gives her some bread and water, and then whispers to her about Djelal and Zareh—that they are in Aleppo, that this evening she'll see them both, that she needs to hold out only a little longer.

Azniv doesn't seem to be listening. She drinks greedily and quickly hides the bread Nazim has given her, muttering. Her youthful beauty has faded, and she's missing two front teeth. But then she stares at him, she recognizes him, and the weight of reality suddenly flattens her.

"Who are you, friend, reminding me of the land of the dead?" she asks with sudden clarity. "Give me a little more water." And then, whispering softly, "You must not speak to me of Zareh or the other. I am no longer anyone. Save the children."

Nazim thinks of the waste of that budding youth, of that smile (*better to make a wife of her, better the wife of a beggar*, whispers a mocking voice somewhere far away inside him), and of the villains who threw to the wind the belongings and the lives of so many good citizens of the Empire. But no need to mention any of that to Djelal;

the lieutenant must simply have his romantic dream rekindled, spurring him to act.

On the other side of the camp, various things are happening at once. Ismene is there, having circled around, and grasps the situation in a flash. She sees that an officer has arrived on horseback, and that suddenly the guards are all on alert and have begun shouting orders to the deportees. She sees Nazim bending over someone, apparently comforting her, and also the officer staring at him, already turning his horse in that direction and raising his riding crop. Ismene suddenly grabs hold of the bridle and begins shouting in the jargon of wailers, with a few Cherokee curses thrown in as refrains.

"Who is this crazy woman?" asks the officer, who has no love—who does?—for the curses of wailers but harbors a superstitious respect for their task.

"I'm Greek, and I'm very good, effendi," Ismene retorts. "Looks like you're in dire need of me and my companions—you'll have to pay us extra." She laughs, impudent.

"Don't joke, woman," the officer growls. "You could be next." Ismene straightens and stiffens in her garish rags, holding his gaze, and her unspoken curse hovers, alive, in the air between them. And suddenly the man's skin feels the breath and the gaze of all the living dead around him; he doesn't push the point, asking only, "What do you want here?"

"I was looking for my husband, that starving man,"

shouts Ismene, triumphantly, racing over to Nazim. She presses a coin into Shushanig's inert hand and whispers, "Tonight. Tonight we're coming for you. Stay together. Tonight."

But the official is eyeing her, vaguely suspicious. "You two, get them out of here," he says to a pair of *zaptiehs*. "Nobody, and I mean nobody, is to be allowed in the camp today. And as for them"—he sweeps his crop around to indicate the camp—"make sure they're ready to leave for Dayr az Zawr. We're sending them on as soon as possible."

ESCORTED ROUGHLY OUT of the camp, Nazim and Ismene stop behind a majestic plane tree, long known among wayfarers for casting its shade over the idle and the weary near the East Gate of the city. With instinctive patience they wait for the officer on horseback to leave. They have already grasped that he is one of the Itti-hadists, the zealous overseers of the deportations, but he is certainly not the man in charge of the camp.

Rumors have been flying regarding dissent within the military here at Aleppo. A minute later, the officer comes by, not noticing them there in the shade, and spurs quickly away. Nazim and Ismene can now get down to business.

A guard appears, lame like Nazim, hopping quickly

toward them. Wounded in the war, he has been sent to work here.

He confronts them at once: "You were looking for someone, my friends. Did you find them?" Nazim asks what became of the fellow he was dealing with before the convoys crossed the Taurus, but his new friend doesn't know. "Could've been the guy who was killed by the Kurds, over spoils," he says impatiently. "But now you've got to deal with me. Amid this horror, I'm the only man, along with the camp's commanding officer, Major Selim, who can still discern and appreciate the tinkle of a nice pair of coins."

Ismene looks at Nazim, for once unsure of herself. Everything hinges on this moment. The world holds its breath around them. Nazim, searching for inspiration, notices two beggars squatting beneath the tree, trying to listen in on their conversation. And he makes up his mind.

"We're going to trust you, comrade. And we'll pay you and your commanding officer handsomely. But don't try to double-cross us. See those two beggars under that tree? They were sent by the Brotherhood. The Brotherhood owes a debt of honor to a certain family, whose survivors are in that camp. We're going to free them tonight. And may God help you if you cross us. Beggars and knives, they're everywhere."

Nazim has taken a huge risk. Ismene looks at him,

impressed at last. ("Oh, we could live in such peace, my people and yours, in this blessed land," she thinks. "We Greeks come first, of course, then everybody else, but we're all God's creatures," she concedes.) The lame guard says, "You'll have to hurry. Tomorrow may be too late. We're sending them all into the desert, to Dayr az Zawr. And there," he gestures significantly with his hand, "they've got trenches that feed into the Euphrates. The guys from party headquarters will oversee it themselves. They're sending us away, we're too softhearted." His only soft spot, really, is for money—"but better to love money than blood," Ismene thinks.

Ismene and Nazim quickly part ways with the guard, agreeing to meet again under the plane tree at two in the afternoon, a time when only the dead, according to the proverb, wander the streets.

The guard is supposed to get his commanding officer's approval and quietly tell Shushanig to remain at the ready in a certain place. He's also supposed to bury Veron, somehow—Ismene takes the cross from her neck, kisses it devoutly, and gives it to the man along with a stream of advice. "It's just a dead Armenian—don't get so worked up," replies the guard, whose name is Selciuk. But when he looks into Ismene's eyes, he shuts up.

Ismene turns her rags inside out so as to pass as Nazim's wife, and they both agree to go straight to Zareh. It's not the appointed time, it's a risk, but at this point Nazim and Ismene must stake everything. They've nearly forgotten Isaac; more a hindrance than a help, he has been assigned to keep an eye on the goats, and to pray.

Meanwhile, Zareh and Marie-Joséphine have prepared the carriage and briefed the coachman. Marie-Joséphine has emptied her kitchen and, *vite vite,* she and the Norman cook have brought a heap of provisions to Zareh's house, along with a small cookstove. And they must get the cellar ready for those poor creatures: provide beds, linen, furnishings . . . Marie-Joséphine is glowing with generosity and excitement.

Emerging, *vite vite,* from the front entry of Zareh's house, they might easily have overlooked the two mendicants off to the side, in the shade, if one of them (who but Ismene?) had not asked, in a submissive but firm tone, "Madame, please take us to the doctor. It's urgent."

It's a voice that resonates with Marie-Joséphine; it reminds her of her Breton wet nurse, a grandmotherly woman one would never disobey. "Come with me," she replies, as if in a dream, showing them into the carriage. To the coachman's great astonishment, she brings them all the way to the consulate.

Zareh is sitting alone on the patio, in a corner, like a spent windup doll. He, too, is waiting, can do nothing but wait, like every Armenian. "It was wise to confide in Marie-Joséphine," he thinks, as he wonders what it must be like to be born French, protected by the "Marseillaise."

Just then the carriage comes flying at full speed into the stables. Marie-Joséphine jumps down, her face red and intense, and with a sweeping gesture offers her hand to someone in the shadows, inside. Zareh looks on, nervous. Ismene quickly steps out, and behind her a filthy-looking individual with a vaguely shifty air and a limp. It's that Turkish beggar, Zareh guesses, the famous Nazim, the keystone of their whole plan. An irrepressible mistrust rises in him, like stomach acid, like nausea, but he fights it back.

Marie-Joséphine quickly brings them all into her parlor and serves refreshments, as if to aristocrats. She is delighted by her role as a conspirator, happy to play a part in a plot to aid injured virtue while stepping on the toes of a few of those unbearable Turks. Boredom has vanished; this is a life-or-death matter—which is exactly why they must act skillfully and very, very quickly.

The rendezvous in the camp is scheduled for two in the morning, but time is passing and no one is thinking clearly. First they need to take stock of their resources: Zareh, Marie-Joséphine, the carriage, and the coachman—these constitute the rescue's core operating unit. But how will they get those poor creatures out of that camp? And them alone?

They debate and speculate as the moment draws nearer. ("And also," thinks Nazim, "Djelal will be waiting for me at ten o'clock, and I'll have to tell him an exact plan, as well as something about Azniv. The idea would be to give her to him, so he could hide her, maybe marry her

later." Nazim recalls clearly the evening when Djelal
knocked and kept knocking, looking for his little dove,
ready to do anything for her. But he hasn't, of course, said
anything about this plan of his to Ismene or Zareh.)

Soon it's time to go meet the guard. Ismene and
Nazim find themselves again in the shade of the plane
tree near the East Gate, far more bewildered than they
were a few hours earlier. The sun beats down and their
hearts ache: the smell of death is everywhere, and the gendarme is nowhere in sight. The deportation camps stretch
as far as the eye can see; the thick stench clings. Here and
there dark smoke rises.

At last something moves, in the distance. It's the
lame *zaptieh* making his way toward them, furtively, indirectly. Behind him, as if coincidentally, they see a fat,
scruffy man, breathing heavily: the commanding officer.

And finally the wheels begin to turn. He's the one,
this older officer apparently disgusted by the task that has
been assigned him and desirous of profiting from the situation, who comes up with the best idea—simple, easy,
feasible, with everyone getting what they want. As soon as
Ismene mentions that a diplomatic carriage is at their dis-
posal, since the French consul's wife is the friend of the
Armenian doctor whose relatives are among the deportees, the commanding officer strokes his chin and declares,
"The doctor will come to treat me. My liver, as a matter
of fact, has been bothering me terribly. My orderly, who

is an ardent Ittihadist, will call in person to ask my old friend the consul's wife to recommend a good doctor, one who will pay a visit to the camp this very night, around one.

"You'll arrive in the consul's carriage, in which you will have installed a false bottom. And you'll put these people in there while the doctor attends to me. I don't want to know who or how many. I don't want any noises, alarms, or questions, or we'll all suffer for it. I have liver trouble, and I want a good doctor—that's all I know, and all I care about.

"Tomorrow, when it's all over, I want five hundred gold sovereigns. (As you can see, I come cheap, but I'm feeling old these days, and the goods are damaged.) You'll hand them over to my wife, Leyla, who lives in the modern two-story house near the fish market. Everybody knows her. I'll be on the road with what's left of these wretches. For all other details, you'll have to come to terms with Selciuk here. As for him, he'll need ten sovereigns."

A fleeting look of nausea (or sadness? or guilt?) passes over the officer's flabby face, and he seems to want to add something, but then he turns and walks quickly away, lighting a cigarette as he goes, as if out for a little postprandial stroll. His face really does have a yellowish cast, and he keeps his right hand pressed into his liver.

Nazim thinks that perhaps he really is ill, and Ismene thinks that perhaps they could have haggled regarding those five hundred pounds. But it's too late now for any more dealing; time is speeding by.

Ismene, Nazim, and Selciuk glance about, suspicious, then sit down beneath the tree. Ismene, having planned ahead, takes out two figs, a round of bread, and a flask of water. They eat and talk, and five gold coins change hands. ("The other five tomorrow, my friend," whispers Nazim. "Go to the leader of the Aleppo Brotherhood, he'll give them to you.")

Selciuk nods gravely. The reliability and secrecy of the Brotherhood of Beggars is legendary in all the Empire. Their affairs may be obscure, but their word, once given, is crystal clear. Selciuk might be able to double-cross them, and might make more money doing so. But inexplicably he feels that God himself has assigned him this task, him and Nazim, the two cripples, dregs of the earth: the lowliest soldier in the camp and a beggar. And besides, he's afraid of Nazim, but he also likes him. And in Ismene he detects, beneath her many-colored rags, an iron resolve.

Ismene says, "Be back again in three hours. A man will be here, his name's Isaac, and no one saw him in the camp this morning. But my lady, Madame Shushanig, knows him well. Bring him with you, say he's your cousin, and take him to her. She knows him and trusts him. Give her a little water, a little bread, the children, too, and Mademoiselle Azniv—but nothing else, so no one gets suspicious. Isaac will bring her comfort, and he'll help you when the time comes. Tell people he's mute, or has taken a vow of silence, but don't let him talk. They'd know him right away for a Greek."

Now they must hurry back to Zareh, who's tucked in a corner of the carriage, waiting, two streets away. It's a little risky, and might arouse suspicion, to leave the French carriage standing in the sun, empty, for so long. But nothing else could be done. There was no other way to keep Zareh safe, and Marie-Joséphine cannot be seen with him in public; she would be risking not only her reputation but that of France, a nation at war, after all, with Turkey.

The hyperalert Parisian coachman, Jean-Philippe, is keeping watch from beneath his lowered beret. Though everything seems tranquil, he's ill at ease. As soon as he sees Ismene turn the corner, followed by the panting Nazim, he whips the horses into motion, without bothering to warn Zareh. When he slows abruptly in front of Ismene, Zareh, shaken from his lethargic gloom, guesses that he ought to quickly open the door while the carriage is still in motion. Ismene jumps in, then she and Zareh lean out and grab Nazim, lifting him bodily from the pavement. Just in time. As the carriage rounds the corner, three gendarmes appear at the other end of the street; one of the area residents, suspicious, had sent a boy furtively, via a back door, to fetch them.

Luckily, it's siesta time; the boy had a hard time finding anyone at the prefecture, and an even harder time getting the gendarmes to follow him back. Now they hear only the sound of a carriage galloping away, and nothing can induce them—at three o'clock on a July afternoon in that stifling city, in that diseased heat—to risk catching the plague by running after it.

Thus Ismene and Nazim are able to fill Zareh in, and the three of them race, breathless and desperate, to Marie-Joséphine, who takes charge of the situation. She tells Jean-Philippe, *vite vite*, to track down planks and nails and a hammer to transform the carriage. *Vite vite*, she and Zareh and Jean-Philippe set to work on the false bottom, which is no easy task. *Vite vite*, Ismene and Nazim are sent off with the cook, a strapping, fearless Norman woman who knows Aleppo like the back of her hand, to prepare Isaac and take him to the camp. The cook will stay behind to keep an eye on the goats and the donkeys, armed with a butcher knife and the large cane she uses for running errands and keeping prying eyes at a distance. She wields it with remarkable skill.

Isaac embraces his new role, happy to finally be of use, and he accompanies Ismene to the plane tree at the appointed time. Nazim, meanwhile, goes back to the leader of the Brotherhood of Beggars; he must now tell him the whole story and pay him for his protection.

"I found the Armenian doctor," he begins, carefully. "But I didn't tell you the truth yesterday."

"I know you're staying with two Greeks, my friend," the man replies. "And I'm sure you had good reasons for lying to me. But now, you know, you have to tell me everything. It's in your interest."

And so Nazim really did tell the old leader of Aleppo's beggars everything, from his original sin to his work as a spy to his devotion to Shushanig.

When he finished, the man remained quiet for a while, then said, "Rest easy, we'll help. Give me the five sovereigns for Selciuk, the lame *zaptieh*, and pay me what you owe the Brotherhood for our help. Ten of my men will be there tonight, from midnight on, near the Gate. Don't look for them; they'll be there, ready to intervene if necessary. My man who works for Djemal Pasha will be at his post and will let me know if anything unusual happens. And an expert carpenter and his sons will show up at the French Legation within the hour."

"My friend, one more favor," says Nazim. "I still need to find those five hundred gold sovereigns for the commander's wife. Can you help me convert our money and precious stones and jewelry into sovereigns?"

"I can, and I shall," replies the leader of the beggars, who knows every money changer in the city. "And I'll do right by you. This story needs a happy ending. To demonstrate my good will, I'll start getting the gold together even before you bring me all the money and jewels."

Nazim empties his pockets and hands over his portion of the treasure without counting it. Then, his burden eased, he shares a bowl of opium with the old man, each of them feeling like one of Harun al-Rashid's knights.

Then, *vite vite*, the endless day begins to race along again. The carpenter and his sons, tight-lipped and able, quickly take over the task that Marie-Joséphine, Zareh, and Jean-Philippe had begun to botch.

In a few short hours they complete a solid false bottom with a counterbalanced door at the rear of the carriage, well disguised by the application of volutes and vine motifs. A number of holes have been drilled in the newly raised floor, each masked by a little movable diamond cut from a darker wood, which Ismene, hiding in a corner inside the carriage, must open as soon as the fugitives have entered beneath her.

Everything in the carriage interior has been adjusted accordingly: the sumptuous leather seats; the graceful shawls from Kashmir, which Marie-Joséphine uses to make the carriage feel more French; the portable tea service in its case, replete with a thermos of cordials, another of coffee, and a box of light cookies.

They put Zareh's medical bag, their official pretext, on one of the seats, but then decide it would be preferable for Zareh to bring it with him after being summoned by Marie-Joséphine, as every good doctor does.

Isaac and Ismene in due course emptied their pockets for the leader of the beggars, though Ismene prudently withheld one little bag of gems and valuables, for everyone's future. She looked the leader of the beggars in the eye; he understood completely, and neither said a word.

Zareh and Marie-Joséphine were running hither and
thither, never far from each other. They will always
remember that day as the zenith of their happiness. In the
moment, they could see nothing ahead of them but
anguish, the desperate horror of looming failure, and the
risk that they wouldn't be ready in time. They didn't realize that those risks and that anguish exalted their bond,
lent their lives flavor; if Zareh was the knight, Marie-
Joséphine was the chatelaine, Melisende to his Jaufré.

It's the slow year ahead of them that will eat away at
their hearts, revealing the differences between the French
beauty from the nation that won the war and the little
Armenian doctor who was doubly marked by defeat, both
as an Armenian and as a Turk, and who on top of that
was suddenly burdened with the terrible responsibility of
a secret family.

The others—Ismene, Nazim, Isaac, the Norman
cook, the French coachman, the beggars, the lame
zaptieh—all take care of their own tasks, cooperating
splendidly.

Around eight, everything grows calm. Now they
must simply wait for the camp commander to keep his
promise. Deciding that the officer he sends must find the
consulate full of activity and cheerful bustle, despite the
lateness of the hour, they stage a game of bridge. They
invite enough guests to make two tables, with the consul
strolling genially between them. Benoît de St. Lazare is
much older than Marie-Joséphine, as indulgent and ami-

able with her as he is shrewd and sly with the Turkish leaders and the city's Arab inhabitants. He likes Zareh and esteems him as a doctor.

The Confiserie Sicilienne delivers trays of its gelato, the best in the city, along with Eastern pastries, crumbly cat's-tongue cookies (the latest rage), cubes of candied honeydew, little marzipan watermelons, and, for the servants, fresh watermelons and casaba, chilled in a well.

No shame in eating when you're pleased with yourself. Everyone's appetite is whetted by the anxiety and the anticipation surrounding the coming night, and a little breeze of optimism begins to blow.

Meanwhile, Isaac waits beneath his plane tree. He's waiting humbly to do what Ismene has ordered him to do, which indeed he has a talent for: offering consolation. He rummages nervously in his pockets, fingering his canteen and the pieces of bread. He hopes to be up to the task. "At least, since I'm not allowed to speak," he thinks, "I can't say anything stupid." No one is farther from the thought of giving sermons than this uncertain priest, who feels acutely guilty—and alone. Widowerhood is not, he thinks, for him, and by now he has grown attached to Ismene. "Can a priest marry a wailer?" is the question he is idly turning over in his head, like a piece of straw between his teeth, as he waits.

"When all this is over" (he, too, feels something like

a whisper of optimism in the air, a murmur, he thinks, that comes from the good Katerina and young Dimitraki, happily reunited at last) "and I have been forgiven, I want to put on my blue simar again, regrow my pigtail, and go back to being a priest. People will need them, the liturgies, after the war, and I at least have a good voice, and I know all the songs."

At that moment the lame *zaptieh* appears, handing him a filthy uniform of some sort. "Get dressed and let's go," he whispers, "there's not much time left. Your friends had better be well behaved and quick-witted tonight. Luckily, they're fairly isolated. I'll take you there, but you've got to hurry. The whole camp is in turmoil, and the officer from this morning could come back at any moment." Isaac nods, already playing the part of a mute.

"The Armenians are rebelling," the man continues. "It took those cheapskate shopkeepers long enough to figure it out, that there's no escape, that they're bound to die. But tomorrow, before they leave, I'm going to pick me out a nice young boy and take him away with me. Now that I've got a little money, I want out. And this way, I'll be doing a good deed, too."

Isaac makes no reply concerning this good deed. He's enormously afraid, as he was on the night at the Farm, though this time he's better prepared. He's even enormously afraid of Ismene. But farther back within himself, he thinks, "I have nothing left to lose." He tries to convince himself that it's true, and that the miniature

Archangel Michael in his pocket will not, despite everything, refuse to defend him.

THUS THE NIGHT is shot through with salvation schemes.
Isaac finds Shushanig awake and once more alert, half-
lying across her children, whispering frantic orders in
their ears. They are no longer used to obeying, only wandering through the camp in a never-ending search for a
crumb of bread, a seed, a forgotten rind. The world has
closed over them, and they have survived by anxiously
scouring and scrutinizing the earth. No reason to lift
your eyes toward the empty shell of the sky, toward the
scorching, motionless heat; no reason to attract the attention of that fierce God up there who has laid claim to all
your food. (For months after their rescue, the children
will not be parted from their rounds of bread, which
Nubar and Henriette will transform into dolls.)
    Shushanig is assisted by Arussiag, a quiet, rather ugly
adolescent, who has never spoken of the abuses she was
subjected to; she gave little trouble to the soldier who
took her away, but apparently little pleasure, too. And so
he brought her back, saying she just wasn't any good.
    Azniv is sitting apart, lost in herself, eyes vacant.
Isaac goes to her first, gives her water and bread, which she
snatches with quick motions. She does not, however, react
in any way to his words. Sighing, he hurries to Shushanig,
gives her the canteen and the rest of the bread, and whis-

pers, "*Mayrig,* tonight's the night. Selciuk here and I are getting you out. Your brother-in-law, Zareh, is coming with a carriage." Shushanig listens, flashing a faint glimmer of her old smile at Isaac: "You're loyal, Isaac. The children and I thank you. But more than that, it's Sempad who thanks you, and our other sons."

On the orders of the officer who has arranged the departures, the deportees are now being watched much more closely. The city of Aleppo is full of vexation and upheaval. The Arabs are restless and quarrelsome. No one likes to be surrounded by this foul tragedy, to be touched personally by these horrors, to smell death all around— and to be unable to do a thing about it. The *zaptiehs,* with equal firmness, keep both the compassionate and the curious at a distance.

Thus at a certain point Selciuk quickly drags his "cousin" Isaac away and sits him down to guard his donkey. Isaac says nothing. By now it has become a habit for him to spend entire days, mute, with donkeys. He doesn't really mind. He prays and drowses.

IN THE MEANTIME, Nazim has informed Ismene—and her alone—of his rendezvous with Djelal. As for Ismene, even she doesn't understand why Nazim wants to meet with Djelal; she just assumes that the officer was one of Nazim's regular benefactors. By now she has come to trust Nazim. In any case, he will return to the consulate on time; meanwhile he tells himself, justifiably, that by having him run into Djelal, God has already given him a fairly clear sign. So he borrows a docile mule and sets out, into the teeming Aleppo night, to weave another strand of salvation. But what should he tell Djelal? How much should he tell Djelal?

Everything hinges, for Nazim, on those distant protestations of love that he overheard from his hiding place. But a river of time and blood has passed since then.

Djelal is already on the street, waiting. Since the previous day he has awaited Nazim like an emissary of destiny. Djelal is a strong, modern spirit—he isn't superstitious. But when he looked the beggar in the eye, he saw and judged himself.

How could he have abandoned his little dove, she whose hands he held beneath the fragrant pergola? Terrible, truthful images weigh upon his heart. She didn't really reject him, it was just her virginal modesty that made her jump to her feet and withdraw. She never actually said no to him. And he—he abandoned her, with her undefended beauty, to gendarmes, to soldiers, to *zaptiehs* . . .

A precise awareness of what has doubtless happened crushes his heart like a vise. His little dove, his rose of May . . . He suddenly recalls the scent and the dark velvety color, almost an omen, of the pergola's roses. How could he have wiped all that out, losing himself in

Aleppo? And what might she be like now? Is she, first of all, alive?

"Yes, she's alive," Nazim tells him as soon as he arrives. "Azniv's alive," he repeats (and Djelal doesn't think to ask how it is that Nazim knows all this with such confidence). "And Madame Shushanig and her daughters are alive." (Best not to speak of Nubar, the surviving male, for now.) "We found them. Only a few from our little city made it this far."

Immense compassion for this contaminated woman fills Djelal's heart, along with secret relief that he might still be her savior, romantically carry her away at a gallop, nourish her, heal her, and then have her all to himself without her fits of pride: submissive and grateful. She's a woman, after all. At this point nothing and no one can stop him from taking her for himself, though his dreams of marrying her and running off to Paris now seem indecent, worse than naïve.

The conqueror's ancient pride regarding subdued women (the same pride felt toward subdued cities) resurfaces intact from beneath Djelal's Western veneer, and he quickly abandons the shards of his romantic dream.

Nazim reads his face, and in truth he approves. Djelal's home seems to him a fine refuge, and many Armenian women are being saved in this fashion. And so, brusquely, he decides what to say: that the surviving family members will be brought out of the camp during the night, by a relative. If he wants Azniv, he should wait after midnight with a pair of friends and horses beside the East Gate, near the great plane tree, with blankets and cordials. Nazim will alert him when the time comes.

Giving Djelal no time to reply, and with a slightly uneasy conscience, Nazim brings his mule sharply about and trots away. Azniv's motionless eyes are weighing on him, and he fears Ismene and her inquiring look, but he's also proud of how everything is coming together, and of the part he has played.

AND THAT IS HOW the never-ending day came to an end. The hot July evening was quickly upon them. The carriage was ready; Nazim and Ismene were crouching inside it, perfectly silent, as Jean-Philippe sought refreshment with a good meal. Her watch over, and having said goodbye to the donkeys, the Norman cook returned in time to set out dainties.

Zareh and Marie-Joséphine have not taken the consul into their confidence, but he gathers from their conspiratorial air that something is afoot. Benoît just smiles, convinced that in that terrible city, besieged by war and by the Armenian horror on its doorstep, Marie-Joséphine is in need of diversion. He's also convinced that, even so, she would never do anything to tarnish his reputation, or France's—best, then, not to know. He guesses it is some small intrigue; he could never imagine what his carriage will be used for that night.

THE GAME BEGAN. They all appeared merry and giddy, but they were not. The stench of death plagued the city. They ate, they drank, they joked. And a little before the appointed time, the Turkish officer arrived on horseback, asked for Marie-Joséphine, and conveyed the greetings of his commanding officer ("whom you, Madame, know very well; and now he has fallen ill, a liver attack. He's in a great deal of pain, and he is confiding in you because he knows that you know the best doctors in Aleppo").

"The best is right here, sitting next to me," said Marie-Joséphine, adding, "Wouldn't you like to take a seat and have some refreshments?"

The officer hesitated, tempted, but he had precise orders. And after all, France was an enemy nation (a perceptive thought crossed his mind: "Why in the world would the commander turn to her for help?"). He declined the invitation, and Zareh rose and got his medical bag. "Please excuse us, we must leave," he said, trembling—trembling as if he were out there in the camp, just another Armenian.

"Should I come, too?" asked Marie-Joséphine, as if in afterthought.

"Oh no, Madame, those camps are no place for you,"

replied the officer, scandalized, and Benoît gave his wife a brief, almost timid, glance. Zareh can't take her with him, and the French carriage, amiably offered, is already at the door.

And so Marie-Joséphine, that sweet butterfly without whom this scheme could never have succeeded, now leaves our story, only dimly aware of herself as a needle of destiny. Zareh would like her company, not thinking of how terribly humiliating for Shushanig, Azniv, and the girls would be the sight of this Western beauty, this perfumed apparition—a Frenchwoman, no less.

Now the carriage speeds away, and at the consulate they finish their game of bridge. Feeling sympathy for his disappointed wife, Benoît takes Zareh's seat and smiles at her.

ISMENE AND NAZIM have been hiding in the carriage. Jean-Philippe, who claims he can see in the dark like a cat, is ready in the driver's box. "Such efficiency!" thinks the officer, mildly suspicious. But recalling the yellowish face of his commander, he soon forgets and slips into more pleasant thoughts. "Maybe this doctor will prescribe bed rest, in which case perhaps I could take command myself," he thinks, "and make a good impression on the leaders back in the capital. These old officers don't like this sort of dirty work. They'd rather do actual battle, with real enemies." To him, getting rid of the Armenians is a duty like any other; one doesn't even need to act directly, just give orders. These inferior, passive races must be gotten rid of, for the good of the Empire. And thus shall it be.

The carriage flies behind the officer's horse, over roads that by now they know well. Ismene and Nazim confer quietly, but without making overly precise plans. They'll play it by ear. "But Zareh," thinks Ismene, "is too pale; his head is rocking, his hands are shaking, he's quickly becoming just another Armenian, ready for the slaughterhouse."

"Dr. Zareh," she says, taking him by the hands, "they can smell fear. You are not afraid, Dr. Zareh, you live in Aleppo. But you're the head of your family now. Think of your brother Rupen, who as yet knows nothing of this; think of the professor in Italy. They're counting on you, and so is Marie-Joséphine. You are a knight to her, and also now to *Mayrig* Shushanig and your sister Azniv. And of course little Nubar." And with a flash of her indomitable spirit, she adds, "We'll fool them all, the damned dogs. And God is on our side, that much I know."

Zareh stares at her, dazed, trusting her. He squeezes her hand nervously and stops shaking. He even sits up straight, and when the officer slows to point the way, he gestures from the window, an authoritative gesture, he hopes. The gesture of a capable doctor.

At the camp gates, the officer slows slightly, as does the carriage. When the officer stops and dismounts,

Zareh gets out and follows him, not looking back, to his patient.

There isn't much light. A few *zaptiehs* are scouring the camp, lantern in hand, to prevent escapes, a measure adopted in advance of the departure, planned for morning.

Jean-Philippe climbs down from his driver's seat, as planned, pretending to close the carriage door left open by Zareh. In the shadow of his tall figure, Ismene and Nazim slip out and disappear behind the carriage, leaving the camouflaged, counterbalanced rear door propped slightly open, ready for use. Isaac and Selciuk are ready in the shadows.

The coachman leans against the side door lazily, takes a cigarette from his pocket, and begins to smoke with an impassive air, peering around from beneath his beret and muttering curses. In the semidarkness around him, weak moans, footsteps, furtive movements, and every now and then a yell. The smell of death and corruption is choking.

Then everything speeds up. A thicker shadow behind the carriage, starting to wobble. A child's brief cry, a rash movement. From the other side of the camp, two figures begin running; someone lights a stronger lantern. And everything would have been lost had not Azniv, the sweet sister, making her way last toward salvation, grasped the situation and drawn all the attention to herself.

"Ov sirun sirun," she begins to sing, standing proudly

erect, rediscovering in her sudden sacrifice all her innocent, serene audacity. "*Ov sirun sirun*, you bastards, I dare you. You'll never kill us all."

A mad wind blows through the camp. The other women begin to scream, their hands raised skyward, like withered flowers seeking revenge. The *zaptiehs*, caught by surprise, rush toward Azniv, shining their lights on her, and she continues to sing until a sword severs her head. Goodbye, sweet Azniv; goodbye, Armenian dove.

In the dark, Shushanig and the children are pushed into the carriage's false bottom, and the door clicks shut behind them. Ismene, Isaac, and Nazim hasten to take cover in the carriage, flattening themselves against the floor, then opening the air vents and whispering some comforting words. Just then Zareh, pale as a sheet, emerges from the commanding officer's hut, shakes his hand, giving him one last piece of advice before climbing slowly, as instructed, back into the carriage.

"All set," Jean-Philippe whispers mercifully, closing the door with ceremony. He jumps into his seat, whips the horses, and quickly leaves the camp.

But outside Djelal is waiting, with his friends. Nazim shudders, though he knows he has to tell him, partly because he has already told him about this escape from the camp. But stopping the carriage now is out of the question; he can't discuss it with Ismene, and Jean-Philippe is racing like the wind. And so he simply slides toward Zareh, opens the door, and rolls out, curled, as they pass the East Gate. Zareh automatically closes the door, then collapses onto his seat. Ismene takes his hands again and tells him how Azniv died. She tells him both that she used to sleep in the desert wrapped in a piece of damask that he, Zareh, had given her, and also that she died a rebel, singing her song.

"Oh, little sister," Zareh would like to cry, but there's no time. The poor creatures beneath him require all his attention.

AND SO, PATIENT READER, we have come to the end of this journey, and of this story. Sempad's daughters survived—and Nubar, too, as had been foretold. For a year Zareh kept them all hidden in his cellar, and he would not have been able to feed them were it not for the kind assistance of Marie-Joséphine and dear Ismene, and the widespread efforts, on the part of the people of Aleppo and the foreigners who lived there, to help Armenians.

Eventually he managed to put them on a boat bound for Venice—and for Yerwant, who took custody of them. Shushanig outlived herself all that long year, but she was in decline, and she died of a heart attack her first night on the boat. Only when she had finally departed for Italy with her small tribe could she cast off her fear and smile again at Sempad. What, then, became of her children, of Yerwant and his countess, and of Yetwart and Khayël? That will be another story.

Ismene and Isaac stayed in Aleppo with Shushanig until her departure, and then they moved to Smyrna, together. That, too, is another story.

Nazim remained in Aleppo with Zareh, postponing his departure. Then one day he disappeared for good, gone perhaps to practice his profession in Mecca. He certainly didn't go back to the little city.

Nazim found Djelal on the famous night; no one knows what he told him. But a few days later, as if by chance, Djelal ran into Zareh, and they mourned together—which is to say they drank coffee and played backgammon. And in the end it was Djelal who found a ship and German passports for Shushanig's small tribe, and this same Djelal was among the witnesses at the trial of those responsible for the Armenian massacres, in Constantinople, in 1919.

No one, patient reader, ever went back to the little city.

ACKNOWLEDGMENTS

I OWE A GREAT DEAL to a great many. I must first thank those who spoke to me: Sempad and Shushanig, Ismene and Isaac, Nazim the beggar, and Yerwant, with his neat Pirandello goatee. And then Azniv and Veron, the great-aunts I never knew; funny, tiny Henriette, who spoiled me; Zareh and Rupen, my legendary great-uncles. I thank my audacious, whimsical mother, who raised me unleniently; Khayël, my serious, sly father, who worried about everything; my uncle Yetwart, and my cousins Yerwant, Ermanno, and Teresa; my little brother Carlo; and my other eccentric and beloved siblings and their children.

I'm grateful to my brilliant friend Siobhan Nash-Marshall for the initial push; the voices spoke to her before they did to me. To Boghos Levon Zekiyan, dear friend, for the rediscovery of my roots and the joy it brought. To Paolo, recipient of my first stories, for a vigilant eye and an ancient love; to Cecilia for the sweetness and the stormy understanding of a true daughter. To Dario Giangolzian-Agopian, for shared Armenianness and for the name Pharmacie Hayastane; to Chiara

Acknowledgments

Haiganush Megighian and Afò Hemmat Siraky, for their wise guidance, word by word, through the incandescent poetry of Daniel Varoujan.

To the many people who heard me tell my stories over the many long years, thank you for listening: the Campel Alto battle unit (Marta, Francesco, Angelomarco, Mariasilvia, and Andrea); Anna Folli, my alter ego, and Piersandro Vanzan; Mario and Fiorenza; Luisa one and Luisa two (and Limpopo); Giovanna the Sheep, Marina, Carlo, Francesco, and Little Alessandro; Mimina, Laura, Cesira, and Natalia; Luigina and Betti; Adriana and Marisa; Lina, Stefania, Sonja, and Roberto; Gianna; Paolo; Leo in Crete, Francis in Tolo; Andrea on the Lido; Luca in Capalbio; and also Margherita, Annalisa, Manuela, Donatella, Flavio, Elisa, Victoria, and all my other cherished students; Big Alessandro and Silvia; Fabio and Carla; Maria Teresa and Clara; and those whose names I don't know—friendly companions on trains, on buses . . .

And then my heart's small creatures: Vanana, Lefantino, Bright Lefante, and Baby-Girl Lefante; Bright Baby-Boy Lefante and Gloomy Dark Junior, who crosses oceans gathering seeds; the Girl with the Boots; Miss Gone Away; the Knights; and all the ones who come and go, never leaving me alone.

And thanks to my friends and companions at Eastern mass, and to Padua's small core of Armenians, with whom even I manage to sing full-throated.

Thanks to Angelo Guerini, who has always been a trusting friend; to Roberta Brivio and Sandra Cossu, friends and partners in crime; to Annamaria and Piero Kuciukian, Fernanda Di Monte, Laura Pisanello, and Beppe De Santis; Gi. Lu.; Arminé and Anahid, who in various ways made me begin to write this story; and thanks to all the gentle, daydreaming Armenians who, in Milan and Rome and the world over, welcomed me and nourished me with ancient images and unforeseen kinship and gave me the gift of treasured memories.

Thanks also to Adele Saravalle, Renato Parenzo, Dario and Aida Foà, and Achille Viterbo, for sharing with me, in many ways, their valuable Jewish wisdom; to Suren Zovighian and Aldo Ferrari, learned and curious friends, experts on things Armenian; to Vartuhi Pambakian, who introduced me to the art of Armenian lacework and embroidery; to Ruth Thomasian, high priestess of photographs of the Lost Country, who re-creates periods, manners, and atmospheres—and creates calendars; to the fantastic architectonic visions of Lucy Der Manuelian; to Haikaz Grigorian, psychiatrist and mysterious soul mate.

I owe a great debt, finally, to the witnesses and historians of the Armenian genocide, including Claude Mutafian, Vahakn N. Dadrian, Robert Melson, Donald and Lorna Miller, and Richard G. Hovanissian, who allowed me to understand more fully the terrible warp and weft of events and thus to better interweave the real and the realistic.

I am also indebted to friends across the ocean—Teodolinda Barolini; Timmie Vitz; Gwendolin Herder; Joe Koterski; Mary and Tona; Maria and Vita; Uxue; Gary; Sandy; and Leora—and to cities across the ocean where some of the characters in this story became real: New York, beloved for that window overlooking the river and the barges and the big chunks of dark ice; for Evanghelos and his restaurant, the Tudor Grill, on Tudor City Place; for Grand Central Station, Place that Protects Me; and for the orange juice and muffins at Zaro's; and St. Paul, Minnesota, for that building across from the Farmers' Market on which CRANE is written in lovely nineteenth-century letters, which always made me think of "Grunk," the nostalgic song sung by Armenian emigrants; and for those thick, tasty soups at the Black Dog Coffee and Wine Bar.

Thanks to my friends in Minnesota, my lake country paradise: Koko and Joanne; Massis and Chaké; Kathie and Jaffar; my rediscovered Kardashian cousins; Lou Ann Matossian; Hanna Kerkinni, Assyrian and Maronite cobbler. And to my students at St. Thomas University: Aaron, Jim, Rachel, Molly, Rougina, Beth, and Kathryn.

To Marilisa Andretta and Vartan Mardirossian I owe affection and gratitude. I am grateful to Roberto Santachiara for his marvelous ear; to Ale, Laura, and Cris for their energetic support; and to the Rizzoli cafeteria for its *riso in bianco* and its phenomenal frittata.

One final affectionate thank-you goes to Mrs.

Donatella Biffignandi, of the Museo dell'Automobile in Turin, for her valuable and proficient consultations, which aided and confirmed my childhood memories, and to all those who are in my heart but have slipped my mind.